About the Author

Emma Coray was born in Crantock, Cornwall and raised in Milton Keynes. She now lives in Qatar with her husband. *Struck* is her first novel.

I dedicate this book to my family for their love and support. First and foremost to my husband Jason and my children Kristina, Holly and Pierce. And to Sheila Louise for being such a good friend.

Emma Coray

STRUCK

Copyright © Emma Coray (2015)

The right of Emma Coray to be identified as author of this work has been asserted by her in accordance with section 77 and 78 of the Copyright, Designs and Patents Act 1988.

All rights reserved. No part of this publication may be reproduced, stored in a retrieval system, or transmitted in any form or by any means, electronic, mechanical, photocopying, recording, or otherwise, without the prior permission of the publishers.

Any person who commits any unauthorized act in relation to this publication may be liable to criminal prosecution and civil claims for damages.

A CIP catalogue record for this title is available from the British Library.

ISBN 978 1 78455 174 2 (Paperback)
ISBN 978 1 78455 177 3 (Hardback)

www.austinmacauley.com

First Published (2015)
Austin Macauley Publishers Ltd.
25 Canada Square
Canary Wharf
London
E14 5LB

Printed and bound in Great Britain

Contents

Tuesday Morning	11
The Bully	18
The Best Friends	25
A Chance Meeting	30
An Unfortunate Accident	40
Mums the Word	47
At Casualty	54
The Bad News	56
The Plan	59
What Jack Did	69
A New Day	73
The Nosey Neighbour	84
Liar Liar	87
The Bloody Clothes	94
The Painful Truth	101
Friday Morning	119
The Proposition	123
Inspector Campbell	131
CJ Makes Tracks	140
The Home Watch Meeting	144
Morning Has Broken	154
What Happened With Barry	158
Back to School	167
Monday Afternoon	176
The Service	180
At Thomas's House	183
'Mother Cluckers'	194
Breaking Point	198
The Morning After	208
Getting Even	213
At the Children's Ward	221
Home Sweet Home	224
Kat's Story	235
After Summer	238

CHAPTER ONE

Tuesday Morning

Jodie was sleeping restlessly.
 The nightmare had come again.
 That feeling of intense heat as though her whole body was engulfed in flames. She was standing on the beach below the pale blue sky, her long auburn hair flaying around her face. The blue ocean stretching out as far as the eye could see. Jodie walked into the sea. The wet sand seeped between her sinking toes and frothy white salt water sweeping around her ankles. Walking deeper and deeper, stroking her finger tips through the low rush of the waves. The salty sea air drifting through her nostrils, filling her lungs. Her strides taking her deeper and deeper until the last drawn out breath of fresh sea air became a stream of salty liquid and her feet could no longer touch the velvety floor. Jodie was falling into darkness. The deceiving blue ocean swallowing her into an inky blackness. Her drowning body drifting helplessly into a bottomless pit of darkness.

She woke with the feeling of alarm. The heavy curtains masked the morning sun but Jodie did not feel the usual urge to snuggle back down and snooze for another five minutes. She switched off her alarm quickly so not to wake Jack and lay still for a while trying to shake off the lurid feeling of her dream. Then turned to look at Jack. Her husband lay beside her, his mouth wide open. With each heavy breath came a grunting noise and a smell of stale cigarettes. She thought it was disgusting. All love was lost. Gradually it had faded over the years and turned into nothing less than repugnance. Saddened that a conversation with her husband was not an option she relinquished the thought and reflected on speaking with her best friend Kat.

Jodie got out of bed, gently tossing aside the duvet and slipped her feet in to her comfy mules. It was six forty-five and Jack was stirring. He would be awake soon expecting his breakfast to be ready and she was afraid to disappoint him. Throwing on her dressing gown, she made her way across the landing to CJ's bedroom and went in.

"Hey honey, it's time to get up," she said as she opened the curtains letting in the bright morning sun. CJ mumbled and moaned as light flooded his room telling him it was that awful moment when he had to get up and get ready for school.

"Wake up honey … come on."

Shuffling around his bed and pulling his Man United duvet over his head, he eventually said, "Alright Mum, I'm awake." His muffled voice just audible beneath his quilt.

"Okay get dressed, I'll go fix you some breakfast."

By seven thirty Jodie had made a plate of pancakes. It had taken years of practice to make them exactly how Jack wanted. The exact size and thickness had to be right. And the fresh coffee was brewed to the exact time required, the cream was just the right temperature and served in a white bone china coffee cup. The sugar bowl was filled with the tea spoon on the side and the Portmeirion butter dish with the butter knife on the side. Placemats, plates, cutlery, a jug of fresh orange and glasses all placed accordingly as though Jodie was making breakfast for the king himself.

Jack and CJ were dressed and had joined Jodie in the kitchen, and as they sat eating breakfast together they looked like a normal loving family. But as always, the air was thick with a heavy tension.

Jack's face was buried behind *The Times* newspaper, folded in half and held clumsily in one hand. Jodie didn't mind this. It was the noise he made when he was eating she found irritating. He shoved way too much food into his mouth and had the bad manners to talk before he'd finished eating. In between mouthfuls of pancakes smothered in syrup and butter he began to give Jodie her orders for the day. He did this without taking his eyes off the paper and with a mouthful of food.

"Jodie I need my suits collecting from the dry cleaners." he said with an annoying chomping sound. "They phoned yesterday to say they would be ready."

"Right ... okay," said Jodie feeling both vexed and panicky at the same time. She was trying to force herself to eat breakfast but her real appetite was to add a large measure of brandy to her coffee.

"And the gardener is expecting you to pay him today." continued Jack, still with eyes on the newspaper. Jodie wondered if he was actually reading it.

"Okay I'll do that today. Dry cleaners and gardener. Got it," said Jodie obediently.

"... And for God's sake will you ask that damn woman to do something with her tree. And you're going to need to put the car through the wash today ... what have I told you about keeping the car clean? It's embarrassing ... this is not some council estate Jodie."

"Sure. I will ... get the car cleaned ... and I'll speak to Christine today if I get chance."

"If you get chance? God damn it woman ... make time Jodie ... you do nothing else all day." retorted Jack.

The words burned a feeling of irritation and anger, as he knew they would. Jodie tightened her hands around her coffee mug as she tried to inhibit them from shaking. It probably wasn't the best time to announce her best friend Kat had asked her to meet her for lunch, but nevertheless, she took a deep breath and nervously said, "Kat's asked me to meet her for lunch today."

CJ grimaced fretfully. He took a bite of his pancake and sunk back in his chair. The very mention of Kat in front of his dad was cause for a ruckus. He was fully aware of his dad's feelings towards Kat. And he too could feel the weight of the air in the room.

"I see," said Jack. Jodie watched him anxiously as he angrily turned the pages of the newspaper, his face still hidden behind the broadsheet. She glanced at CJ and caught his worried look.

Here we go thought Jodie. Kat had been her best friend all through school. They had both turned up late for their first day in art class and had sat next to each other at the back of the room. There was an instant click and they soon formed an affable relationship. A closeness that Jack could never understand. Jack objected to their friendship. He hated Kat with a passion. She was an extension of Jodie that he could not dominate or oppress, which over time spawned an unfathomable resentment.

"Why have you arranged to meet that woman? I told you before, I don't want you having anything to do with her. Damn it Jodie, why can't you just do as I ask?" Jack continued to snap. He looked clumsy as he attempted to fold the newspaper, shaking the pages so that it would fold neatly. There was a glisten of irritation in his wild green eyes as he glared at Jodie and began to rant for the next few minutes. His voice low, controlled and daunting. Jodie only watched his lips move, paying no attention to the words. This was all too familiar. Jack didn't want Jodie to meet with Kat because he knew that Kat would try and get Jodie to leave him, and he would be right. In her mind's eye she pictured picking up the jug of coffee and pouring it over his head. She warmed to the vision of seeing fear in *his* eyes, scalding him with the boiling liquid. She wanted to pick up the Carrara marble sculpture of a naked lady and smash it over his head. Jack finally stopped his tirade and the image faltered and fury suppressed. Jodie got up out of her chair and managed to find her voice, albeit a little shaky.

"Jack, I haven't seen Kat in ages. I want to see how she is. It's only going to be for an hour. I'll still get all my chores done." Jodie began tidying the kitchen, quickly occupying herself hoping that neither Jack nor CJ would notice her body trembling. She desperately wanted to see her friend. There had been urgency in Kat's voice when she had asked to meet up and Jodie had felt compelled to say yes, despite the repercussions from Jack. *Why is it so hard for Jack to let me have a friend? Why am I tormented every time I arranged to see Kat?* thought Jodie.

Jack was slurping his coffee. He had been watching his wife with a cold look of disappointment. Jodie caught Jack's stare and turned away quickly, continuing to tidy up. There was an awkward silence which amplified the sounds of the clattering dishes as Jodie loaded the dishwasher. CJ was still sat silently at the table. Too scared to defend his mum, yet too afraid to leave her on her own with his dad. He ate the last pancake, even though it had gone cold. He wanted to appear that he had not finished breakfast so that he could remain seated at the breakfast bar. He glanced at the clock. The school bus will be arriving soon. He didn't have much time. He wished his dad would leave for work.

A few minutes later, much to CJ's and his mum's relief, Jack announced grumpily he was going to work. As he picked up his brief case from the corner of the room he was still glaring at Jodie disapprovingly, but she had been avoiding eye contact.

"I'm telling you," he said forcefully, "you better not meet Kat today. That woman has no place in our lives." Jack didn't have to shout to sound frightening. The tone alone carried a heavy weight. A horrible silence hung in the kitchen. Jodie and CJ stared at each other in anticipation as they waited for the resonant sound of the front door closing signalling Jack's departure. Jodie's heart was pounding. Then she heard the front door close and as if by magic the air felt fresh and she could breathe easily. Jodie looked out the window. It was always reassuring to see Jack drive away. And for the first time that morning she noticed the pleasant sun shining brightly. There were wispy white clouds in the pale blue sky and her colourful begonias that filled the window boxes, swayed in a mild breeze. *I am going to see Kat,* she thought defiantly. *How will he know?*

"Mum, why d'you tell Dad you're meeting Kat? He's not gonna know what you do when he's at work ... so long as you do your, (*he imitated speech marks*) '...chores'."

"Because ... just because, alright," said Jodie turning to look at CJ. She didn't really know why. She was just scared of the repercussion of going behind his back. There was an invisible hold, a control that only she could feel. She wished that maybe he would accept that she needed her friend, but deep down she knew that was just never going to happen.

"Well you're just gonna have to learn to not get caught. I'm not gonna tell Dad if you meet Kat Mum ... am I? And I don't get why he has a problem with her. Kat's nice. She's like an aunty to me." CJ was gathering up his school books and putting them in his rucksack.

"Your dad doesn't like Kat, because Kat doesn't like him," said Jodie "But ... you know ... I've got to see her today. I have the feeling there's something she wanted to tell me. Something important."

"I've gotta go to school Mum or I'll miss the bus. Are you gonna be okay?"

"Yes honey I'll be fine. Go. You get yourself to school. Here take this." She handed CJ some loose change as she ushered him out the house and watched him walk up the front path. He looked disgruntled, shuffling along awkwardly carrying his rucksack over one shoulder. He gave the nosey neighbour Christine Hunt a polite wave as he walked past her and through the shadow of the towering silver birch tree. She was wearing oversized garden gloves and her bouncy grey hair looked like it was fresh out of rollers. Bright red lipstick had been applied to her thin lips and she was dressed in a summer frock and wax jacket.

Dressed for gossip thought Jodie. Christine Hunt probably had plans to stay out in the garden for most of the day. She was pruning her rose bushes, or at least pretending to prune them. It was something that only needed to be done once a year once the climbers had been trained into a basic framework, but Christine liked an excuse to be out in her garden so that she could search out any frivolities on Mottrom Road.

"Good morning Christine," called Jodie politely. Masking the fact that she disliked her nosey neighbour.

"Morning dear," replied Christine with a joyful wave.

There was not an argument, incident or event that Christine Hunt was not aware of. She was notorious with the locals for being a scandalmonger. Jodie shut the door quickly. There was plenty of time to confront Christine about pruning her silver birch and she was not about to do it in her dressing gown. Right now Jodie needed a drink to calm her nerves. Without hesitation she walked through to the dining room to where the drinks cabinet is kept, poured herself a double vodka and drank the liquid fast. *Just one more,* she said to herself quickly pouring another double measure. She walked out of the dining room, through the French doors at the back of the house which lead out onto a beautifully dressed veranda. It was a cool morning with clearing blue sky and the sun was already blazing, bringing promise to the day. Wisteria climbed the walls like floating clouds of white flowers and Myrtle trees said to represent the emblem of love stood in terracotta pots. Elder flowers heralding the start of summer blossomed in the dense shade of the veranda. Jodie took a deep breath filling her lungs with the delicious smell from the sprays of hundreds of tiny white flowers and drained her glass. She felt the calmness sweep through her body and a rosy glow dashed her cheeks. Now Jodie felt ready to face the day ahead.

CHAPTER TWO

The Bully

The school bus driver had already pulled up on the corner of Mottrom Road. There was the usual bustle of traffic and impatient drivers trying to manoeuvre their vehicles around the bus into oncoming traffic, forcing cars onto the pavement and the senseless beeping of horns. CJ could see from the short distance three year seven students about to get on the bus, also dressed in the Kings High School navy blue trousers and white collar shirt with the logo of a lion's head wearing a crown. He hurried along the path past the last three houses with their beautifully kept gardens and vibrant green lawns. The cool breeze was refreshing to his skin and the fresh smell of grass was pleasing. He jumped on the bus and was greeted by the usual driver. He had a thick silver grey moustache and unkempt thin silvery shiny hair with a bald patch on his crown. He welcomed CJ with the usual friendly smile and nod. CJ quickly scanned the seats looking for his friends Kelly and Thomas. They lived at the other side of the Mottrom estate and although it's only a short distance away, the bus driver does a scheduled pick up on the corner of their street. Evidently today they were not on the bus. *Shit they're not here; they must've actually bunked off school* thought CJ as the bus jerkily pulled away causing him to stumble a little. A driver was beeping as he had tried to steer his car recklessly past the bus. CJ took his seat at the front, where he found comfort away from the school bully whom always occupied the back seat.

At Kings, the school bully was called Wayne Dear, but his name was not fitting of his character. He had only been at the school for a few months after joining Kings following the

Christmas holidays. It was rumoured that he had been excluded from his previous school for beating a boy so badly that he had to go to hospital. But that was just a rumour. The truth was that his dad had come into some inheritance and moved from a rough neighbourhood at the centre of town to the Mottrom estate. Wayne had confidently walked into the classroom on his first day, his head high in the air looking haughtily, not turning out like your average new kid in school. His arrogance was out of sorts with the way he was dressed, for although he wore the required uniform, he was so large that each and every button on his shirt could pop off at any moment and the sorely fitting navy blue cotton trousers hugged his thighs. His broad frame and height made him by far the biggest kid in year seven and possibly in year eight too. (*Besides the fat boy they called 'Cake' whose mum and dad own the local bakers. His real name was Paul Barrett, but everybody called him Cake and he was extremely popular with everyone in the school as very often he brought in doughnuts, danishes, and cream cakes that he would willingly share.*) Wayne's perfectly round shaped chubby face was spoilt with pimples and he had a dimple on his chin. His mid length hair was very dark and fell onto his face, parting like curtains to reveal his astonishingly dark brown eyes.

"I'd like you all to welcome Wayne Dear," announced Mrs Edmondson as she stood at the front of the classroom beside the new boy, looking shorter than usual. CJ observed the bedraggled spectacle before him and wondered how someone could look so disorderly yet wear a conceited expression. CJ's desk was at the front of the class in the middle of a line of three rows. He was sat next to Thomas who was busy rummaging through his rucksack looking for his timetable. CJ gave him a nudge with his elbow imploring him to look at the new kid. Thomas gave a snigger, hiding his face behind his timetable hoping to go unnoticed.

Mrs Edmondson was wearing one of her many long floral dresses that made her look like a fat fairy. Her thickly applied make-up became even more apparent as she lowered her head glancing over the top of her half-moon glasses. From CJ's position he could see smudges of blue eye shadow and her mascara was clumpy. Kelly, who was seated at the desk next to CJ, leaned over in his direction and whispered, "Weindeer?" in a questioning fashion, just audible enough for CJ and Thomas to hear. This triggered a memory of Kelly singing Rudolph the Red Nose Reindeer in the primary school Christmas play, which had been somewhat amusing to hear as she has the speech impediment rhotacism. Forgetting where he was for a moment CJ let out a loud uncontrollable laugh. It was infectious and set Kelly off into a fit of giggles, and Thomas sank back in his chair still attempting to hide behind his timesheet. Before long the whole classroom had erupted in complete fits of hysterics that could be heard in the neighbouring classrooms. Those who sat close by could faintly hear CJ muttering "Weindeer", holding his side with one hand and hammering on the desk with the other. Mrs Edmondson, whose glasses still rested on the end of her nose, glared at CJ with a stern disapproving look. Wiping tears from his eyes, CJ caught sight of his teacher's stare, and still chuckling to himself he realised he had earned himself a detention.

Wayne said nothing, but his conceited look had now changed to a cold hard stare filled with resentment and malice.

Gradually the classroom quietened down and Mrs Edmondson then spoke with equanimity.

"I expect my class to behave in an appropriate manner when we welcome a new student." She was addressing the entire class yet kept a fixed eye on CJ and continued. "I have no idea what you find that is so amusing and I suggest that you bring your manners to school. Any more of this carrying on and you will all be facing detention. Is that understood?" There was the occasional whisper and muffled snigger and then the room fell silent again. Mrs Edmondson pointed to an empty desk toward the back of the room and asked Wayne to take a seat.

She had no choice but to put CJ and Kelly in detention. She knew very well why they were so amused at the name of the new boy, but as she had told them, "You need to have more self-control, I expect better from you both."

Wayne took an instant dislike to CJ and his decision to teach him a lesson was the start of an ongoing spell of bullying. Two days later during morning registration Mrs Edmondson asked for a volunteer to help take down the Christmas decorations. Anyone who knew that you got to take home any chocolates and candy that had been left on the tree put their hand up.

"I will Miss." CJ raised his hand in the air. He would miss the school bus, but he didn't mind the walk home.

"Thank you volunteers," said Mrs Edmondson giving CJ an acknowledging smile. "CJ you can stay behind and help with the decorations. I will contact your mother and let her know that you will be late home today."

A big sigh of disappointment was made by the other volunteers. Wayne was not disappointed. Far from it. This was an opportunity he was not going to miss. Even if it meant that he also would miss the bus home.

CJ walked out the school gates on that cold winter day with a big smile on his face and pockets full of chocolate coins and candy sticks. There was crisp snow in the ground that crunched beneath his shoes upon each step and there was an icy chill in the air. He shoved three chocolate coins into his mouth, pulled his woolly hat over his ears and put his hands in his fur lined parker pockets and started the walk home. His rucksack thrown loosely over his shoulder. His head down watching his freshly made footprints in the snow and his breath threw out a misty cloud. He didn't see it coming until it was too late. Wayne had been waiting patiently round the back of the school where the boiler room fan threw out a constant supply of heat through the air vents. A perfect view was had through the warped and slightly parted fence panels that stretched past the school entrance. As soon as he spotted CJ walking out of the school grounds he made his way through the car park and climbed over the wall to meet CJ coming down the alley.

"Hey CJ, you slimey little maggot!" shouted Wayne in a menacing tone. He was standing in front of CJ now. He had crept up like a dark shadow. The crisp coldness in the air did not seem to bother him. Without hesitation he took a full swing and punched CJ hard in the face. CJ winced in pain as he took the unexpected blow on his nose. He could taste the blood that had trickled down his face.

"What the fuck is wrong with you?" screeched CJ completely stunned. He touched his face. His fingers were wet with blood.

"You think you can take the piss out of me do you, maggot?" hollered Wayne giving CJ an almighty shove that sent him staggering backwards. "You better watch your back CJ. I'm telling you there's more where that came from."

CJ had lost his footing on the icy ground and was lying on the floor. His hip caught his fall with a thud. He then felt the force of Wayne's hard boot in his back.

"Aaaahh!! You're` fucking mad Wayne. What the hell have I done to you?" A sharp pain surged through his ribs. Drops of blood from his nose splattered scarlet on the hard snow. CJ was anticipating another hefty boot from Wayne's size eight kickers when he suddenly heard the sound of voices. A couple was walking through the alley towards the school. Their voices were a saviour. CJ looked up. His heavy breaths pouring out steam into the bitter wintry air. Wayne's apprehension was warmly felt.

But before Wayne made his swift exit he bent over CJ and said, "No one laughs at me gets away with it. You hear me CJ?"

He grabbed a handful of chocolates that had fallen out of CJ's coat pocket during the scuffle and took off.

Six months had passed since this incident. Wayne was sat at the back of the bus along with his two equally unruly sidekicks. Wayne had befriended the Haywood twins, whom were as rough around the edges as he was. The three boys had become known as the 'Nomads'. So called after a geography lesson on nomadic people. Their under developed minds had liked the idea that they were hunter gatherers moving from place to place. Hunting down vulnerable year seven students and gathering all their lunch money.

Today CJ was sat on his own. Kelly and Thomas had decided to play truant and go to the woods at Squirrel Hill. Although, bunking off school was completely out of character for both Kelly and Thomas alike. They were typically model students from a loving home and CJ was taken aback when the two of them had yesterday suggested skipping school.

"Come with us," Thomas and Kelly had pleaded, but CJ worried more about what his dad would say if he got caught than having his lunch money taken from him by the Nomads. He didn't think they would actually do it. As CJ sat staring out of the window his mind drifted and he began thinking about his mum. The view from the bus window was obscured by dirty water marks, but the memory of coming home from school on that cold winters day with a bloody nose and bruised back, was as clear as the brilliant blue sky above.

"I fell on the ice," he told his mum. It was a plausible explanation. His trousers were wet from lying on the snow and he did actually slip on the ice, with a little help from Wayne. Even at the age of thirteen, CJ had learnt that he needed to protect his mum from needless worrying. He could handle the abuse from Wayne and his two sidekicks as long as his mum was not worrying about him. She had enough to deal with from his dad.

CJ heard his name mentioned in conversation from the back seats. A sudden reality check and his focus was now how to avoid Wayne for yet another day which would make it a record two weeks since school reopened after the half term break. But today was going to be different. He was without his best friends Kelly and Thomas. He checked his watch. Eight twenty-six. The bus pulled into the school car park and CJ was already standing up, rucksack thrown over his shoulder, ready to jump off. There was a loud shuffling of feet behind him as the other students started making their way out of their seats, and the usual foul smell of diesel that always irritates CJ just as he's getting off the bus. The engine rumbled harshly, there was a shushing sound and the doors were open. As quick as he could CJ made his way through the school doors, down the corridor towards his form room and into the classroom where he was met by Mrs Edmondson, sat, as usual, behind her desk, a large mug of tea in one hand, glasses resting on the tip of her nose, reading *The Guardian*. And CJ knew that he was safe. For now.

CHAPTER THREE

The Best Friends

The brilliant sunshine bounced off the shiny metallic blue paint of the S Type Jaguar as it screeched round the bend. The road ahead stretched out for several miles before merging with Woodbank Road. The driver accelerated with a rush of adrenaline breaking the stillness of the road with the solitary sound of the car's engine. A fair distance away two friends were hiding in the peace and serenity of the woods.

Kelly was very petite for her age. Soft light brown hair bounced on her shoulders and her pale skin warming in the sun made her blue eyes look vibrant and alive. The oversized school uniform made her look skinnier than she really was. Despite her small frame she was very fit and full of energy. She loved playing in the woods and the excitement of today fuelled the teenagers with even more vigour.

Thomas had bright red hair that he kept cropped very short. He had a cheery freckled face and a joyful personality to match. He too was small for his age, but only in height. He was quite plump and not at all fit like Kelly. This very disposition was the reason he too was singled out at school and was the subject of bullying by the infamous Wayne Dear. Kelly had a problem pronouncing her Rs which unfortunately made her a target for Wayne too. Today though they had decided to meet round the corner of the bus stop, wait for the school bus to leave and then make their way through the wood, straight to the top of Squirrel Hill.

Squirrel Hill was set aside vast woodland, home to many grey squirrels. And at the top of the hill there was a small clearing in the thicket leading to an opening where sparse woodland mounted the area like a balding spot. Some of the land was privately owned and some was under conservation and was owned by the National Trust, but there was still a wealth of woodland besides to be explored. Mostly you would see people out walking their dogs or jogging along the various dirt paths, winding through the dense trees, which would all eventually bring you out onto Woodbank Road. And there you could continue along the road for a few miles before entering the Mottrom Estate.

It was now late morning and all the early morning joggers had been and gone, as had the dog walkers. Kelly and Thomas had taken the long walk to the hilltop in the coolness of the morning air. Fresh dew kissed the long blades of grass that stretched around the countless trees and the sun had yet to pour its warmth through the cluster of branches above them. The rustle of leaves could be heard all around as the squirrels scurried back and forth. When they finally reach the hilltop they rested at the foot of a large oak tree. A family of rabbits grazing out in the open on dandelion leaves were suddenly startled by them and darted into the thicket, their soft white tails twitching wildly as they disappeared out of sight. The two friends rested on Squirrel Hill for some time, until they were certain there was no one present in wood, who would no doubt want to know why they were not in school.

The teenagers left the hilltop and the scuttle of squirrels that had been darting around, and headed back into the cool shade of the wood. They sauntered down the hill to a dry dirt path towards Woodbank Road where the foxglove spread in abundance, their blooming purple flowers spiralling up out of their bed of leaves pointing toward the clear blue sky. The sun was finding strength now and broke through the gaps in the trees like a powerful torch, beaming down on the hard soil. The heat unearthed the beautiful essence of the newly blossoming flowers and fresh grass. They continued down the dirt track. They had long been conversing about what their parents might say if they were to find out they did not go to school. Both teenagers were academically very smart and had decided they would easily catch up with any work missed by reading CJ's notes. As luck would have it they were all in the same classes. The peacefulness and serenity of the wood was working its magic. Thoughts of relentless torment of the past six months of Kelly's speech impediment and the constant persecution of Thomas's fiery red hair were being obliterated from their minds. Today they would not have to endure any torment. The scents and smells had stirred their psyche into a beautiful place of calmness. They felt safe and happy and without the uneasiness they carry every time they get on the school bus and hear Wayne's voice calling them 'slimy maggots' from the back seat.

They continued to make their way towards Woodbank Road. There was a thicket at the other side of the road with narrow dirt paths that passed through the trees and brambles and eventually lead down to Alderley Brook. It was still a long walk, but they had unfound energy. The sounds of rustling leaves, twigs snapping beneath their feet and bird calls from high in the treetops all played their part making Thomas and Kelly feel relaxed but at the same time energised.

They laughed and joked about what they wanted to happen to Wayne as the approached the end of the track.

"Maybe his mum and dad could drive him round the safari park and open the window when they go through the lion enclosure."

"Hey Thomas that's so cwuel!" laughed Kelly.

"Or how about we put some laxatives in his drink when he's not looking? I bet my mum has a stack of supplies that she brings home from work. I could sneak some into my school bag and slip them into his drink when he's having lunch. We should definitely do that, for sure." Thomas spoke serious for a moment. Kelly turned to look at his round face and cute freckles and serious green eyes. All she could do was laugh some more.

"Why are you laughing Kelly, I'm serious," said Thomas, moving thin branches out of the way that obstructed their path.

"And how are you going to slip laxatives into his dwink without him noticing?" asked Kelly in amusement.

"I don't know ... but how cool would it be? Imagine how embarrassed he would be?" In unison they both said " ... shitting himself!" Then they fell about laughing.

"Then we'll see who's the slimy maggot," said Thomas.

"Oh I wish CJ was 'ere ... It would be such a laugh," said Kelly fervently.

"Yeah ... I know it's a shame. Wonder how he's getting on keeping away from Wayne."

The two friends pondered over CJ as they continued their walk. The pleasant bird calls sang high above their heads in the tree tops, a mild breeze wafted through the wood and the grey squirrels went about the business scampering up and down trees.

"We should do something back," said Thomas gravely. "Retaliate ... Humiliate him in front of the whole school." Thomas was feeling gutsy with all the talk about revenge.

"And how are we going to humiliate him?" asked Kelly.

"Oh I don't know. I did read somewhere that one time the teachers at a school made the school bully stand up in assembly and apologise to all the kids that he'd picked on. The kid was so humiliated that he never picked on anyone again."

"Yeah ... that's a nice story Thomas," said Kelly sarcastically, "but how are we going to get the teachers to make Wayne apologise to everyone?"

"I dunno," said Thomas shrugging his shoulders. "Just a thought."

"I like the idea of the laxatives. There's nothing more humiliating than sitting in a classroom full of people with poo running down your leg." They burst out laughing again and almost tripped over a stump of wood, momentarily losing their footing.

Kelly and Thomas were deep in thought of revenge on Wayne, feeling like they had been fed confidence from the tranquillity of the wood, day dreaming of a time when Wayne would become their victim. They felt adventurous and brave. *Were they really capable of outsmarting the school bully?* They wondered. They were certainly clever. Probably the two smartest students in their year. They were daring enough to bunk off school. That was something they had never done before. Could they draw some courage from today and keep it with them to carry out an even more daring task? Could they pull one over on Wayne? As they questioned themselves dreamily, they did not realise that they had stepped off from the safety of the muddy pathway and walked out onto the main road toward the opening in the thicket on the other side.

It was only a matter of seconds when the sound of the powerful engine came screeching upon them before they could make it across to the other side. They would not paddle in the stream at Alderley Brook today nor would they see the brook lampreys swimming on the soft sediment of the stream. Today their parents would not be cross with them for skipping school.

As their limp bodies lay in the road, the car sped off.

CHAPTER FOUR

A Chance Meeting

"Hiya Jodie." Kat's distinctive Manchester accent travelled the entire canteen floor. Jodie had spotted her standing beside a table at the far side of the entrance close to the concession stand. She was waving frantically expressing her surprise and excitement that Jodie had actually turned up. (Jodie often changes her mind at the last minute.)

The hospital canteen was as busy as ever. Jodie wondered how they were ever going to talk amongst all the noise. She zigzagged around the occupied tables and when she eventually reached Kat she was greeted with a friendly hug and kiss on the cheek. Dressed plainly in the unappealing navy blue nurses' uniform with her long dark hair pinned back in a high pony tail, Kat still looked remarkably stunning.

"I'm so sorry I'm late," said Jodie taking a seat. "I … erm … had to put the car through the car wash. Yer know… it was one of my chores for the day."

"Oh that's okay. No problem … I'm just glad you could make it. So how yer doing babe? It's good to see you," said Kat cheerfully.

"I'm good, yeah I'm okay," lied Jodie, trying to appear confident. The alcohol had given her cheeks a soft red glow and her hands had stopped shaking.

"So did you tell Jack you were meeting me?"

"Oh yes … I had to … I can't lie to him … He sees right through me. But he did say that I wasn't allowed to see you."

"He's a shit … what right as he got to tell you who you can and can't see. I mean for fuck's sake, it's not like you're having a bloody affair or anything." said Kat with a sorrowful expression.

The two friends were seated at a typically wobbly square table. On which was a worn out brown tray with two coffees served in small white porcelain cups and saucers. Sachets of brown sugar and mini cream cartons on the side and there were two large baguettes wrapped in white paper. Kat pushed a cup of coffee and a tuna baguette in front of Jodie.

"So Kat," began Jodie trying to brush off her husband's insistence that she should not see her friend, "sounded like you had something important to tell me."

"Oh my goodness Jodie, have I got some fantastic news for you? You are going to love this." Kat was beaming with enthusiasm. "The Senior Charge Nurse in the children's ward is looking for a mural artist to paint the ward for the kids. As soon as I heard, I said, d'you know, I know just the person. I told her all about you, how you used to paint those fantastic murals, about the one you did in that nursery ... with the giraffes and the canvases you used to paint."

Jodie had anticipated a reason for the meeting beyond the social aspect, but she had not been expecting this. She listened alertly above the chattering and noises around her. Sighing inwardly as Kat continued.

"We were thinking of maybe some sort of jungle theme. Lots of big bold bright animals. Something cheerful to make the kids feel better." Kat spoke quickly and excitedly making her typical hand movements and raising her finely plucked eyebrows. "What do you think? Please say yes. It will be a chance for you to get back to work ... earn some money and leave that arsehole of a husband."

"Jesus Kat. Really? Ahh I dunno." said Jodie smiling ruefully. Kat could read the concern and apprehension in the depth of her eyes. They were swimming with sadness. Although Jodie had not painted for many years the burning passion to pick up a paint brush was as much alive as the sun's solar flares. She had been forced to give up painting by Jack. One of the many sacrifices she had made for him in his neediness for control. He liked to use the word 'guarded' but his intentions were always to control. She fell into silent thought.

"Jodie you would be perfect. I know how good you are. I've seen your work. You are wasted sitting around in that big fancy house of yours. And you can't kid me, I know you miss painting. It's not right that you can't do what you want. You have a life too you know." Jodie was looking directly at Kat as she spoke with pleading eyes. There was a compliment in her statement, however Jodie felt slightly offended.

"You can work while CJ's at school. Jack doesn't even have to know."

"I don't know Kat ..." said Jodie after finishing chewing a bite from her baguette. She needed much more reassurance and persuasion from her best friend than what had been freely given. "What if Jack was to find out? It's taken me all my guts to come here today and meet you. My life wouldn't be worth living if he was to find out I was working."

"All the more reason for you to work. It's the only way you're ever gonna be able to leave him. And anyway that's why he doesn't want you to work. He knows that he might lose you. Honestly Jodie, I don't understand why you ever married him."

"Yeah well ...believe me I've been asking myself that very same question."

"Does he still burn you with the teaspoon?" asked Kat.

"You mean after he stirred a hot cup of tea? ... no ... I can't remember the last time he made me a cup of tea. But he still hits me on the knee with the TV remote ... He thinks it's really funny if he hits my reflex." Jodie knew where this was leading.

"What about the underwear thing? Does he still go mental if your underwear doesn't match?"

"Absolutely. He hates that," said Jodie, remembering all the unpleasant times she had encountered. The list of extremities to Jack's personality was endless and Jodie didn't want to dwell on them. She knew that Kat had brought up the subject of Jack's strange and mean traits to sway her decision.

Her heart knocked as fear of deceiving her husband had her in a tight grip.

"Does he still ... "

"I don't want to talk about Jack," Jodie interrupted. "You know what he's like. I've told you enough times," she said soberly.

"So work ... earn some money and leave him. This is a great opportunity for you. You are the best Jodie and I'm not just saying that because you're my best mate. I have never known or seen anyone who can paint as good as you. Seriously. You will be mad to turn this offer down. And how will he find out? Who's going to tell him? Eh?" Kat spoke so matter of factly, she made it sound so easy.

Jodie intuitively wanted to say yes but inside she was twitching violently. She breathed in with the hopelessness of a drowning woman. She felt her husband's invisible hands holding her down. A grasp that even Houdini would find it hard to break free from.

"At least come over to the children's ward with me and have a look!" Kat leaned forward put her hand on Jodie's knee to wheedle her some more. "I'm not due back on the Ward for a couple of hours and if there's an emergency I'll get paged."

"Alright, I'll come see the children's ward, but I'm not promising anything."

They finished their lunch, casually chatted, avoiding discussing Jodie's marital misery. Jodie was grateful she had some food inside her shrunken stomach to soak up the alcohol. She had become an expert in hiding her secret obsession to drink. She would never admit it to herself, but Jodie was alcohol dependent. Her good looks and figure also helped hide the drinking. She still had her youthful complexion and although age was starting to show around her eyes, trips to Harley Street surgery for Botox injections kept the years off. She was blessed with beautiful olive skin and only had to put on a small amount of makeup to highlight her bone structure to look eye-catching. Today she had spent sometime after drinking the vodka to apply a little make up and style her long auburn hair and had chosen a modest long tunic dress with strappy sandals and a cashmere cardigan.

Jodie found herself following Kat through the never ending white washed corridors away from the noise and chaos of the hospital cafeteria. The voices in the canteen rattled in her head. Merging from all directions into one heavy echoing sound. It was becoming too much for Jodie, but as they distanced themselves from the vocal sounds Jodie welcomed the cold, white, clinical feel of the hospital corridors. They walked through large weightless two way double doors that looked heavy yet swung open with ease. Then through a second set of doors, up two flights of stairs and finally they entered the children's ward.

"And here we are, this is my ward. These children are in recovery. There is another ward for the terminally ill patients but thankfully I get to look after these wonderful bunch."

Moving through the ward Jodie observed the patients. They were of all ages. Young ones were sat up in their beds playing with games and toys. Some of the older children were reading magazines and books. Despite the smell of illness and the slight fumes of urine, the children were smiling. And those that were not shy shouted a polite, "Hello nurse Katrina." The hospital radio was broadcasting well wishes to those who were well enough to go home. . Jodie's intention had been only to look. To indulge her friend's enthusiasm. However she could not have been more surprised. The close personal connections in the ward appeared to suck her in and take a hold of her humility. Some of the privacy curtains had been pulled around the beds. She wondered if these children were asleep or just shy or maybe the nurses were sat with them. The drawn curtains hung loosely with bold colourful pictures; elephants, zebras, giraffes and lions. Jodie assumed this was the reason Kat had suggested the jungle theme painting on the walls. Distracted from her fears she absentmindedly began picturing a Noah's Ark theme, a continuous display of animals filling the void. Images of animals walking in two by twos stretching from end to end and at the far side toward the nurses' desk there was space, a blank canvass large enough to paint the ark.

Her mind continued to wonder further as she reflected on a scenery full of trees which would give the feel of being in the heart of the jungle. A wilderness filled with different animals and birds. And a waterhole with hippos, alligators and snakes.

"So now you've seen it, what do you think?" said Kat. Her big brown eyes gleaming as she sensed a spark of zeal.

Jodie quickly became aware of the implications of what she had been considering.

"I would love to say yes, but I have to consider CJ and Jack …"

Before Jodie had chance to finish her sentence Kat interrupted with a flair of conviction.

"Ah come on Jodie … What's there to consider? CJ is more than old enough to look after himself. You don't have to worry about doing school runs. And as for Jack, well he's never home. You could fly to the moon and back and he wouldn't have a clue. So long as when he comes home from work his dinner is on the table he's not gonna know anything … is he?"

Listening to Kat, regardless of truth, did not lessen the doubt in her mind. Something about it scared her. *What if she was seen by someone who knew her husband?* The pure fact she would be deceiving him gave her a cold chill of dread. Jack did not want Jodie to work. He had made that clear when CJ was born. 'A women's place is at home' he had told her. The thought of her interacting with people Jack didn't know would torment him incessantly. And to lie or go behind his back would bring about a punishment Jodie dared not even think about. It was this fear and this fear alone that gave realisation this was her chance. Kat was right. Jodie needed a way out. Her will to leave had to be stronger than the fear of remaining trapped in a marriage filled only with torment and suffering. *Could this work?* Jodie asked herself this question over and over.

"Come on let's go in the nurses' office and talk about it. We'll grab a coffee on the way. We're going up in the world. Did you know you can get mocha from vending machines now?"

"Sure. I would love a mocha," said Jodie and they walked to the new vending machine situated just outside the ward.

"Hey this is like a mini version of Starbucks," she said sarcastically. The machine was lit up, sandy in colour, a picture of a large white cup of creamy frothy coffee on the front, with a means to tempt the passing person. Bizarrely this image prompted Jodie to recall her dream. She remembered standing on the beach, a feeling of extreme heat and the overwhelming sensation of emptiness.

"I had the strangest dream last night," said Jodie completely out of the blue. She did not mention it had been a reoccurring dream. She took the hot drink from the cup holder of the machine and watched Kat punch in the numbers for another mocha.

"Go on," replied Kat, always interested in Jodie's weird and wonderful dreams. It was an interest they had both shared since high school. A fascination that had lead them to predict the meanings of many dreams, and nightmares. Jodie proceeded to explain her dream. Even adding the part of waking up next to Jack snoring and stinking of tobacco.

"You know, you can spare me the details of what Jack looks like in the morning," laughed Kat.

From behind them came an amusing chuckle. Neither had noticed the police officer standing a few feet away but still within earshot of Jodie's story. He was unable to place the sound of her soft accent but never the less it was pleasing to the ear. He couldn't help admiring her alluring swelled breast pushed up against her dress and her cleavage just modestly hidden beneath a low buttoned up cardigan.

"Sorry girls, I'd just like to get some coffee if you don't mind?" said Matt Campbell with a cheeky grin. Almost reaching six foot tall with short dark hair, dressed favourably in uniform, he portrayed the classic case of a 'tall dark and handsome man'.

"Afternoon officer. Are you here on business or visiting?" asked Kat in her usual polite and nosey manner, stepping to the side to give him some room.

"Unfortunately ... " Matt Campbell quickly observed Kat's name badge. "Nurse Katrina, I'm on duty ..." He rummaged around in his uniform trouser pocket and pulled out some loose change. As he fingered through the change looking for the right money to feed into the vending machine, standing very leisurely and looking incredibly relaxed, he continued conversing. "Looks like a hit and run on the Woodbank stretch of road out by the woods at Squirrel Hill. Two kids got hit. Ambulance brought them in about an hour ago. I have the unfortunate job of notifying their parents. I'm Inspector Campbell but as you are a nurse here you can call me ... Inspector Campbell." He let out a snort and glanced at Jodie expecting a reaction. He was certain he caught a smile, although she did not look up at him. Instead she sipped her coffee allowing Kat to talk to the policeman in her familiar composed way.

"My God, two kids. And do you know what happened? Are they okay? Do you know who did it?" Although Kat thought Inspector Campbell was amusing, she spoke very seriously. It was her job to look after sick and injured children and she couldn't help but feel concerned.

"It's shocking," replied Inspector Campbell. "Poor kids had been skipping school. They are both unconscious and in a critical condition." He spoke softly but with a firm tone that you would expect from a policeman.

Kat had been working on the children's ward for seven years and she was familiar with hit and runs, although this did not happen often, but for two kids to be hit was something that she had never experienced before.

"Can you tell us their names?" she asked.

"Sorry nurse, we are still trying to identify them." Inspector Campbell picked up his coffee and pointed down the corridor towards the theatre room where he imagined the small fragile teenagers were being treated.

"Now I don't know where you're heading after this ..." Inspector Campbell was now addressing Jodie, "but Woodbank Road has been closed. The police are treating it as a crime scene."

Jodie could sense Inspector Campbell's advances on her like an invisible force. His intrusion on her body with his admiring eyes and nervous laugh made her feel complimented without the need for words. Kat could see the attraction a mile off as she watched the policeman desperately trying to make eye contact with this beautiful woman.

"This is my friend Jodie. She's an artist," she said.

Officer Campbell held the hot coffee in his left hand so that he could hold out his right hand to make a polite introduction to Jodie. He could feel the heat of the coffee coming through the polystyrene cup.

"Pleased to meet you Josie," he said at last looking into her eyes and thinking how fantastically beautiful she was.

Jodie looked up into Matt Campbell's eyes as she gently shook his hand.

"It's Jodie, my name is Jodie not Josie." The moment felt paused as she took the time to really appreciate how incredibly handsome this man was. She could not help her credulous grin, surprising herself at how comfortable she felt meeting a complete stranger and feeling completely at ease. Normally a very shy and nervous person around people she did not know, Jodie was poised and relaxed. Of course she had drunk an awful lot of alcohol which helped with the calmness.

She was accustomed to men's admiring stares. That she didn't mind so much. The lecherous intent looks she had learned to ignore. The watchful gaze from officer Campbell however made her feel different. She had been inviting him to look without realising she was even doing it. She was now looking hard into his eyes. Drinking him in to her mind.

As an artist she could see deeper than most people. She could naturally observe fine details and she was liking observing the fine details of Inspector Campbell. He had a slight suntan which had brought out faint freckles around the bridge of his nose. She noted that he had shaven in a hurry as tiny bits of stubble was left unshaven around the side of his jaw line and there was a slight nip above his lip where he had caught himself with his razor. His hair was gelled so that the short stands stood upright and cushioned some very expensive

Ray Ban sunglasses. She could not decide if his eyes were green or brown. The two colours seemed to mix in a fantastically unusual way. He had light wrinkles around his eyes and forehead. Jodie placed his age in his early thirties. *Probably around the same age as me* she thought. He was smiling at her showing immaculate teeth. Perfectly straight and white.

Inspector Campbell said, "You can call me Matt."

Releasing her hand he quickly changed the hot coffee into his other hand. He had been feeling the heat penetrating through the cup and scolding his fingers.

"Ouch, that coffee's hot," he said shaking his hand as though it would help.

This time he did get a reaction from Jodie. She laughed in amusement at Matt's discomfort. He liked her laugh. She had a wonderful smile and at that very moment they both had the strangest feeling they would see each other again.

"And you already know my name, but my friends call me Kat."

"Pleased to meet you Kat," said Inspector Campbell quickly shaking Kat's hand.

Suddenly the police radio that had been silently sat in its holder on Matt's uniform belt came to life. It made a high pitch crackling sound and then a voice came through.

"Matt, do you read me?" Both Jodie and Kat respectfully watched as Matt retrieved his radio and quickly responded.

"Hi Carl I read you."

"I have an ID on the two kids. The school has confirmed two children absent that fit their description."

Matt graciously excused himself from Kat and Jodie.

"Okay Carl go ahead."

They reciprocated with an understanding nod and wave and headed off to the nurses' office. They were just out of ear shot when the reply came through on the radio.

"Kelly Jones and Thomas Bradshaw."

CHAPTER FIVE

An Unfortunate Accident

The school bell signalling lunch break seemed to ring louder today than usual. CJ was keeping his wits about him as he was feeling incredibly vulnerable without Kelly and Thomas. He had spent the morning concentrating on avoiding the Nomads and so far he had managed it. Other than the form room where registration was taken, CJ and the Nomads were not in any lessons together. CJ, along with Kelly and Thomas were in top sets, whereas the Nomads with their brains the size of a pea, resided in the bottom sets.

CJ's tactics for getting from his form room to his first lesson was to simply leave the form room ahead of Wayne and keep close to any senior student or teacher he could find. Because he sat at the front of the room and Wayne and his sidekicks sat at the back, this plan of action was not too difficult. He was always the first to slip out the classroom ahead of Wayne, but lunchtime proved harder to escape the Nomads.

It was during the spring break when the three friends had been plotting how they were going to dodge the lunchtime bullying when Thomas came up with a plan. He had suggested they sneak back into their classroom and hide out. This seemed like a good idea until they realised that the classrooms were locked up during break. After much discussion it was eventually decided that they could climb through a window, so long as they remembered to release the window latch, which would enable the window to be opened from the outside. Recently they had spent several lunchtimes sat on the floor of many a classroom, eating their lunch and whispering their conversations, giggling amongst themselves and feeling triumphant. By trial and error their plan only worked with the classrooms that were located away from the canteen area and the playground. And situated on the ground floor of the building, so that they could slip in through the window unseen. Ideally it needed to be the last room they used right before lunch, as they found out to their annoyance; windows they unlatched had later become locked again.

Spanish lesson was now over and CJ deliberately packed up his books slowly and spent time sorting out his stationery until, besides Miss Mendes he was the only one in the classroom. Miss Mendes, the Spanish teacher disappeared in the stationery cupboard, as she did after every lesson, so that she could store away the Spanish dictionaries. CJ took his opportunity to swiftly lift the latch on the window so that it could be opened from the outside just as Kelly had done the week before. The room was on the ground floor overlooking the playing fields at the back of the school grounds. It was an ideal classroom to hide in.

CJ knew Wayne would head straight for the canteen with a quest to be the first in the dinner queue. And if he didn't make the front of the line, he would certainly try pushing his way to the front. CJ left the classroom feeling forlorn. He was missing his friends' company and the feeling suddenly became stronger now that he was hiding out on his own. He paused and took a moment to glance down the hallway that echoed the sound of shuffling feet and chattering. The hallway was gradually emptying as students meandered along mostly in the direction of the canteen. CJ needed to walk to the end of the hall past the corridor leading to the canteen and out through the main double doors. He hated himself for having to sneak around the school like a frightened mouse. His father would be ashamed to have a son who would not stand up to bullies. He took a deep breath and proceeded down the corridor, past the GCSE artwork that colourfully decorated the otherwise dull magnolia painted walls and prayed for the day when Wayne could move on from his first day at Kings when CJ had uncontrollably laughed at his name.

Besides a small group of students skulking around outside their class room, the hallway was almost deserted now. CJ looked back and gave a smug smile as he caught the sight of Miss Mendes locking the door and walk in the opposite direction toward the staff room.

'*Me has ayudado mucho*'

He had a fleeting look in the direction of the canteen as he passed by. It was overcrowded but CJ could still spot Wayne and the Haywoods, Tweedle Dum and Tweedle Dumber, sat at their usual table busily gorging on burgers and chips. Even though he was feeling sure of himself he felt a sudden pang in his chest. A reminder that the indignant Wayne was still around and the harm and damage he and his two sidekicks could cause was real and frightening.

'*que estupendo*'

CJ hurried out of the doors away from the strange aroma of poster paint and chip fat and round the corner of the building where the playing fields on his left were quiet but for a handful of seniors kicking a football around and a group of giggling girls watching admiringly. CJ took a deep breath, anticipating his triumph. The cool smell of grass was refreshing. He sauntered casually unseen, past the classroom windows sporadically peering into each one until he reached the Spanish room.

'*te encontre*'

He pushed the unlocked window. It was a little stiff at first. CJ gave a heavy upward push and was thankful when it opened. He took a momentary look around to check that he was not being watched.

'*si facil*'

Satisfied it was safe he awkwardly attempted to bundle his school bag through the window. It took all his effort to push the heavy bag through the gap. The weight of the books and stationery made a thud as it hit the tiled floor. Putting his hands on the sill he lifted himself up. Arms straight holding his weight and keeping his balance he lifted his right knee up to the sill and ineptly found a foot hold. Still balancing rather clumsily, he got his right leg through the window and was able to shift his balance to edge himself in, his foot a little away from the floor. *"Yes I'm in,"* he muttered. Then he tried dragging his left leg through,... *"Ouch! What was that?"* Something was ripping into his skin on the inside of his thigh. All his weight was now on his right side allowing him only to move forward, but the pain was excruciating. He wanted to scream out loud. Biting his lip hard he momentarily somehow managed to prevent himself. He felt his skin rip like a slash from a sharp knife. A cold dread gripped his heart. He lost his balance trying to grab hold of his leg and finally let out an uncontrollable scream as he fell, landing hard on his shoulder. The window slammed shut with a clatter.

The pain that he felt in his shoulder hurt badly but the pain in his leg was far worse. He was laying on the floor next to his crumpled school bag his hand clutching his thigh as though the tighter he held it the less painful it would be. Water began to flood his eyes as the sting in his leg intensified. Blood trickled through his fingers as he lay on the floor in agony. *"What just happened?"* he asked himself. He had to look at his leg. He needed to know what damage he had done. He sat himself up. His shoulder still throbbing, but that was not what he was concerned about. He peered down in between his legs. His school trousers were torn and blood damp. He had a deep gash and desperately needed help. Grabbing his school bag he rummaged inside anxious to put his hands on his mobile phone.

"Where are you? Damn! Where are you phone?" He fumbled frantically feeling for the smooth flat shape of his mobile. Finally in desperation, emptied all the contents of his back pack on the floor. Quickly he found his phone, picking it up he was just about to dial his mum when he suddenly asked himself, *"What am I doing? How can I explain to my mum why I am hiding out in a locked classroom?"* He needed to think fast and come up with a story. His head blurry, engaging only with pain, he battled with himself straining to think straight.

"Okay I don't have to tell Mum that I climbed through the window of a locked classroom. She just needs to know that I'm hurt. But she will want to know exactly what happened. Maybe

I could call the staff room and have Miss Mendes come and unlock the door. Maybe she will feel sorry for me and won't be mad that I sneaked back into class. She is a nice teacher. She likes me. It's better than my mum finding out why I was trying to hide. Or worse still ... my dad." As CJ talked himself into a course of action he tied his PE shirt around his leg in an attempt to stop the bleeding, grimacing under the agony as he tightened the fabric to apply pressure. Then with an unsteady hand punched in the phone number of his school.

"Kings High School, good afternoon, how can I help you?" The polite telephone voice of the school receptionist suddenly panicked CJ, as the reality of what was happening was starting to sink in.

"Er erm please can I speak with Miss Mendes?" said CJ managing to keep a calm voice.

"I'll just see if she is available. Whom shall I say is calling?"

CJ suddenly had an attack of nerves and immediately killed the call. *"Shit! Shit! What am I doing?"* The pain sensation in his leg was like a burning sting, his shoulder was throbbing hard and his head was spinning in a mad fuzzy whirl. *"I have no choice,"* he told himself. *"I'll have to phone Mum."* Still holding his phone in his right hand, he pressed hard on his wound with his left hand, wincing under the sheer pain. Pulling himself together he gathered up the courage he needed to phone his mum.

As the phone starting ringing his heart began pounding even harder. For a moment he felt like he was going to pass out. He realised he was sweating hard and besides the pain from his wound, his body was now aching from sitting on the hard floor of the classroom. He stared around the room, observing the pictures of the Spanish coastline and the bull fighter and the flamenco dancers. Keeping his focus. Aware that his light headedness was a sign that he might blackout. This time he was not going to hang up.

"Hi honey, is everything okay?" Jodie very rarely received a phone call from CJ during school. And usually when she did it was because he had forgotten homework or his PE kit. CJ felt immediate comfort in hearing his mum's voice. He wanted to scream out down the phone. His palm was sweaty as he held the mobile and the piercing sun was burning through the windows. He couldn't think clearly and wanted desperately to give his mum a believable explanation to what had happened. But instead, in his panicked and wounded state he began rambling in a choked up voice uncontrollably down the phone.

"Mum, I'm in pain. I need you to come and get me from school. I'm locked in the classroom and my leg is cut really badly. And I've also damaged my shoulder. I don't want to move. I can't stand up, it hurts. Mum are you there? Mum? Mum?" CJ held the phone out in front of him, staring down at the display only to find, to his complete horror and disbelief, the call had ended.

"No please no!" CJ wasn't sure how much of the call his mother had heard before the signal was lost. He paused for a moment trying to hold back the tears. *"How the hell did I get myself into this mess? What an idiot?"* The blood from his leg was started to seep through his PE shirt and his hand was covered in blood. He tried to pull himself off of the floor and onto a chair. He wanted to move out of the direct sunlight. But it was impossible to move without the pain in his leg worsening and even putting pressure on his shoulder caused agony. It would be another half an hour at least before Miss Mendes would be back in the classroom and CJ had no idea what she would think when she finds him. All of a sudden a voice spoke through the open window.

"Are you okay in there?"

He looked up with burning eyes. A senior was peering curiously through the window. CJ had been more vocal than he realised in is moments of pain and frustration and an older girl had heard his moans as she strolled past the classroom. Holly's efforts to push the window open had gone unnoticed by CJ as he sat pitifully on the floor fraught by his fruitless victory. Not really knowing what to say, and clearly he was looking like someone who was in a lot of pain and in need of assistance, he managed only a blunt reply.

"No, no I'm not okay." CJ lifted his arm to wipe the sweat and tears from his grimacing face. Holly caught sight of his bloodstained hand. She stood on her tip toes and stretched through the window to get a better look. As she gazed down she saw the PE shirt wrapped around CJ's leg tinged with crimson red that she knew to be blood.

"Oh my God, what the hell happened to you?" But before CJ had chance to answer Holly, she hastily added, "Stay there, I'm gonna go get some help." And as quickly as she had appeared she was gone.

"Of course I'll stay here, I can't go anywhere," said CJ managing a smile of relief.

CHAPTER SIX

Mum's the Word

The nurses' office was a small cluttered room chaotically furnished. Venetian blinds hung scrappily at the window and beneath, a tattered wooden desk stood facing the doorway. Behind the desk was an uncomfortable looking weathered chair. A filing cabinet almost touching the ceiling stood in one corner of the room and on the other side there were piles of papers and folders neatly stacked upon a long unit with three cupboards. Shelves filled most of the remaining wall space, hoarding an array of grey box files and medical books. The sad looking spider plant on the sill brought little cheer to the room.

"My boss is on the ward at the moment. She said it was okay for me to use her office," said Kat as they entered the room, still every bit as enthusiastic. "I told her all about you and she knows that you are visiting me today." Kat had not lost the excitement of the prospect of her best friend working at the hospital, despite just learning of the hit and run. She spoke with zest as she pulled out the two worn out terracotta chairs that were tucked in front of the desk. They took up the little remaining space that was left in the room.

"Sit down hun," she said. "After meeting that tasty police inspector I think you need to rest."

The cheerless shadows in the room made Jodie feel gloomy and she could sense the effects of the alcohol wearing off. Although the surge of the warm gooey feeling she had got from Matt did not ebb.

"Well if that's the sort of guy you meet in a place like this, how can I refuse?" She said wittily, taking to sitting down begrudgingly on the threadbare fabric of the chair. But no sooner had she sat down when her mobile rang.

"Oh it's CJ. I'm sorry Kat I need to take this. Hiya honey is everything okay? Honey I can't hear you, it's a bad line, can you hear me ... CJ?" Glancing at the display Jodie realised her battery had died.

"Oh great ... my battery's dead," said Jodie in an erratic tone, still eyeing her phone wanting it to spring back to life.

"Something happened at school?" Kat asked. Her big brown eyes lighting up with concern."

"Yeah but ... I don't know what ... I got cut off. All I heard was something about being in pain and wanting me to come get him. I'm sorry Kat we're gonna have to do this another time. Can I think about the job and let you know?" Kat looked like a child that had just been told she couldn't have a puppy.

"You can use my phone to call him back?"

Jodie realised this would be sensible, but she found the room depressing and was glad of an excuse to leave. As well as feeling the effects of her liquid breakfast wearing off.

"No ... it's okay thanks ... I'll put my phone on charge in the car and call on hands free. I just need to get going," replied Jodie as she hung her bag over her shoulder and gripped onto the leather strap with both hands hoping Kat would not notice them start to shake.

Kat's puppy dog eyes could not hide the disappointment of Jodie leaving.

"I would love to say yes," continued Jodie as the two friends left the room and headed back down to the main entrance, "but I need to think about it."

Still relentless in her efforts, Kat made attempts to talk her friend round as she escorted Jodie out of the hospital. But nothing she could say would make Jodie feel less scared of her husband. They reached the car park and quickly said their goodbyes.

"Let me know what's up with CJ," shouted Kat, remembering the reason why Jodie had to rush off so suddenly.

"Sure, will do. And let me think about the job. I'll phone you later." Jodie hollered back as she hurried to her car.

Jodie knew she had to get to the school quickly, but as she climbed into the driver seat of her shiny blue S Type Jaguar her mind was now plagued with dark thoughts and she had to pull herself together quickly if she was going to be able to concentrate on driving. Another panic attack was starting. The usual signs, hands shaking, the nervous rash and those awful chest pains. She reached into the cooler compartment in between the front seats and pulled out what looked like an innocent bottle of orange juice. She drank quickly to calm her nerves. The shaking stopped but the vodka and orange could not eliminate the horrid thoughts. Her head was swamped and confused. *Job offer, police inspector, CJ hurt and worst of all two innocent children victims of a hit and run were laying in hospital beds in a coma. Still have the dreaded Christine Hunt to face. And what does Jack have in store for me when he gets home?*

"Come on girl pull yourself together, you need to go and fetch CJ." Jodie's gentle self-persuasion fuelled with more alcohol coaxed her into action. She plugged her phone in to the charger, waited a few seconds for the mobile to come to life then called CJ. The call was diverted to his answer phone. Confused and troubled she still had to drive to the school. At this moment she knew it was the most important thing. *Just drive nice and slow girl and take it easy on the bends.*

~~~~~~~~~~

Several minutes after Holly had appeared at the window, CJ heard the echoing sound of voices and the key turning in the lock. The classroom door swung open. Miss Mendes, Holly and Miss Hettrick the school nurse hurried in. Their presence alone gave short term pain relief, but he could not escape from the shame. Nurse Hettrick carried with her a small plastic green case. Immediately she rushed to kneel down beside CJ, whose face had now become white and pasty. The only redness now was not from hotness and embarrassment but the dried blood which made him look even more pitiful. The nurse was a pretty lady with a friendly smile and her aura oozed reassurance.

"My goodness you've got yourself a nice little wound there." The nurse very gently removed the blood soaked shirt to take a closer look at the injury. The tear in his navy blue trousers exposed a deep flesh wound that was bleeding heavily.

"Oh dear ... oh dear ... yes ... I see," said Nurse Hettrick as she inspecting the damage. "You're going to need some stitches young man. Yep, trip to Macclesfield General for you laddie." Nurse Hettrick gave a charmed smile as she opened her first aid box and took out a pair of scissors. She then swiftly cut the trouser fabric so she could attend to the wound. First she cleaned the wound with a disinfectant wipe which made CJ cry out in pain, then she applied some tape to close the cut and finally wrapped a tight bandage around his leg. CJ watched dejectedly as he was patched up, wincing in pain the whole time but said nothing during the whole episode.

"We need to get this young man into the med. office and contact his parents. And then we'll have a little chat about how this happened," said Nurse Hettrick, addressing the Spanish teacher, whom had walked over to the window to close it, and had noticed part of the sill was coming away from the window. A rusty nail was exposed, protruding nastily from the sill, telling signs of exactly how CJ had come about his injury. Holly had stood over CJ watching the nurse in fascinated horror with a cursed look on her face.

"There you go laddie ... all done." Nurse Hettrick smiled sweetly. Miss Mendes was not looking so sweet. Her ominous smile gestured that his ordeal was far from over.

Thirty minutes later Jodie was outside the schools med. office after being met at the reception by Miss Hettrick. She had learnt from the phone call she'd received on route to the school that CJ had a deep cut on his leg and would need stitches and also required a tetanus injection. A very peaky and sorrowful looking boy sat in a wheelchair in the medical room, half a trouser leg missing where the nurse had cut it so she could dress the wound and his shirt damp from sweat and grubby from the classroom floor. His blood soaked PE shirt had been put in a clear plastic bag along with the leg of his trousers that had been cut off. CJ had no idea why this was given back to him to take home. He thought maybe the school had some weird policy they were not allowed to dispose of clothes covered in blood. He perked up when he heard voices outside the room. *Mum's here at last.*

"As I explained to you on the phone, Mrs Vickers, your son climbed through my classroom window. I have no idea why. He's not really telling us much. I don't want to push him ... you know ... he's in a lot of pain. Take him straight to the hospital. Mrs Hettrick has already phoned ahead, they are expecting you."

Mrs Hettrick, gave a nod and a smile as though to reconfirm.

"They'll fix him up. Give him some pain killers and stitches. It could've been a lot worse ... you know ... he's lost a lot of blood and if Holly McShane had not 've found him when she did ... ooooh God knows what state he would've been in. Our nurse Hettrick, she's marvellous, absolutely marvellous. She's been a complete godsend to Christopher I must tell you ... "

"MISS MENDES!" Jodie hollered louder than intended. She cleared her throat and spoke in a softer voice, "Miss Mendes please I just want to collect CJ ... Christopher and get to the hospital."

Miss Mendes, surprised at Jodie being standoffish was instantly silenced and Nurse Hettrick smiled sweetly as her cheeks flushed with embarrassment. Jodie's head still plagued with the morning's events did not want to listen to her son's Spanish teacher going on and on and on. She didn't even have a pleasant accent. And certainly wasn't Spanish.

"Oh ... well yes ... of course ... please he's in here," said Miss Mendes in a cheerless tone and looking sombre.

CJ's delight at seeing his mum did not show on his pained face. Jodie hugged her son and gave him a kiss on the forehead and taking hold of the wheel chair she pushed him out of the room, mouthed a polite thank you to the nurse and made her way the car. The Spanish teacher said nothing as she trotted alongside Jodie and watched CJ struggle to climb into the passenger seat before taking back the wheelchair. Now Jodie had to focus on the thirty minute drive back to the hospital.

"There's been an accident on the Woodbank Road near Squirrel Hill," she told him. "I'm sorry honey but I'm going to have to take a diversion to the hospital."

All CJ could manage as a reply was a feeble, "Oh."

He sat quietly in the passenger seat, his face pale, his eyes red and his now bandaged leg still in extreme pain. Despite his predicament he couldn't help tormenting himself further, wondering what reaction he would get from his father. How could he explain climbing through the window? A sickness was sinking right into the pit of his empty stomach like the feeling of falling from a great height. He thought about Kelly and Thomas, imagining them hiding up in the woods. He thought about Wayne, wondering if he had been seen, being pushed out of school in a wheel chair. *How many students would already know? Who would Holly McShane tell?* His hot and clammy head was pounding and his throat was dry.

"Mum, please don't tell Dad that I did this climbing through the window." CJ was only too mindful of what his dad's reaction would be. Their father and son relationship was far from ordinary and past experiences had taught him to be aware of his dad's skewedness to opinions. The obscured vision of judgements and feelings that an ordinary mind could not grasp, but would make a challenging subject for a psychiatrist.

Approaching the traffic lights they turned to red. Jodie brought the car to a stop. Her thoughts during the ten minute journey had surprised her. Out of all of the events of the day that had beset her mind, she had found herself wondering if Inspector Campbell was still at the hospital. Hands still gripping the steering wheel but her eyes were now fixed on CJ. His pale despondent face filled her with anguish.

"Honey let's get you to the hospital eh? It will be okay." Jodie's heart was beating rapidly, spurred by the worry and possibilities of what torment the rest of the day would bring.

CHAPTER SEVEN

At Casualty

The resounding sound of the clock ticking was irritating to say the least. *What was happening to CJ?* The look on the nurse's face had frightened Jody as CJ was led from the waiting room, down the corridor and into a cubicle where the pale blue curtain had been fully drawn for privacy. Jodie had remained seated in the casualty waiting room, pointlessly scanning the pages of an old magazine she had picked up from a nearby table. She was now on her third cup of coffee and the taste was not getting any better. It was still bitter.

CJ felt his body trembling from tip to toe as his leg was stitched. Against his own will he had watched the shots of anaesthetic around the cut area and the cleaning with a large washing syringe. And now he watched the doctor put one stitch in the middle of his wound, then another in both halves. On either side of that another stitch and then the middle of those halves and so on until they all met. Twelve neat stitches were needed to fix his leg. And just when the dressing was applied and he thought it was all over and he could go home …
"We just need to give you tetanus shot. Can you remove your trousers and your underpants?"
Oh shit, oh shit, oh shit! He wasn't sure if he was speaking out loud or just thinking the words. But as he warily started removing what remained of his bloody ripped trousers that hung loosely round his thin legs, he uncontrollably became aroused. A nurse had accompanied the doctor while CJ had his leg stitched. She was young and pretty. Her bronzed face, dark hair and brown eyes captivated CJ. Her eyelashes were long (probably false CJ had thought) and her full lips were glossy

pink. CJ was feeling no pain in his leg from the anaesthetic and was able to stand freely and comfortably.

He stood naked from the waist down. Bloody clothes around his ankles. Blood rising beneath his flushed skin. He looked down and could see his own hardening. He was completely out of control of his own body. *Oh dear God ... No! Surely this can't be happening.* He had looked through many porn magazines with Thomas before. They had once stumbled across some hidden in the garage. He remembered being pleasurably excited, but this felt different. Swiftly came the unexpected flick from the nurse. Her fingers quick and sharp right on the end of CJ's tiny erection. As quickly as the incredible stimulation had stirred in his loins the sensation was gone. He watched his penis go limp as he felt an injection into his left buttock.

"All done my lovely." The nurse spoke sweetly and softly as though nothing out of the ordinary had happened.

CJ scrambled to pull, what remained of his pants back up. Fumbled nervously with his zip. He desperately wanted to escape the shame. His cheeks burned scarlet red and his left buttock was stinging.

The nurse, who was ahead of CJ, opened the privacy curtains.

"Are you alright?" she asked noticing his distressed look.

"Uh yeah, I think so," he said, head hung low, eyes on the floor. He didn't want to look at the nurse. Instead he wanted the ground to open up and swallow him whole. *Is all this real? Has today really happened?* He just wanted it all to end. To vanish. *Was today the result of six months of being bullied and tormented? Was Wayne accountable for today's events?* CJ thought so. And as these thoughts flooded his mind he was no longer upset. Now he was angry. He needed to see Thomas. His best friend. This was a problem he needed to solve with Thomas. Thomas would understand.

CHAPTER EIGHT

The Bad News

The sun's rays shone brightly through the window, catching the specks of dust that floated weightlessly in the warm air. Besides the odd sounds of footsteps from the nurses and their mindless chitter chatter, the ward was peaceful and calm. A heavy scent of disinfectant mixed with an undesirable musty odour hung in the air. The warmth from the sun poured onto Thomas Bradshaw as he lay still in his hospital bed. His bandaged head rested on two fluffy pillows with crisp white cotton sheets and his limp bruised body was loosely covered with a white sheet and pale blue blanket.

Down the corridor Thomas's mother had been asked to take a seat in the family room. The room was cosy and cheerful, decorated with floral wall paper and furnished with lime green fabric sofas and fluffy orange cushions, designed to make visitors feel comfortable before they are told the conditions of their loved ones. Mrs Bradshaw sat anxiously, perched on the edge of the sofa. She was not taken in by the falsity of the room and could not commit to leaning back and relaxing, and taking advantage of the small luxury the room had to offer. Only minutes had passed by, but the time seemed to have slowed right down before finally a middle-aged man entered the room clutching a file.

"Mrs Bradshaw?" asked the doctor.

"Yes I'm Thomas's mum." She rose promptly and formerly held out a shaky hand.

"I'm Doctor Patel." He reciprocated and shook her hand. It felt limp under his firm grip. Gesturing her to sit back down, he perched himself on the edge of the seat, leaned slightly forward to fully engage with his patient's mother, then went straight to the point.

"Thomas has received a strong blow to the head and it's what we call a closed head injury. There are complications. The injury has caused intracranial pressure which means there is swelling on the brain. I'm so sorry to have to inform you that your son is in a very serious condition. He has slipped into a coma and has been put under constant care and supervision. We are hopeful that he will wake but we will not know the full extent of the damage until he is conscious."

There was distance in her eyes.

"Mrs Bradshaw do you understand what I am telling you?"

"No, this isn't happening." Thomas's mother muttered out loud to remind herself that she wasn't dreaming. Although her eyes portrayed distance from the words, she understood perfectly what the doctor was saying. She understood that there could be damage to the brain tissue. She understood this could mean Thomas could suffer brain damage or even worse he could die from his injury. She understood perfectly. She just didn't want to believe.

"I want to see him," she said. Tears already running down her cheeks.

"Yes of course. Please, Mrs Bradshaw, follow me."

He escorted Thomas's mother the short walk down the corridor and into the ward to her son's bedside. She caught sight of two forensic detectives. They were wearing the distinctive long white coats and latex gloves. She recognised her son's clothes and watched as they put them into evidence bags.

"What are they doing with my son's clothes?" she said fretfully.

"It's normal procedure with hit and run victims," began Dr Patel, "there may be traces of car paint. This will help police identify the car that hit your son".

At that moment her eyes were on her little boy lying helplessly in bed. To her despair, she couldn't see his beautiful fiery red hair through the bandage and his cheeky freckled face was bruised and swollen, as was his left hand, but that was from the drip that he was hooked up to. She held tight on to his right hand wishing with all her heart that he would squeeze her hand and give her a sign that he was aware of her presence.

"Thomas darling, I'm here with you. It's Mum. I'm here and I'm not going to leave you. You are going to be fine. Do you hear me? You are going to be fine. It's all going to be fine."

She fell onto the bed and buried her head in the blue blanket and sobbed uncontrollably never letting go of his hand. Never giving up hope.

Kelly's mother and father were at their daughter's bedside. They had arrived only a few moments earlier, having already received the agonising news from Doctor Patel. Kelly too had suffered a severe head injury and was unconscious, fighting for her life. She looked soporific, as she lay a short way away from Thomas, unresponsive to her mother's sobbing. Unsure how to respond to the news, Kelly's mother remained with her hand over her mouth, clutching a tear soaked handkerchief. Her other hand delicately holding her daughter's hand. Kelly's father sat rooted to the chair next to the bedside, his mind deep in a state of disbelief and confusion, wondering, *how the hell did this happen? What the hell was Kelly doing in the woods with Thomas? Why was she not at school? And most importantly – who the hell did this?*

Rising abruptly from the chair, he paced back and forth, hand cupped in his chin, trying earnestly to find a reason how this happened, but going nowhere with his thoughts. His wife remained clutching Kelly's hand praying hard for her daughter's recovery. Her eyes burning as she could not hold back her tears of anguish.

CHAPTER NINE

The Plan

It might have been the fact that Jodie had not bumped into Inspector Matt that made her feel disappointed. Merged with the feeling of apprehension of her husband's return home from work and sorrow for CJ's traumatic day, she was more than ready for her next intake of alcohol. She was thankful though that CJ had not yet quizzed her about her meeting with Kat, for she did not know what to tell him. She did not think it was wise to mention the job offer. The ride home from the hospital had been strangely quiet. CJ's urgency to talk to Thomas was eating him up. He was still red faced from his embarrassing episode with the delightful nurse. Jodie however was pleased to see CJ had some colour back in his cheeks. This was an improvement from the pale despondent face she was met with when she arrived at the school.

Before long there was the familiar sound of the stones crunching under the tyres as Jodie pulled onto her driveway. She spotted the ever watchful Christine Hunt out of the corner of her eye. She had lost the wax jacket and was wearing a ridiculous straw hat that seemed to bounce on her curly grey hair. She had made her way across the front lawn toward them and before Jodie had even had chance to turn the engine off, Christine was stood beside the car door, one hand on her hip and the other holding a rake and still wearing garden gloves.

"Oh my goodness young Christopher. What in Devil's name has happened to you?" Through the car window she glimpsed a sight most unexpected. CJ shared his mother's lack of enthusiasm when it comes to Christine Hunt. She was an obstacle that got in the way. Another issue of the day that he wanted to avoid. A mild one compared to today's events, but she was a problem all the same. A widower of three years and retired, Christine Hunt took pleasure in engaging in everyone else's lives. Poking her nose into other people's business. The nosiest of all nosey neighbours.

"Hi there Christine. CJ's fine, he just had a little accident at school that's all," said Jodie tautly, stepping out of the car.

"A little accident? But he's covered in blood. My goodness Jodie how can you call that a little accident? His trousers are all ripped. The poor boy. What on earth has happened to you dear child?" CJ's appearance became more apparent as he stood on the driveway absentmindedly holding the bag of bloody clothes. Christine's jaw dropped at the ghastly sight of the blood soaked clothes. CJ made a poor effort to cradle the bag and hide its contents, but his attempt came too late.

"CJ is fine Christine, it looks worse that it is," announced Jodie trying to stay calm despite her neighbour's screechy high pitched voice. She gave CJ a stern glare imploring him not to tell Christine anything.

"My word Christopher you look like you've been through the wars."

"I'm fine Mrs Hunt. Really I'm fine. It's just a small cut on my leg."

Christine followed them both to their front door inelegantly carrying her rake like a walking stick and her straw hat flapping around her overly concerned face. Jodie fumbled nervously with her keys.

"What happened to your leg? How did you cut it?" continued Christine. Inside she was screaming out to know what had occurred.

Jodie was screaming inside for her to disappear in a puff of smoke and leave her the hell alone.

CJ could see his mother was edgy. He observed her shaky hands as she unlocked the door.

"It's like my mum said, it looks worse than what it is," he said, stopping himself from saying too much.

"Well if there's anything I can do ..." Christine Hunt was still pressing CJ and Jodie as they entered the porch and edged the door shut.

"No, we're okay thanks." The door clicked shut. CJ and Jodie looked at each other. They both felt a release of pressure . Though not amused by their interfering neighbour, they smiled nevertheless.

"Cum on hun, let's have a cup of tea," said Jodie as if tea was the answer to everything and tea would make all the troubles go away. Jodie put the kettle on as she battled with her inner self to keep a brave face. In spite of being somewhat shaky, she appeared to CJ as being less distressed now that there were bricks and mortar between herself and the meddling Christine Hunt. But she was really afraid. That canny little voice inside your head that lets you know when we have something to fear was giving Jodie the danger signals. She thought she would only have one problem to deal with when Jack got home from work. A tricky problem of talking her way out of having lunch with Kat. Now this had escalated. She had to come up with a story to protect CJ from his father. She too was well acquainted with her husband's failure to nurture, care and understand. His failure to love and his dexterity to somehow legitimate an argument. She had to think of a good story as to how CJ cut his leg. And she still needed to confront Christine Hunt about her silver birch tree. *But how can I talk to her now? It would be impossible without getting the third degree about CJ's accident.* And Jodie didn't want her knowing what happened.

CJ had left his mum making tea in the kitchen and gone to his room to get changed. Jodie took advantage of having a moment to herself and she discretely took a swig of vodka from a bottle she had stashed behind the waste bin in the cupboard underneath the kitchen sink. It was a trick she used regularly to hide her drinking. She had filled the bottle with only a tiny amount, enough for a couple of mouthfuls and then placed the bottle behind the bin. As she was usually the only one to take out the rubbish it was cleverly hidden. And if anyone did find it, they would assume that it had fallen out of the bin and the bottle would just get thrown away. No one would suspect that the clear liquid was not water.

Jodie's nerves were momentarily calmed. She made both herself and CJ 'a nice cuppa tea'. CJ had changed out of his blood soaked clothes and in no time at all was sprawled on the sofa watching TV. The anaesthetic had not worn off so he was not in any pain.

"There you go hun." Jodie placed the tea besides CJ and then sat down with him.

"So now that your leg is all fixed up," she said patting him in the thigh, "and you're okay ... are you going to tell me why you climbed through the window?"

"Mum, please do we have to talk about this now?" His tone worn thin with fretting.

"Yes we do," she said firmly. "You know your dad's going to want to know what happened today."

CJ knew telling the truth was not an option.

"I just needed to get back in the classroom, that's all ... Please Mum ... don't tell Dad."

"That's all! ... CJ you hurt yourself really badly today ... I want to know why you climbed through the window."

CJ's brain was racing trying to think of a plausible explanation. He was reluctant to speak in case he said something he regretted. He said nothing for a few moments. But the weight of his mum's stare made him realise he was going to have to give some sort of an explanation.

"I just needed to get back in the classroom and Miss Mendes had locked the door."

"Okay and what was so urgent that you couldn't wait until after lunch?"

"I ... I ... I left my bag ...You know it had my lunch money in it ...and I wanted to buy lunch."

"If that's the only reason then why are you being so secretive?" The questioning stare seemed to be locked on to CJ. "Is it a girl? ...Were you meeting someone? Why weren't you with Thomas?"

"No Mum. I wasn't meeting a girl," he said sheepishly. " And Thomas wasn't in school today."

Jodie cupped her hot tea, sat back upon the soft cushions on the sofa and took a big gulp. *Did Jack really need to know?*

"I don't think your dad will be mad at you for wanting to meet a girl. Maybe he won't be best pleased that you tried to meet in a locked classroom ... so who's the girl?"

"Mum please! There is no girl."

"Oh really?" said Jodie quizzically.

Alright I'll tell you." Began CJ in a huffy voice. "I left my bag in the classroom, but it was on the table next to the window. Miss Mendes locked the door and then disappeared into the staff room. I remembered the window being open next to my desk, so I walked round and leaned through the window to reach my bag and caught my leg. I fell through the window and couldn't get back up." The stroppy teenage attitude was something that Jodie didn't see very often. She dismissed the manner in which he spoke, putting it down to the events of the day. There was a moment's silence. Jodie wanted to be sure that CJ had finished his little rant before she asked any more questions. Careful not to exacerbate the situation.

"And that's it ... ?"

"Yes."

"So why all the secrecy?"

"I dunno mum, I just felt stupid."

"Okay, okay no more questions."

"So are you gonna tell Dad?"

To say yes would be like wielding an axe. It was impossible for Jodie to be so ruthless and put CJ in the fate of his dad. CJ's panic was lessoned by the warmth in his mum's eyes. Her look changed so quickly from a harsh stare to one of compassion, that it gave him hope the answer was a 'no'. Although he could not be absolutely sure. CJ felt some relief that he was able to keep hidden the real reason for hiding in the classroom. For now anyway. Miss Mendes was sure to give him the third degree when he returned to school. He decided he would try for some sick days. He knew his mum would allow him to stay at home until his leg was better. Realising school would soon be finished, he knew in a short while he could phone Thomas. There was so much to tell him and he wanted to know how his day went with Kelly. For the time being he made himself comfortable propped up on large soft cushions, switched on the TV and drew his attention to a programme on Discovery Science. It helped take his mind off of things.

Jodie felt comforted that CJ had opened up, albeit only a little bit. Even though her mother's intuition told her that he was still keeping something from her. But she wouldn't press him anymore. He had gone through enough. Instead her attention was on the sick feeling in the pit of her stomach. The nagging nervousness that sits, lingering like a warning sign for the danger that was to come. Only drink could help control it. It was always the same. If Jodie and Jack had argued or had any sort of disagreement in the morning it would continue when he came home from work. The argument this morning was because of the meeting with Kat. *Maybe CJ's predicament would make things worse.* Jodie didn't want to take that chance. For her own sake as well as CJ's she thought about not disclosing his accident to Jack. She was succumbing to the idea of keeping it a secret even though she knew what the consequences would be. *You're just gonna have to learn not to get caught.*

Jodie wasn't sure how long she had sat clutching the empty cup. She had drunk the hot steaming tea on auto pilot while CJ had been sent to sleep by the calming voice of Morgan Freeman as he narrated 'Through the Wormhole'. She was too preoccupied to be watching TV. Instead her eyes had been fixed on something else.

The Thomas Moss clock that sat on the marble fireplace had survived for more than two centuries and as many world wars. It was one of many household items that spoke as a silent grandeur. Standing only fifteen inches tall this restored regency brass ball mounted mahogany bracket clock gestured that Jack Vickers was distinguished, impressive and inspiring. Jack liked to be surrounded by such splendour to represent his success, or magnify it. On the other hand, if the clock could speak, it had borne witness to the countless times Jodie had taken a slap, punch, kick, push and as equally harsh verbal abuse, that it would more likely say it is indignant of its purpose. Still it kept perfect time. Jody liked the white painted arch dial with Roman numerals and the brass spade hands. It was this object that she had been staring at for the past hour. Thinking about another life. A life without Jack. Without trepidation. Maybe a life without the booze, but one step at a time. Jodie knew she needed the drink for the time being. It was her only source of courage and confidence. Yet her mind was made up. She would take the job and she would leave her husband. And when that day came, she would take the Thomas Moss clock with her.

Jodie almost jumped out of her skin when the telephone rang. CJ was unresponsive. Picking up the receiver, she was expecting to hear Kat's voice. Usually Kat was too impatient to wait for Jodie to call. Shock hit her when she heard the sound of her husband's voice. His tone surprisingly short, sharp and courteous.

"Hi it's me. It's going to be a late one tonight so don't make me any dinner."

"Oh. Okay ... how late?"

"I don't know exactly. There are changes to my forecast reports. I have to have them finished for my meeting first thing tomorrow. I'm working on them with Mikey and it's going to take some time. It's going to be a late night. I'll order some food from the office. Don't wait up. Bye love." *Click*

Bye love? After she'd hung up she knew at once why he spoke so agreeably. Mikey was sat with him. But how fortunate she felt at that moment. Maybe she would escape an evening of torment. Eyes were back on the clock. Four thirty. CJ was sleeping soundly on the luxurious Knole sofa. For a second Jodie admired the damask fabric. All these fine things she would have to say goodbye to when the day came. She knew it would take lots of careful planning, concealment and most of all guts.

You're just gonna have to learn not to get caught.

Jodie went into the kitchen. She couldn't risk CJ waking up and hearing her conversation with Kat. She took out her mobile from her handbag and as calm as death she punched in Kat's number. Almost immediately Kat answered the phone. She sensed a change of attitude in Jodie's voice when she said, "Kat I need to talk to you."

"Sure. What's up? You want to talk about the job?" Kat's shift at the hospital had finished and she was now at home sank into her favourite chair with her laptop on her knee. She had been attempting to research Jodie's dream.

"I need you to do me a favour," she told Kat. "I need a pay as you go mobile. I can't let Jack track any of my calls. Can you get me one."

"He checks your phone?" said Kat. She had no idea why she was surprised.

"Yeah of course. He has the home phone and my mobile calls itemised."

"Does this mean you're gonna take the job?"

"I need to get out of here and Jack must never find out." She tamped the urge to cry as reality of what she was doing kicked in and she went on. "So can you get me a phone?"

"You can use my old phone. What else do you need?"

"An email address … work email address …so that Jack can't access my emails."

"Okay. Shouldn't be a problem. You can always use mine. I guess you've thought of everything."

"Well not quite. But for the last hour I've been trying to figure out how I can get away."

"Well you know I'm here for you. Anything you need, just ask. Okay?"

"Okay. Thanks Kat."

"Oh and by the way. I did a little research about your dream," Kat was saying brightly as she proceeded to read from her laptop, "Apparently if you dream about the sea it brings hope, a new perspective and a positive outlook on life no matter how difficult your current problems may be. And there's more. To dream that you are hot signifies passion and heated emotions. It may reflect a situation that is potentially dangerous or a relationship where you are getting burned. Alternatively the dream may represent a person who is great looking or perhaps you are lusting over someone. Like a certain police inspector," laughed Kat and then continued, "To see or taste saltwater in your dream symbolises tears and heartache. It may also indicate some emotional outburst or suffering. And the symbol of the drowning points to serious problems often caused by lack of planning, to helplessness and a too low self-confidence."

"I think I'll just stay focussed on the 'new perspective and positive outlook on life'," remarked Jodie. Not losing sight that CJ was still in the next room, she added, "Kat I gotta go. I need to check on CJ. I don't want him to know about any of this. I can't risk Jack finding out." Jodie's voice changed to a whisper at the thought of CJ waking.

" You can do this you know. I know it's not gonna be easy ... Jack is ... well he's ..."

"Controlling," whispered Jodie.

"I was going to say ... an arse," sniggered Kat. Then remembering that CJ had an incident at school, she asked, "Hey, is CJ alright?"

"Yeah he seems alright now. He had a pretty bad accident at school. Needed some stitches in his leg." There was a groan at the other end of the phone. "I'll tell you more when I see you."

"Why don't you come and meet me again tomorrow? "

"Okay. Lunchtime?"

"About one? You can pick up my phone, we'll go through some stuff about the mural and you can fill me in on CJ."

"Alright. I'll see you then. Bye Kat."

"Bye Jodie."

Click

A quick check round the lounge door to find CJ was still fast asleep. Jodie gave a sigh of relief. It had been a tiring day. Jodie was thankful that the evening without Jack would give her time to collect her thoughts. It had been many years since Jodie had painted a mural. But the words about the dream were now ringing in her head. *Symbol of drowning points to serious problems often caused by lack of planning, to helplessness and a too low self-confidence.* Jodie had not told Kat that this was a reoccurring dream. She wondered how significant the meaning was. *It must be a warning. I need to make sure my plan is foolproof. Jack must never find out I am planning to leave.* Jodie felt a stabbing pain in her chest. It was another panic attack. She fixed herself a Jack Daniels and coke and sat in the dining room gathering her thoughts, plucking up the courage. She knew what she had to do. The plan had begun.

You're just gonna have to learn not to get caught.

CHAPTER TEN

What Jack Did

By the time Jack returned home, Jodie was in bed, as was CJ sleeping soundly under his Man United duvet. But Jodie was stirred by the soft rumbling of the engine and stones crunching as the car pulled up on the driveway. Then came the faint noises; the key in the lock, the front door opening and closing. Solitary sounds amplified in the stillness of the night. She listened hard to the noises coming from downstairs and in her mind's eye pictured Jack's movements. He was taking his shoes off and hanging up his suit jacket on the iron coat rack. His footsteps soft and faint, but Jodie could just make out that Jack was now in the kitchen. The fridge door opened and closed. The ice-maker hummed and rattled. Then the sound of the ice clinking in the glass. He was fixing himself a drink. Probably a Jack Daniels and coke. Seconds passed, then the TV came on. Loud at first then the sound was lowered. Jack was winding down after a long day at work with a nightcap. Jodie didn't move. She continued to lay still waiting for the landing light to suddenly shine through the thin gap at the bottom of the bedroom door where she would inevitably see the shadow of Jack seconds before he would enter the bedroom. Panicked and scared she lay still and pretended to be asleep. Her stomach was in a knot and her breathing heavy. The uncomfortable feeling of knowing that his anger from the morning had been brewing all day was hitting Jodie like a stabbing pain in the chest.

She tried to predict his actions. *Will he come to bed and fall asleep? Will he know that I am awake and pin me down on the bed forcing me to listen to another tongue lashing as he had so often done in the past? Is he going to sit on my abdomen with his knees pushed into my arms and hold my hair scrunched up in the palm of his hand as he holds my head on the pillow?* Jodie imagined Jack's cold hard spirit. He'd tell her how ungrateful she is, how selfish and disrespectful she is. The full weight of his strong body on top of her. Unable to move, her face would feel the spit as the hurtful words showered down on her. No, he would come to bed so tired after working late he will just want to go to sleep. The whisky will relax him and he will just fall asleep. *Oh God, please let him just fall asleep.*

The TV went off. Jodie was so tormented by her thoughts. The landing light was now on. Footsteps on the soft carpet were unheard. But then the landing light shining warmly under the rim of the door suddenly darkened. Jack was the other side of the door. Like a shadow man, lurking and praying on the weak. *Oh please God don't let him hurt me.* The door opened. Jodie's eyes shut tight, yet she could make out the brightness from the hall light. A flick of the switch and the room fell back into darkness. Jack entered the bedroom. Jodie's small slim body lay rigid and helpless. She kept her eyes squeezed tight feeling the solace of falling into her own darkness. If she couldn't see him she could pretend he wasn't there. The 12 tog duvet was making her feel hot, but despite this she dared not to move. The unpleasantness of the heat was at the same time making her feel a sense of protection. *Oh dear God, he knows I'm awake. Don't move. He's looking at me. Shit. What's he doing?* Jodie could feel her heart beating so hard she was positive Jack could hear it. There was movement around the bedroom as Jack undressed. Jodie heard the shower running. *He's in the shower. Oh thank God. Does this mean that he will leave me alone tonight?*

Jodie relaxed albeit only for a few minutes. For just as she thought all was well, Jack was climbing into bed. She lay on the edge of the bed in a foetus position. Her back towards Jack. His damp naked body pressed against hers. He hadn't dried himself fully after showering. The sweet smell of soap did not disguise the not so sweet Jack. His mouth pressed up to her ear. The minty toothpaste only just masked the smell of cigarettes.

"I know you're awake," he whispered. "Do you really think I'm going to let you get away with what you did today? Have a nice time with Kat did you? Been talking about me have you? Telling her how terrible your life is with me. Eh? When I give you everything." *Here it comes. You're just going to have to learn not to get caught!* Jack spoke in a soft whisper but with malice. He was controlling with everything that he said and did. "And don't even think about lying to me and telling me that you cancelled your little meeting because I know you went. Didn't you?"

Jodie winced as Jack's hand smoothed her hair away from her face and was crumpled in his hand forcing her to turn her head towards him.

He knew? How did he know? There was no use trying to deny it. She just had to take what was coming to her.

"I swear I don't talk about you Jack. I don't know why you would think that." Her eyes finally opening in defeat. Her voice weak.

Still with a soft whispery voice Jack said, "I don't like her and I don't want you to see her again. Is that understood?"

"Okay ... okay ... Yes, I promise I won't see her again. Now please let me go to sleep."

Jodie tried to take Jack's hand away from her hair but his grip was too strong. He had no intention of letting go.

"Jack please, you're hurting me."

"Let's kiss and make up then shall we?" Jack smiled a conceited smile that was as hostile as his actions.

His control did not stop at dictating to Jodie whom she could be friends with. He would control the sex too. This cruel and frightening personality had slowly, oh so very slowly, crept up on Jodie, gradually worsening over the years. Jack had changed from the sweet loving, hardworking family man to a narcissistic husband. To Jack his relationship with his wife was all about power and command.

He pressed his lips hard against her mouth pulling on her hair. Jodie felt Jack's other hand on her thigh, squeezing at first then move in between her legs, lifting up her silk nightdress. Jodie was compelled to lie motionless as Jack roughly inserted two fingers into her. She tried to recoil but this just made Jack more excited. He drew his head back to observe her face as he held her soft brown hair tightly in his hand keeping her head on the pillow, the other hand continued to play with her vagina. He kicked the duvet off admiring Jodie's sleek body. He tasted his fingers, made them wet with spit and inserted his fingers again. Jodie squirmed and tried to twist her body as Jack pushed his fingers hard into her. She arched her back in an effort to fight the feeling. Finally Jack released her hair and his hand moved to her breasts, squeezing and pinching her nipples through the silk fabric of the nightdress. Jodie wanted to squeal, but instead she bit down on her bottom lip and closed her eyes tight knowing that it will soon be over. Too scared to yell, to fight back, too scared to say no. Jack pulled the straps off her shoulders to reveal her perfect size thirty-six breasts. He climbed on top of her. She could feel the full weight of his body. He was heavy and strong. She couldn't move from beneath him. He prized her legs wide apart with his knees and held her hands either side of her body. She felt his hot lips on her breast, his tongue licking her nipples until they were hard. He began biting each one in turn. Occasionally looking at Jodie's face as she grimaced in pain. Then he entered her. Still holding her hands either side. Still in command. Still smiling.

CHAPTER ELEVEN

A New Day

The chirring sounds of the blue tits nesting on Christine's silver birch were joined in the dawn chorus by the band of robins, blackbirds and song thrushes. But Jodie would need more than a tune from mother natures feathered singers to get her through the day. She needed all her strength alone just to get out of bed. She'd had a restless night and felt like she had hardly slept. She didn't want to get up. She didn't want to move. Her body ached, her head ached and her breasts were sore. And all this aside, she awoke with sudden horror that she had forgotten to set her alarm. Luckily Jack had left for work before the first delightful bird call to welcome sunrise, otherwise this could have caused her further problems. Jack still had no knowledge of CJ's accident and he would have wanted to know why she was not getting up to make breakfast before CJ went to school. She knew if her plan was to work she needed to be on her guard and not let anything slip. She remembered the meaning of her dream. The drowning, it signified problems caused by lacking of planning. She had to be more careful.

It was going to be another hot day and Jodie would have to dress to cover up the bruises on her arms and legs which was not a good prospect. Despite the overwhelming feeling that every ounce of energy had been drained from her body, she managed to shower and dress, conscious that she needed to be ready before CJ was up. She could not allow him to see her in her delicate state. She had to be strong for him as much as for herself. But of all the things on Jodie's mind, to her the most trivial one required the most deliberation. What to wear? After careful consideration she decided to wear her maxi dress with a long sleeved lace shrug. She fixed her hair and make-up, using lots of concealer. And feeling as satisfied with her look as she did listening to the cheerful twittering coming from the garden, she crept quietly across the landing to CJ's bedroom, opened the door quietly and peeped in. He was snug under his duvet, breathing deeply and snoring quietly. Satisfied that he would not wake up anytime soon, Jodie began filling her empty water bottles with a small measure of vodka and hiding them around the house. She hid one in her favourite hiding place, behind the bin underneath the kitchen sink. She put another in the cloakroom cupboard under the sink behind the cleaning detergents and another in the utility room behind an extra-large box of washing powder. And finally she refilled the bottle of orange that she kept in the car. Christine Hunt was, as usual, in her front garden, but she was engaged in conversation with one of the residents. So Jodie was free to run to her car without being spotted. When she'd finished creeping around the house like a secret agent on a mission, she took another sneaky look at CJ. He was still sleeping peacefully. Jodie then proceeded to make herself a large mug of coffee with an added touch of whisky for good measure. She drank while resting on the sofa, feeling relaxed and jubilant she fell into a much needed deep sleep.

By the time CJ was out of bed, most of the morning had passed. He was ravenous now for he had hardly eaten the day before. He hobbled around the kitchen making himself some toast, still feeling sorry for himself. And he was wishing that his mum was not fast asleep on the sofa. He was eager to find out what she had told his dad about his accident, if indeed she had told him anything. And he was intrigued to know what Kat wanted to tell his mum. He would not have minded her making his breakfast either, so that he could rest his leg. The wound hurt like a prickly sting that seemed to throb relentlessly and the sickly feeling in his stomach was still actively making him feel nervous. The thought of the consequences of his dad finding out that he was hiding out in a classroom was too much for CJ to handle. But the thought did not curb his appetite. And as CJ devoured a plate of hot buttered toast and drank, almost in one go, a tall glass of fresh orange juice, his focus turned to Thomas and Kelly. *I'll phone Thomas. It will be lunchtime soon* he thought. He was intrigued to learn about their day bunking off school and as neither Thomas nor Kelly had answered their phones from previous attempts, he was desperate to find out what had gone on, and if his accident was today's classroom topic of conversation. But before he made the call he wanted to talk to his mum. He limped pitifully into the lounge and edged himself on the sofa. Jodie looked restful, but CJ could not stop the urge to wake her. He shook her shoulder gently.

"Mum ... Mum wake up." Jodie stirred and sat up, suddenly remembering that she had fallen asleep in the lounge.

"Hey baby how you feeling? You feeling better? You sleep okay?" said Jodie pushing herself up into sitting position.

"Yeh Mum. I'm feeling a little better. My leg is still sore though."

"You taken any pain killers?"

"No not yet. But I will."

Jodie noticed the Thomas Moss clock, it was past twelve thirty. She stretched and yawned trying to bring her aching body back to life.

"Mum did you tell Dad what happened yesterday?"

"No honey I didn't."

CJ's worried look vanished as he heard these words and some pink colour dashed his cheeks as he restored calmness. The thought of his dad knowing that he had climbed through the classroom window had been troubling him more than the pain in his leg. He needed to know for sure that his mum was not going to tell him.

"Mum ... do you think we can ... erm ...not tell Dad about yesterday." He watched attentively for his mum's reaction. "I just think that he might be ... yer know ...be really annoyed with me and ... I just don't need it." Jodie smiled ruefully at her son's noble efforts to persuade her to keep secrets from her husband. Perched awkwardly on the edge of the sofa and evidently still in pain, CJ looked at Jodie with pathetic beckoning eyes. Two mornings ago she was trying to act prudent and worrying about spending an hour having lunch with her best friend. And now here she was contemplating hiding the fact that CJ had twelve stitches in his leg, as well as planning to go to work so she could get some money and leave her husband. *What the hell! In for a penny on for a pound!* thought Jodie.

"I guess it would make life easier if your dad didn't know," she said finally, much to CJ's pleasure.

"Thanks Mum," said CJ feeling much relieved of worry and settling himself down on the sofa."

"I need to go out," added Jodie. "Will you be alright on your own for a bit?" Jodie was conscious of the time, yet trying to sound casual.

"Sure Mum. I'll be fine. I'm gonna try phoning Thomas again."

"Okay, but before you phone Thomas go and take those pain killers," suggested Jodie as she got up from the sofa. "I won't be long."

"Alright Mum," replied CJ completely ignoring her and switching on the TV.

Jodie grabbed her handbag, slipped on her sandals and jumped in the car, somehow managing to avoid Christine Hunt. Although she thought she heard a shrill sound come from the direction of her neighbour's house. Too fixed on meeting Kat, she averted her eyes from that direction and set off. She drove down Mottrom Road and onto Woodbank Road. A cold shudder ran through her body as she passed a police notice asking if anyone had any details about an accident that had occurred on the morning of 16 June. She reached the hospital feeling a little jittery and couldn't get out of the car until she had drunk liberally from her secret supply of vodka orange. Thankful that she'd had the chance in the morning while CJ slept to refill the bottle. Now she felt more at ease and able to handle the day better and think more clearly. She took several deep intakes breath. Each one felt like a wave passing over her and washing away the nerves and anxiety.

Then feeling cool and calm, she talked herself through the mental notes she had made. *I need a pay as you go mobile, an email account and bank account that Jack can't track. I need to obtain art supplies for the mural without Jack finding out. Make sure CJ doesn't get into trouble from his accident and run the usual errands for Jack without him becoming suspicious. And deal with the neighbour from hell. And all this without losing my head?* Jodie began to laugh. *Not impossible. Just need to be smart.*

You're just gonna have to learn to not get caught.

Pushing the thoughts of last night to the back of her mind, Jodie was now more determined than ever. She knew her plan could work. It had to work.

Jodie met Kat in the usual place, the hospital canteen. It was equally as noisy and as busy as the previous day and Kat looked just as stunning. She was fresh faced and grinning with an infectious excitement that seemed to illuminate the whole canteen with a glow of happiness. The two friends hugged and had their coffee and baguettes while Jodie filled Kat in with the events of CJ's accident. Then they made their way straight to the senior nurse's office. Kat pushed the door shut so they could have some privacy. Being back in the pokey little room gave Jodie a feeling of solace, unlike the previous day when Jodie had an attack of nerves. Her mood today had taken a complete turn. Maybe CJ's accident had something to do with it. And maybe last night's attack on Jodie had been one too many.

"Oh my God Jodie you have no idea how glad I am that you are here?" said Kat with elation. "So you're really going to go back to work and leave that egotistical, self-absorbed arsehole."

"Yep. I'm really going to do it," said Jodie smiling with amusement. "But please don't let anyone know that I am working here okay. I can paint during school hours and no more. Weekends are definite no working days. I can give you a list of all the supplies that I will need and I need one of your staff to pick them up. I cannot risk being seen buying this stuff."

"No problem," interrupted Kat. "We do all the ordering on line."

"Okay great. I'll need aprons as well. I'll take my breaks during visiting hours so that no one I may know sees me."

"I know, I know. It's okay ... we wouldn't want you to be painting anyway when there are visitors. I've made some enquiries and you can have use of one of the computers here. I'll give you my logon details and you can use my email address. Here is my old mobile." Kat handed Jodie a Nokia 311. "It's a pay as you go, so you're gonna need to buy a top up card."

"Thanks Kat."

"Listen Jodie, it's not just the children's ward they want painting. There's talk about the geriatric ward and the maternity ward. All you need is to give us a quote for the work and then they want you to invoice us. We have to hire you as a private contractor not as an employee. The best way to do this is to give an hourly or daily rate and complete a timesheet each week. This is signed off and you get paid monthly. You can provide an estimate on how many hours you expect to take to complete the work and we'll work out your daily rate. I reckon on your hours being 10 a.m. until 3 p.m. as this is after and before visiting hours and fits in with school. You can take a thirty minute lunch break. "

Jodie listened intently.

"Shit Kat. Really? I have to do the quote and the invoicing. How the hell can I pull that off? I am not a businesswoman." Jodie started to panic.

"Jodie it's okay. You don't have to be VAT registered or anything. Just provide a sheet of paper with your name and your bank details. That's all we need. Just so we can identify expenditure."

"I thought that I was being paid from expenses." Jodie had remembered their previous conversation.

"Yeah me too hun, but the amount of money they will pay for a mural artist is too much to come out of expenses. You should easily make enough for a deposit on a new place and then who knows. You can get a contract with other hospitals, schools or nurseries even.

"Yeah, that's the plan," said Jodie with a sigh. "But I'm gonna need some help setting up a business. I don't know where to start."

"Well firstly my dear, you gotta think of a business name, and then register with the HM Revenue and Customs. Once you've done that apply for self-assessment and then get yourself a business portfolio. The Senior Charge Nurse will want to see it along with a quotation. The job sheet is then signed off and we get you in to start work. Remember this is all confidential so Jack has no way of finding out. Use my old phone as a contact number and my email address ... Just be careful of using your home number. You can specify contact by SMS or emails nowadays with the banks."

"You make it sound so easy," said Jodie

"It is easy. You can do most of this online. Use this computer if you want." Kat rolled her eyes toward the flat screen monitor on the desk. "How long have you got?"

"Maybe an hour or so before I need to head back home."

"Okay, let's do it now."

Without a moment's hesitation, Kat was seated behind the tattered wooden desk under the small window that barely let in any light. She pulled the keyboard toward her and typed in 'www.hmrcgov.uk'.

"What shall we call your business?"

"How about 'Wall Art by Jodie'?"

Jodie was surprised at how quickly and straightforward it was to register her business. After thirty minutes of filling out forms online Jodie had her business set up and was registered. Setting up a new bank account was going to be tricky. To use a different postal address Jodie needed to provide utility bills. There was no way of getting round it. She made a request with her bank to receive electronic statements, but not before she changed her personal email address to Kat's and updated her contact number to Kat's old phone number.

"I think you're ready Jodie." Kat gave her a hug.

Before heading home Jodie made several stops. This would make her later than she had planned, but nonetheless she had to run by Dickens' Nursery to pay the monthly gardening bill. Trying hard not to engage in conversation so as to be as quick as possible, which was a chore in itself. Then on the same stretch of road, Jodie stopped off at the newsagents to buy her top up card. She also bought an art folder, a copy of Art Monthly and other periodicals she thought would be helpful with putting together a portfolio. She wasn't sure how much original artwork she was able to use, so she decided she would take pictures from magazines. It was important that the pictures she chose for her portfolio were murals that she would be able to paint. She was so focused on her plan that for a short moment she forgot her fears of the repercussions of getting caught. Not forgetting to pick up Jack's suits, Jodie also stopped at the drycleaners on the corner of Hough Street. The All Day Laundry owner was a weird creepy guy called Barry who always ogled Jodie. Jodie loathed Barry and hated coming into his shop, but Jack was insistent that she used this dry cleaners. The idea that his designer suits and shirts were noticed by the locals pleased him no end. Today though she was amused when he was too busy looking at her cleavage that he ineptly knocked the receipt book clean off the counter top and into a customer's raffia shopping basket. The old woman standing beside her did not notice. Jodie left with a smile of both amusement and satisfaction.

Jodie was unusually high-spirited. In light of the past two and a half hours, last night's episode now seemed hazy. Despite the cleverly covered up bruising attesting the cold harsh reality of Jack's temper, Jodie actually felt vivacious. This however would be short lived. Jodie approached her driveway and saw to her complete and utter horror that Jack's car was parked on the drive. Her heart sank deep into the pit of her stomach as she stared at the number plate JV1. She struggled to catch her breath. Pain in her chest, hands shaking, she felt like she was dying. She desperately fought to get the top off the plastic bottle of orange and drank the last mouthfuls of vodka orange. This only just took the edge of her nerves.

She quickly hid the Nokia and phone charger Kat had given her under the car seat. Then shoved the carrier bag of her purchases from the newsagents under the car seat too. She checked herself in the car vanity mirror and took a deep breath before getting out the car. The walk up the driveway was daunting. Even though the sun was burning in the clear blue sky a cloud of doom hung over Jodie as she approached her front door. She was dreading what awaited her on the over side of the door. Jack now knew CJ was off school. Did Jack also now know that CJ had some sort of an accident? If he did, Jodie knew that somehow she would be the one to blame and the punishment did not bear thinking about.

~~~~~~~~~~~

CJ expected that Thomas would answer his phone or at least return all the missed calls. *Not even a text message* he thought *and no answer from Kelly either. What's going on?* Still desperate to off load yesterday's events and equally as eager to hear about their day bunking off school, CJ was at a loss of what to do. Realising he was still hungry he made more toast. Then he tried calling Thomas and Kelly again. No answer. He snuck into his dad's study to use Facebook but still nothing. This was not like Thomas or Kelly. They were his best friends. *Why would they ignore me?* CJ began to feel slightly annoyed. He imagined they were keeping secrets from him. Secrets of their little adventure together. Adventure without him. Because he wasn't brave enough to miss school. *Why will they not share their day with me? Why are they being so enigmatic? And where the hell is Mum? She left almost two hours ago.*

A sharp stinging pain in his leg reminded him he still needed to take some more pain killers. He'd promised his mum he would take them before phoning Thomas but somehow thought that talking to his best friend was more important. As CJ gulped water to wash down two paracetamol he heard a car pull up on the driveway. But to his surprise it was his dad not his mum. CJ's heart raced. He should be at school now. What was he supposed to tell his dad? He had no idea. He just knew that his dad would be more furious at CJ hiding out in that classroom than Wayne Dear was the day he laughed at his name. He also knew that he would be mad that his mum had not told him that he has twelve stitches in his leg. What possible explanation could he give that would appease the situation? It was almost two thirty and CJ wasn't even dressed. As Jack walked through the door CJ felt the blood drain from his face.

"Hi son, what're you doing home? You okay? You look awful. Are you ill?" Jack didn't notice that part of the dressing that covered CJ's stitches was showing beneath his pyjama shorts. CJ's dejected look was because he knew that the dressing was visible. Fortunately Jack mistook the look of pure dread on CJ's face. CJ stood at the kitchen sink holding his glass of water looking pale and peaky not wanting to draw attention to his leg.

He swallowed hard and spluttered out, "I ... I ... I don't feel well". Then after a pause in a shaky voice he asked, "How come you're home early Dad?"

Jack was wandering around the kitchen, opening and peering in cupboards looking for something to snack on. As he passed by he casually placed his hand on CJ's head and ruffled his hair. That was as about as much affection CJ would get from his father.

"I worked till late last night and we got all the reporting done so I came home early. So what's up kiddo? Stomach bug?"

"Err ... Yeah ... No ... Headache. I have a really bad headache so I stayed home. I think I'm gonna go back to bed Dad, if that's alright?"

"Sure kiddo. Where's yer mum?"

"Er ... she ... she had to pop out."

Jack observed the box of paracetamol on the side.

"She had to pop out? What was so important that she left you on your own when you're sick?"

"I don't know Dad. I can't remember what she said. I wasn't really listening. Please don't shout Dad. My head hurts."

"I'm not shouting," answered Jack softly.

CJ hastily left the room. In his moment of dismay he knew he had to get a message to his mum that his dad was home. As soon as CJ was in his bedroom he sent a text message to his mum. *'Mum Where r u? Dads home. Thinks I have a bad headache. x'*

~~~~~~~~~~~~

The beeping of Jodie's phone caused her to pause on the doorstep. Holding the dry cleaning in one hand she rummaged with the other hand frantically through her handbag for her phone. She read the text message from CJ then as quick as she read it she deleted it, dropped the phone back in her handbag, took a deep breath and opened the door.

CHAPTER TWELVE

The Nosey Neighbour

Neither Jack nor Jodie had caught sight of Christine Hunt in her front garden. But Christine, although today busy filling her flower beds with Alchemilla (lady's mantle) and Astilbem (false goat's beard) she had not failed to spot Jodie leave hastily around 12:30. And when Christine had moved on a little later to cutting back her Phlox, she watched Jack arrive home early shortly followed by a very worried looking Jodie. Perhaps the reason she had not been spotted was due to her flowery dress which blended so well into her blooming garden. She was now busily watering the soil where her Phlox were flourishing in the corner of her garden. The spot carefully chosen to allow for just the right amount of sunshine. Cheerfully she hummed to herself deep in thought, puzzled at the goings on at the Vickers's house. Then suddenly she was stopped in her tracks. Still holding the hose pipe pumping out water she gazed unreservedly as a police car pulled up outside the Vickers's house. Today was getting really interesting for Christine Hunt. The familiar voice of her friendly neighbour from the other side called out from over the garden fence.

"I wonder what that lot are doing 'ere ... eh."

Albert and Christine watched intrigued as two uniformed officers mooched around the Jaguar and then approached Jodie's front door. Within a few moments they had disappeared inside the house. Christine immediately piped up and began running through her account of yesterday, witnessing CJ's bloody clothes as he got out of the car.

"And can you believe it? That woman said it was just a little accident. Little accident? They didn't think I would notice, but you could tell he'd had stitches. Kept saying he's fine, he's fine. I tell you she doesn't know how to look after that boy. Do you know he's been left all on his own today and with an injured leg? I say, all I wanted to do was help and d'you know she closed the door right in my face she did. And now the police are here. Makes you wonder what goes on in that house and how young Christopher got his injury, doesn't it Albert?"

Christine was indeed grateful that Albert had shown up. Now she had someone to gossip to. And what better time than on a beautiful spring afternoon amongst the blossoming flowers and a police car on your neighbour's driveway.

Albert leaned on the fence engaging in chitchat.

"Ah, stitches you say. Must be a real nasty cut if he had stitches. And she wouldn't tell you how he cut himself? Sounds suspicious if you ask me." Albert scratched his wispy white bearded chin as though this action might help him find some answers.

"Oh it's suspicious alright." replied Christine as she turned off her hose pipe realising that her Phlox was getting overwatered.

"So why d'you think the police are here? You reckon it's got something to do with young Christopher's accident?" Albert continued to stroke his chin whilst deliberating.

"Ooh yes," replied Christine with some emphasis, "Don't think that was an accident at all. Well how can it be? Police wouldn't be here if it was an accident would they? And Jack's home early today. He must 'ave known the police were coming."

"Well I don't mind telling yer Christine, if anyone would know it would be you. You see more than most folk around 'ere." Albert hesitated and not wanting to offend he added, "And that's why you have the best garden on Mottrom Road."

Christine's cheeks took on a colour that even her roses would envy. She fanned her chubby smiling face with her hand and took the compliment as was intended.

"Aww Albert you are too kind," she chuckled.

"Well my dear, as much as I'd like to, I can't stand 'ere chatting all day. I've got stuff to be getting on with."

Christine was a little disheartened that she couldn't continue the mindless gossip with Albert, but her spirits were lifted when she spotted Audrey coming from her house across the road waving rather foolishly trying to get Christine's attention.

"Well I'll be seeing yer Albert. Mind how you go now."

"You too my dear. Bye now."

As fast as Albert left, Audrey was at Christine's front garden. A little out of breath she said, "Oooh I say Christine what in heaven's name are the police doing at Jack and Jodie's?"

And so the gossip continued and before the day was out most of the residents of Mottrom road had speculated that CJ had been attacked, probably a knife wound and had no less than twenty stitches in his leg. Now it was construed that there was a mad man on the loose. The idea of a home watch scheme was suggested by one of the residents of Mottrom Road and Christine Hunt had jumped at the chance to hold the first meeting at her house at the weekend. She looked forward to paying Jodie a visit, when she would invite her neighbours to a home watch meeting. The perfect opportunity to partake in gratuitous blather, drink lots of tea and eat cake, not to mention quench Christine's curiosity.

CHAPTER THIRTEEN

Liar Liar

Jodie had no idea what to expect as she entered her home. It was only by pure luck that she had received the text message from CJ moments before entering the house. The news that Jack had believed CJ was off school due to feeling unwell was welcomed as much as a winning lottery ticket. She proceeded to hang Jack's suits on the ornate iron coat rack. And just as Jack liked her to, she took off her sandals placing them neatly on the rack and hung up her handbag, following the usual ritual taking care not to give cause for Jack to gripe, although her face could not hide the disappointment of seeing Jack home early as she walked into the kitchen. He was sat at the breakfast area with a plate of cold chicken breast, assortment of pickles, an unsliced loaf of bread sharing a wooden chopping board with a large knife and the Portmeirion butter dish.

"Where have you been?" asked Jack with a mouthful of food. He spoke in his usual low unpleasant voice that sent a chill down Jodie's spine. "You left CJ at home when he's sick."

Jodie took an intuitive gamble, based on receiving CJ's text message only moments ago, that Jack had not been home long and guessed that CJ had not told him how long she was out for.

"I went to pay the gardener. I was not out for long," she replied cautiously.

Jack picked up the bread knife and proceeded to cut himself a slice of bread. His technique was a little too rough for Jodie's liking.

Without taking his eyes off the bread he said, "I distinctively remember telling you that you needed to pay the gardener yesterday. God damn it Jodie, if you hadn't been so hell bent on meeting Kat and deliberately deceiving me you would have been able to get your chores done. Do you know how embarrassing it is when you pay the gardener late? And what about my suits? Please Lord, tell me that you did that yesterday."

Jodie hesitated, unsure what to say, but before she could respond Jack resumed, "You did pick up my dry cleaning yesterday, didn't you?"

"Y… y … yes, yes of course I did," said Jodie. "And I got the car cleaned. Full wax, polish the works … Went to that Polish garage. Made sure they were really thorough." Alarm bells were ringing in her ears. "I … I'd better go check on CJ."

She hurried out the kitchen like a frightened mouse scurrying into a hole, grabbing the dry cleaning she had previously hung on the coat rack. *There's no way he saw the dry cleaning, not from the breakfast bar* she thought to herself and ran up the stairs into her bedroom. Her heart was pounding fast and her breathing heavy. She could hear Jack still talking. His voice muffled. She was unable to make out the words. But just the sound of his voice was a mental strain. It sent a shiver of nerves down her spine. She had spent so much time yesterday at the hospital with Kat and then with CJ so, other than getting the car cleaned up, she hadn't done any of the other errands she was supposed to do. Not even asked Christine Hunt if she could get her silver birch tree pruned. And now Jack was angry with her … again. She had no sooner hung all of Jack's suits in his wardrobe when the doorbell rang. From the top of the stairs Jody heard a familiar voice.

"Good afternoon sir. I am Inspector Campbell and this is PC Martin. We would like to ask you a few questions about the Jaguar. Can we come in?"

"The Jaguar? Why officer? What's wrong with the car?"

"If we could just come in for a moment we will explain everything."

Yes of course, please come in." Perplexed yet unnerved by the company of the law enforcement Jack ushered the two policemen into the kitchen. Matt and Carl were escorted into a beautiful country style kitchen. The sun was pouring in through the window highlighting a dark chestnut wooden floor. The kitchen cupboards were the same warm wood colour as the floor with intricately detailed handles. The unusually shaped granite work top in the centre of the kitchen made a curious seating area. One part of the granite top was straight sided overhanging the cupboards underneath and the other side shaped like a trapezium.

Jack pointed to the heavy looking tall chairs tucked under the worktop.

"Please take a seat." The three men sat down. "Now how can I help?"

Jodie was now stood motionless on the landing not sure what to do. She continued to listen with heavy breath as the three men conversed. It was Matt that began talking first. She felt goose bumps all over her body as she listened attentively.

"Yesterday two teenagers were knocked down on the Woodbank Road and both are now fighting for their lives in Macclesfield General. We know from our forensic reports that the car was a blue S Type Jaguar. We also know that there are nine blue S Type Jaguars in this part of Cheshire. We are checking all the owners in the area. It's standard procedure. Could you please tell us where you were yesterday around the time of 11.30 a.m?" Matt's voice was calm and friendly.

Then another voice spoke unknown to Jodie.

"We'll need someone to verify your whereabouts ... I'm sure you understand sir. This is just routine."

Jack replied disdainfully,

"Actually officer, my wife drives the Jag, my car is the Merc. I can tell you though that yesterday from ten thirty until one I was facilitating a project controls meeting in my office."

"Your office sir?"

"Yes, do you know Blanchet's just past the Waverley bypass?" Matt and Carl both simultaneously nodded. "That's where I work."

Officer Martin scribbled down some notes in his jotter. "And your wife, is she here? We'd like to ask her the same questions."

Upon hearing this Jodie tried casually to walk down the stairs and into the kitchen. But she was actually shaking all over. Her whole body trembled and her heart was still beating so hard it felt like it was going to burst right out of her chest. Her emotions were a mixture of nervous excitement of the exceptionally handsome Inspector Matt now sat at her breakfast table as cool as a cucumber, the restless worry caused by her husband and the frightening realisation that she had to come up with a story of where she was at 11.30 a.m. yesterday morning. She desperately wanted a drink to calm her nerves. She was clutching the All Day Laundry receipt she had intended to throw in the bin before she was stopped in her tracks by her visitors. Matt and Carl were sat with their backs to the kitchen door. They did not see Jodie as she uneasily entered the room. Through the kitchen window Christine Hunt could be seen talking to Albert over the fence. *Oh Christine is going to love this* thought Jodie.

"And here is my beautiful wife," announced Jack upon seeing Jodie advancing rather precariously towards them. "Jodie, these officers would just like to know where you were at 11.30 yesterday morning." Jack proceeded to get up out of his chair and offer his seat to Jodie in a gentlemanly fashion. Jodie knew very well this was just for show in front of the policeman and that any anger towards her was being temporarily cleverly contained. She made a failed attempt to seat herself gracefully opposite Matt and hoped that he hadn't noticed. In the split second it took for Matt to comprehend who was now sat opposite him he nearly fell off his chair and then managed to retain his composure with a lot more poise that Jodie. He had hoped after their brief meeting at the hospital he would see her again, but hadn't imagined that it would be under these circumstances or so soon. Jodie noticed straight away Matt's fresh handsome face was today looking tired and unshaven. Although this did not falter the attraction. His dark hair was gelled just as it had been and the Ray Bans still resting on the top of his head looked like they had not moved. Jodie gave a meek smile and prayed their encounter at the hospital was not mentioned. It was probably only a matter of seconds but Jodie's apprehension made it feel like there was a long pause of silence before Carl gave a reintroduction of themselves followed by the rehearsed account of why they had called. Jodie listened as though this was the first time she was hearing this news.

"So if you could just tell us where you were at around 11.30 yesterday morning we should be able to wrap this up."

Jodie's eyes moved from Matt's to Carl's, politely acknowledging Carl as he spoke and at the same time modestly admiring Matt, whilst Jack hovered around picking up a slice of chicken breast and uttering, "Please officers help yourselves!"

Jodie did not know what made her say it, maybe the fact that she was holding the All Day Laundry receipt reminded her that she wanted Jack to think she had picked up his dry cleaning yesterday. Maybe if Jack thought she had done what he had expected it would lessen his anger and appease the situation.

"I would have been at the dry cleaners around that time," said Jodie hoping to sound convincing as she fought to control her shaky voice and tried not to fidget. "You know the All Day Laundry on Hough Street?" Matt nodded politely although amused by this beautiful lady's discomposure but said nothing. Carl continued scribbling in his notebook.

"Well ... anyway ... there's a dry cleaners at the bottom of Hough Street and I ... I called in to ... to pick up Jack's suits and ... and ... then I went to meet my friend for lunch." She glanced at Jack who appeared nonchalant.

"And where does your friend live?" asked Matt. Already knowing the answer he just wanted to hear Jodie confirm that she did not drive down Woodbank Road.

"I ... I went to meet my friend at the hospital." Jodie took another sideways glance at Jack, half expecting some sort of reaction, but he still he seemed unmoved. He was now busy reading emails on his phone. Nevertheless the topic of conversation still made her feel uncomfortable.

"Oh I'm sorry, is your friend sick?"

"No officer. My friend is a nurse." Jodie gave a half-hearted grin.

Then Carl spoke. "So from Hough Street to the hospital you would have taken … "

" … the old road. It's the quickest route to the hospital and the road's always quiet," said Jodie.

"Well I think we have taken up enough of your time," said Carl as he made his final entry in his notebook, flicked his pen, closed his pad and then gave Jodie an artificial smile. Which did not help her nervous disposition.

As Jodie courteously accompanied the officers to the front door, she noticed Christine Hunt was now in full conversation with Audrey, another resident from across the road. It was unequivocal that the chin-wagging was about the police calling at her house. Jodie loathed that her doings were feeding Christine's meddlesomeness like drugs to an addict. Yesterday it was CJ's accident and today the police. The sick feeling already present in her stomach intensified.

"Are you alright?" whispered Matt even though Carl was already now out of earshot as he was getting into the police car. "You're looking really shaken-up."

Jodie was aware that her distress had not been very well disguised. This would easily be remedied once she had consumed some alcohol. She wanted to tell him something. Anything to try and excuse her nervousness. Unsure that anything she said would make a difference she gave a feeble, "I'll be alright," indicating that there was something wrong.

Matt handed Jodie his card.

"If you ever need to talk, just give me a ring … okay." This notion was partly the obvious perception that something in the Vickers household was not right and partly that he wanted to see this beautiful woman again.

"I … I will. Thank you," said Jodie feeling herself flush. Her hand slightly shaking as she took the card, careful not to show the laundry receipt.

After a wave of the hand and a perfect white toothed smile, Matt had joined Carl in the car pondering over how nervy Jodie had been. The engine purred softly as Jodie watched them drive away.

"I think we need to pay a visit to the dry cleaners. I don't know about you Matt, but I get the impression that the lovely Mrs Vickers is hiding something."

"I don't know Carl ... I just don't know ... The car looked clean. And she was at the hospital yesterday. I saw her. But you're right ... she is definitely hiding something."

"The car looked too clean if you ask me. She could have easily put it through the car wash. Well there's only one way to find out," said Carl as he drove down Mottrom Road and headed toward Hough Street.

Jodie watch the police car as it slowly disappeared down the road and turn out of the estate. She wondered vaguely who the other owners of blue S type Jaguars were and if Matt would hand out his card so willingly to them. For some reason she hoped he would not. Holding the card between fingers and thumb she stared at the words '*Inspector. Matthew Campbell. Cheshire Constabulary*'. Warmness burned in her belly like the embers of a fire. For a moment she could not move. It suddenly occurred to her what would happen if Matt found out she had lied. Not only was she lying to Jack she was now lying to the police.

If Jodie could ever justify to herself the right time to have a drink it was now. The ever watchful Christine Hunt had been enjoying the spectacle in her flourishing garden whilst conveying to Audrey and anyone else who was out in the neighbourhood opinions of the Vickers and views of why the police had come to their house. Jodie could hear the mutterings coming from her garden, but dared not think about what drivel was being said. She shut the door. For now she was not going to dwell on her nosey neighbour. Jodie had more pressing matters to deal with behind the closed door.

CHAPTER FOURTEEN

The Bloody Clothes

Jodie had to have a drink and fast. Usually alone in the house at this time of day, fixing herself a stiff drink to calm her nerves would not be a problem. But being restricted by having both Jack and CJ at home, this seemed to make the want for alcohol even stronger. While Jack was still in the kitchen engrossed in email activity, as he had been since Inspector Matt and Carl had left, Jodie snuck up the stairs and in to CJ's bedroom. He had slept soundly and undisturbed during the whole police episode. His cluttered and untidy room was lit with a slither of warm sunlight that shone brightly through the small opening where the curtains had not been fully drawn. He looked comfortable, laying only partly under his duvet with his bandaged leg exposed. He woke with a start when his mum began picking up his dirty laundry that was typically strewn all over the floor. She thought she was being quiet but had managed to wake him all the same.

"Hey Mum you woke me up," said CJ hazily.

"Oh sorry," whispered Jodie. "You been asleep all this time? Didn't you hear the doorbell ring about half an hour ago?"

"No ... why? Who was it? Please tell me it wasn't Mrs Hunt," said CJ. He had been having the same awful thoughts as his mum. He didn't want her coming round questioning his accident while his dad was home.

"No. It was the police," said Jodie trying to sound casual as her voice was still a little shaky. She continued to rid the floor of clothes, noticing the blood stained PE shirt and the bloody torn trousers, still in the clear plastic bag, that were left so openly on the floor. She picked them up half wanting to scold CJ for being so careless, but thought better of it. She wondered if it was her imagination but was certain there was a strong clinical smell just like the smell of hospitals.

"The police? What did the police want?" asked CJ totally unaware of his mum's annoyance.

Jodie retold the story she had now heard three times ... "And apparently the car was a Jaguar S type so they are checking out all the owners in the area."

"Er .... Mum ... did they say who they were ... the people ... I mean who were hit?"

"No actually they didn't," said Jodie.

For the second time that day, CJ's blood ran cold as it dawned on him, *could it possibly be his two best friends that were hit yesterday morning? Is that why he'd not been able to get hold of either of them?* CJ tried to shake this thought out of his mind. But there remained a frightening realisation that this was the reason neither Thomas or Kelly had been answering their phones. And he knew they were on Squirrel Hill which leads down to Woodbank Road.

"What's up CJ? You look like you've seen a ghost," said Jodie as she noticed the colour drain from his face. "CJ? You okay?" But before CJ could answer he leaned over the side of his bed as though he had no control of his body and threw up all over the rug.

"Oh Mum I'm sorry." Tears welled up in his eyes and his stomach was in knots. His body felt like it was sinking into a place of darkness yet he could not explain to his mum what just happened.

"CJ it's okay ... it's probably just the after effects of ... " but before Jodie could finish her sentence she heard Jack's voice as he entered the room.

"Oh dear! CJ m'boy you really are feeling bad today aren't you? Jodie go get CJ a glass of water." Jack had walked right past Jodie as she stood suddenly rooted to the spot. Her eyes wide with alarm, both arms full of laundry and amongst them was the see-through bag containing the blood soaked clothes. Jack sat at the edge of the bed looking at CJ fondly. His eyes almost portrayed a loving sympathetic look that CJ did not often see. Without breaking eye contact CJ concentrated all of his efforts to quickly pull his duvet over himself, mindful of not leaving his bandaged leg on show. Jodie was frozen, rooted on the spot powerless, as she watched CJ's struggle as he tugged hard at the duvet underneath his dad's weight, pulling it up and over his stitched leg with Jack just inches away. She couldn't help but wonder in disbelief at his stupidity, why was CJ not wearing long pants? CJ was now starring at his mum clutching the bloody trousers, sharing the same look of complete horror. A ray of sunlight broke through the gap in the curtains like a spot light shining directly on Jodie. The atmosphere in the room was so tense even the magnolia walls seem to take on a rolling fog colour making it suddenly seem like the blood stained trousers were the only object of colour in the room.

"Go on! What are you waiting for?" snapped Jack.

Jodie was gobsmacked Jack had not noticed the crimson colour emanating from the pile of clothes. She crumpled them together in a tight ball and in a fit of panic hurried out the room and down the stairs to the utility room, dropping odd socks and boxer shorts on the way. *Your just gonna have to learn not to get caught* she thought, as she ineptly shoved all the clothes into the washing machine and slammed the door shut. Flustered, frightened and in her mind, overdue, she grabbed the water bottle filled with vodka from behind the box of washing powder and drank abundantly. She thought she could hear Jack calling from CJ's bedroom. For a split second she felt woozy, but the alcohol was now working its magic. She steadied herself against the washing machine as the satisfying sensation swept through her body like a summer breeze gently caressing the treetops. And as though her whole trembling body had been touched by a healing hand, she reached a pleasant state of calmness. She took a deep elongated breath before quickly running outside to the wheelie bin and ditching the bag with the bloody clothes, hiding it underneath a pile of vegetable peelings. Then fetching a glass of water she carried it up to CJ's bedroom, still sure that she could hear Jack calling out, but no longer felt disturbed by it.

She liked that her hands had stopped shaking and her body had stopped trembling. She liked the way the alcohol washed away her unsettling feelings and anxious worry. What had happened just now almost seemed funny and Jodie had to stop herself from grinning as she handed CJ the glass of water. Jack was still perched on the bed doing a very bad job of consoling his son, as to what he thought was a terrible stomach bug. Jodie was able to ignore Jack's sharp remark at how long it had taken her to fetch a glass of water.

"Thanks Mum," said CJ and as they both looked at each other they exchanged a sweet smile that spoke a hundred words. Jodie then proceeded to clean up the vomit, content and comforted that she somehow had miraculously managed to fool Jack for the third time that day.

The rest of the day was strangely calm. Surprisingly Jack seemed so concerned with his son that Jodie had been left alone without torment and he hadn't even wanted Jodie to cook his dinner. Probably because he had scoffed a bountiful amount of chicken breast and fresh bread. When Jack wasn't reading through emails or taking work calls he was checking in on a doleful CJ whom had remained in his room dwelling on the possibility that his two best friends could be the same two persons lying unconscious in a hospital bed. It was a sad and heartbreaking reflection of life in the Vickers home, when CJ's grief meant solace for his mum. This had left Jodie spending much of the evening reliving the events of the day and in her mind's eye picturing a scene of events that could have transpired had Jack seen what was right under his nose. Moreover, she couldn't stop herself from wondering, *who were the children who had been hit by the car?*

For what seemed like the hundredth time that evening Jodie found herself staring at Inspector Matthew Campbell's business card wondering what consequences one innocent phone call would bring. As desperate and curious as she was to know the names of the hit and run victims, there was a willingness eating away inside her just purely to talk to Matt Campbell. Just to hear his voice. But her own inner voice was telling her that one innocent phone call would have consequences. The risk of Jack finding out that she had phoned another man was too great, so she decided to just keep the business card in her purse. Keep it innocently hidden, like a trophy and just feel happy knowing that she was carrying around something Matt Campbell had given to her. As sad as she knew how her reasons sounded to herself, it was never the less comforting. Then it suddenly hit her like a giant wave crashing against rocks. She had Kat's old Nokia phone hidden under the car seat. She could make any phone call she liked and Jack wouldn't be able to trace it. But to make the call while Jack was home was too chancy she would need to wait until tomorrow. For the meantime, Jodie would leave the phone along with her other purchases, safely hidden under the car sear. And tomorrow, when Jack was at work, she would phone Matt Campbell.

~~~~~~~~~~

CJ's tormented and troubled mind had left him still feeling tiresome. He did not want to leave his room, partly of fear that his dad would see the dressing on his leg and he knew what trouble that would bring. Although he knew that he wouldn't be able to hide his scar forever. He did wonder however how his wound would heal and how much of a scar would remain visible on his leg. Only time would tell. And for now at least the best thing he could do for his own and his mum's sake was not to let his dad find out about his accident. If CJ could keep the scar hidden long enough, he supposed when the time came when his dad saw it, he could make a credible excuse – *Oh that Dad ... I caught myself on one of Mrs Hunt's thorn bushes... it's nothing ... looks worse than it is!* Maybe, just maybe his dad would believe him. He could only hope, as CJ knew only too well that his dad does not stop until he gets to the bottom of matters. He would dig endlessly and thoroughly to the root cause, which in CJ's mind would reach the charming Wayne Dear. The very thought of his dad finding out that for the past six months he was a victim of bullying and had been hiding like a frightened little mouse, would first disappoint and then outrage his dad. This would then be followed by somehow being his mum's fault. *His mum should have known what was going on in school ... his mum should not have allowed this to happen.* His mum would have to suffer too.

CJ's door made a low creaking sound as his dad slowly opened it to check on him for the sixth time since he had thrown up. Same as the previous times, CJ huddled under his duvet, his empty stomach rumbling and eyes shut tight pretending to be asleep. He had no idea why his dad was so concerned. He by no means had an affectionate nature and the caring attitude was becoming more unnerving. The evening slowly crept in and CJ still couldn't help feeling restless. It seemed like he spent hours tossing and turning before he eventually fell asleep.

He was stood by a lake. It was very calm and endearing. A low fog hung over the lake and a frosty mist fell upon the stony ground. There was a rowing boat afloat in the middle of the lake, pure white in colour. It glowed through the fog and was as still as the water. On board sat two people, a boy and a girl. CJ couldn't see their faces, but he felt a deep connection to them and somehow from the distance he could sense their sadness. He felt a strong desire to help them back to shore. He paced up and down the pebbled shoreline. The water licked his shoes and he felt it was icy cold. Too cold to swim out to the boat, yet his longing to help the two stranded souls grew stronger and more desperate. He tried to call out to them to row back, but his voice fell unheard on the wintry water. All of a sudden the grey clouds parted to reveal an immense stream of light that without warning consumed the boat. The brilliant light flickered then faded to a warm sunlit glow. The fog immediately lifted and the glistening sunlight fell on the water with a warm orange glow. The boy and girl had vanished and the empty white row boat bobbed merrily on the lake. CJ felt an emptiness like nothing he had ever felt before. He called out in vain for the boy and the girl to come back ... sobbing uncontrollably ...

"No, come back ... don't leave me ... .please come back ... come back!"

"CJ ... honey ... it's okay ... you just had a bad dream." CJ curled into his mum's arms as though he had regressed to a small child, and Jodie cradled her son reassuringly ... "Shh, it's okay ...it was just a dream."

It took several minutes for CJ to stop crying. When CJ finally dried his puffy red eyes and found his voice, through the sniffles he managed to tell his very concerned mum about his dream. Jodie listened carefully.

"What do you think it means Mum?" asked CJ. The dream had left him momentarily scared with a deep felt sadness. At the back of his mind all he could think about was Thomas and Kelly.

"I don't know honey," replied Jodie. "Try get some more sleep honey, it's the middle of the night." And she gave CJ another heartfelt hug as the thought of the two children in hospital still weighed heavily on her mind. CJ closed his eyes, but he couldn't sleep. His stomach was tight and ached from lack of food, but he could not bring himself to get out of bed and go to the kitchen for something to eat. And the lurid dream was still vivid in his head. Hours went by before CJ finally went back to sleep. Morning was now breaking, but the sun was not as bright for the grey rainclouds clouds filled the sky. CJ slept deeply. Noises from downstairs did not wake him.

CHAPTER FIFTEEN

The Painful Truth

It was a cool Thursday morning. The sun was not shining as brightly as it had the previous two days. The sky was overcast and the weather forecast had predicted rain later. Jodie was stood solemnly gazing out the kitchen window clutching a steaming frothy coffee with a measure of brandy. There were broken plates on the floor by her feet and a shattered glass that was swimming in a pool of orange juice. Jodie ignored the blood trickling down her leg and the dull pain in her head. She took a deep breath and a gulp of coffee. She was tired and weary. The pleasant smell of crispy bacon and French toast disguised the mess that was left by Jack moments before leaving for work.

Jodie heard CJ enter the kitchen. She did not turn around, she just took another sip of coffee and stared blankly out the window at the scenic neighbourhood. Gardens along the street flourishing with colourful flowers, wall climbers, pottered plants and hanging baskets. Each garden with its own quintessential design that was typical English. And thought *how can outside look so vibrant and full of life.* Jodie wanted to grasp hold of the sweet scented freshness and peacefulness of outside and bring it into her home. But instead she stood amongst the shards of crockery and broken glass feeling empty and deflated. She took another big mouthful of coffee expecting to find some strength from it. The fiery taste of the brandy set her a little on her way.

"Mum what happened? What did Dad do?" said CJ tiptoeing around the broken piece of crockery and the pool of orange juice.

"Your dad said that I didn't clean up your sick properly yesterday," said Jodie with a grave sigh. "He said that every time he went in your room yesterday he could still smell it and this morning he told me that he could smell sick in the house and it put him off his breakfast. So ...so he threw it at me." Jodie knew that this time it would be pointless trying to play down the events of the morning. She was thinking that she would certainly need to take CJ's rug to the dry cleaners. The prospect was not appealing, but less so was Jack's temper.

"What? Mum that's ridiculous. There is no smell of sick," said CJ.

"I know ... I don't know ... I can't smell anything. And don't you be doing any cleaning up," added Jodie pointing her finger at CJ. "I just wanted a moment to drink my coffee and collect my thoughts." Jodie finished the coffee with one last big gulp and stuck her empty mug in the dish washer. She took a hard look at the surrounding mess. A jug of milk had been knocked on its side and a pool of milk had run to the edge of the table and was dripping on the floor. There were slops of coffee and spills of sugar over the worktop and Jack's coffee mug had somehow lost its handle. But before Jodie started the bothersome task of clearing up the mess she plated up some crispy bacon and French toast that had remained unharmed on the stove. CJ, who couldn't remember eating anything other than toast for his breakfast the previous day, was again now absolutely ravenous. He had been sharing his mum's gaze around the room with a horrible sense of self blame.

"There you go babe. You must be starving," said Jodie and she passed CJ the plate noticing his eyes were still watery and sore.

"I'm sorry Mum ... this is all my fault ...If I hadn't been sick yesterday none of this... Oh Mum your leg's bleeding. You need to put a plaster on it." CJ looked irritatingly like his father when he spoke with a mouthful of food.

"Don't talk with your mouth full," snapped Jodie more harshly than intended. "And none of this is your fault. Don't even think that."

"Sorry!" said CJ after he swallowed his French toast and his cheek regained normal size.

Jodie paused to take a look at the cut on her leg. It was only a small cut probably caused by a bit of glass.

"It's just a graze honey ... I must have caught it on a piece of glass. It's not that bad," said Jodie candidly as she applied the band aid, more for CJ's satisfaction than her own. A small cut on her leg was the least of her worries.

"Mum ... Dad kept coming in my room yesterday. I thought he was seeing if I was okay, but do you think he was checking to see if my room smelt of sick?" This notion had just occurred to him while he had been mulling over his dad's behaviour of both yesterday and this morning. "I thought it was really strange ... you know ... it's not like he's the compassionate type ... Dad ... is he Mum?"

Jodie gave a snort.

"Er ... no ... compassionate he is definitely is not. Maybe he just has an extra sensitive nose."

"Well at least there's something about him that is sensitive," said CJ and he smiled.

Jodie managed a laugh. Typically she would try and cover up when Jack had had an outburst, but today she was glad that CJ was there. He added humour to a state of unrest. In spite of the lightening mood in the Vickers home, the day turned grey as heavy clouds rolled in and the heavens opened up bringing the predicted heavy down poor of rain. The weather at least would keep Christine Hunt from skulking around outside like a herald for the estate. But the rain did not stop her from calling at the house. Luckily by this time the kitchen was looking as though this morning's occurrence never took place but instead it appeared that the family had enjoyed a pleasant breakfast together and the sweet smell of fried bacon and coffee was still lingering.

Both Jodie and CJ were dressed when the doorbell rang. CJ had wisely worn long pants so that there would not be a repeat of yesterday, when he nearly exposed the bandage that covered the twelve stitches on his leg, and Jodie was dressed casually in jogging bottoms and hoody that also covered up the light bruising.

"Hi Jodie have I caught you at a bad time?" Christine Hunt stood shielding herself from the pouring rain with a huge yellow golfing umbrella and ridiculous green wellington boots.

"Er ... no ... no ... not at all," replied Jodie completely caught off guard. She was not able to excuse herself quick enough and consequently unable to reject Christine Hunt.

The moment CJ heard Christine's voice he scampered up the stairs to his bedroom, as fast as his sore leg would allow him, leaving his mum alone with the neighbour from hell.

"I wanted to invite you to a home watch meeting on Saturday," continued Christine Hunt as she rather violently shook the droplets of rain off her umbrella and retracting it as she walked through the door. "The residents and I think it will be a good idea to start a home watch scheme and ... well ... I thought where better to host the first meeting than at my house." She looked positively delighted by the prospect as she pulled off her wellington boots to reveal bright pink fluffy socks. "So what d'you think Jodie? Will you and Jack be able to come? Oooooh, something smells nice Jodie. You making coffee?" Christine removed her green wax jacket and handed it to Jodie. "I don't know where you want to put that my love it's a bit wet."

Jodie hung the jacket on the ornate iron coat rack. Droplets of rain falling on the Axminster carpet. Momentarily speechless and dazed at Christine's brashness.

"Well Jodie my love, I'm glad you're home because I also wanted to ask how young Christopher is doing. I've been really worried about him see ... Through here is it?" said Christine following the smell of coffee and making her way into the kitchen.

"Oh ... er ... yes ... " said Jodie remembering that Christine has never been in her house before. Even though the layout is a mirror image of her own. "CJ's fine ... Yes he's doing good. Erm ... resting at the moment. You want some coffee Christine?"

"Ooh yes, that would be lovely. Thank you dear." Christine sat herself down. Eyes like a hawk scanning the kitchen. "Beautiful kitchen dear ... yes ... yes ... I really like the design ... it's very nice."

"Oh thank you. Milk and sugar?" said Jodie as she began begrudgingly making coffee.

"Yes please ...two sugars Jodie. Thank you dear," said Christine.

"So you say you're going to start a home watch scheme" Jodie passed Christine a mug of freshly filtered coffee and seating herself opposite her.

"Yes, that's right dear. Can you and Jack come to our first meeting this Saturday? We thought 5 p.m. would be a good time. Not too late then. Some of the old folk say they don't like being out too late. Not after what happened to young Christopher and in broad daylight too?"

"CJ? I don't understand. What he has to do with anything," said a confused Jodie.

"Well he was attacked. Was he not?" replied Christine questioningly, eyeing Jodie with an inquisitive look.

It was at this point when Jodie understood why Christine had called round. It was not to try and get her to go to her home watch meeting but to pry information about CJ. She makes it her business to know everything in the neighbourhood. Jodie wished for the power to snap her fingers and Christine Hunt to disappear. She did not want to be having this conversation and was annoyed with herself for letting Christine's forceful personality defeat her.

"Christine you know CJ was not attacked. I told you before it was an accident," Jodie .

Christine gave a reluctant nod as she sipped her coffee. Her expression was one of guilt.

"Why would anyone think that CJ was attacked? What have you been saying?" She recalled seeing Christine talking to Albert and Audrey but somehow managed to curb her annoyance.

Christine looked appalled at the accusation that she had been gossiping.

"Well I might have mentioned that CJ had a nasty cut on his leg ... but you know what people are like round here Jodie. They make their own minds up and what with the police coming here yesterday. They put two and two together ..."

"Yeah and make five!" added Jodie "The police had nothing to do with CJ. They were here because of the hit and run," Jodie slightly let down her guard and bared her agitation. But she managed to keep her voice calm. The last thing she wanted was to have a row with her neighbour and if she was honest with herself she didn't mind talking about the car accident. The story held more weight with Christine and would defer her from gossiping about CJ. Albeit she would rather not be sat with her drinking coffee in the kitchen.

"Oh, what happened Jodie?" probed Christine, attempting now to change the conversation. Her shameful expression had suddenly changed back to one of curiosity as her eyes sparkled underneath her glasses.

"Well all I know is ... " began Jodie and she retold the story to her attentive neighbour.

"And you don't know who the children are? Well it's gonna be in the paper today ... surely?" said Christine.

Jodie had forgotten that the local free paper was delivered on a Thursday. And Christine was probably right. There would most likely be an article regarding the accident published in today's newspaper.

"Yeah ... I guess so," said Jodie. However she didn't want to wait until the paper was delivered. It would not arrive until late in the afternoon and Jodie still had plans to phone Inspector Matt Campbell the first chance she got. The heavy rain that pounded the window brought with it a dimness that filled the room and there was a chill in the air. Jodie poured some more coffee. More for the warmth than anything. She thought of asking Christine if she wanted a drop of bandy with her coffee but decided against it.

"So what about the home watch meeting ... can you come Jodie?" asked Christine.

"Oh right ... yes ... the home watch meeting." Jodie had restored her inner calmness. She went on, "Well I don't think

Jack will go. It's not really his thing Christine and Saturday he usually plays golf, but I should be able to make it." Luckily for Jodie, Jack would not give Christine the time of day. Or any of the neighbours for that matter. He looks down his nose at them as though they are not worthy to be living in the same street as him, like there is an invisible class structure in which he sees himself above all. He refuses to engage in conversation and they are lucky if they received a reciprocating passing smile. Jodie believed that her presence at the home watch meeting would prevent any rumours and lessen the gossip amongst the Mottram residents. She also wanted to keep on the right side of Christine as she had yet to bring up the matter of her overgrown silver birch. "Oh wonderful!" exclaimed Christine sounding too over excited by the prospect. "Well I'd better get back home and leave you be."

"Oh right okay," said Jodie trying not to look pleased that Christine was leaving as she followed her out of the kitchen, amused by the pink fluffy socks. "Er ... just one thing before you go ... You know how Jack ... Well, er ... he has this thing about your silver birch. The thing is it's getting a little ... well a lot actually"

"Come on Jodie what are you trying to say my dear?" snapped Christine as she threw on her dripping wet coat.

"Jack has asked me to ask you to get your silver birch tree cropped. It's all the leaves you see, they fall right onto our drive and he's ...well he's getting a little miffed that every morning his car is covered with piles of leaves." Jodie could not tell if Christine looked cross or bewildered.

"You have a gardener don't you?" said Christine sounding a little severe.

"Yes. I use Dickens Nursery. Why?"

"Well ask them how much it will cost to prune my birch," said Christine, much to Jodie's relief.

"Sure. Will do Christine," replied Jodie feeling relieved she had finally got that off her chest.

"I will be seeing you then my love." Christine stepped into her boots and she was out the door. The golfing umbrella held high over her head of bouncy grey curls. "And thanks for the coffee." She left with a cheery wave.

"Bye Christine," said Jodie and she closed the door.

"Blimey Mum! What's Christine Hunt doing coming round here?" said CJ a little scared. He was walking down the stairs now he decided it was safe for him to leave his room. "Having a nice cosy chat? That's just weird."

"I didn't want to let her in. She just … well … let herself in," said Jodie amusingly as she followed CJ into the lounge. "She wants me to go to a home watch meeting on Saturday."

"I bet she's asking everyone," said CJ making himself comfortable on the sofa. "You're not going are you Mum?"

Jodie glanced out the window to watch Christine walk through her garden gate looking full of beans.

"I told her I'd go. I don't want her gossiping about me to all the neighbours." Jodie watched the rain drops bouncing off the car, picturing the phone secretly tucked under the seat. The morning had all but passed and she still hadn't phoned Matt. She knew she would need to leave the house to make the phone call. But she had no reason to go out and the weather was by and large preventing it. It was frustrating to say the least.

"CJ do you need anything from the Chemist? Painkillers? Settlers?"

"No Mum I'm okay. My leg doesn't hurt," said CJ as he began flicking through the TV channels. "Ah cool, *The Simpsons*."

"And your stomach?" asked Jodie

"Fine Mum. Unless you poisoned me with your cooking."

"Oh, you are definitively feeling better today. I think you can go back to school on Monday."

Jodie was glad to see signs that CJ's witty and jovial nature was returning. The emotions from his dream appeared to have passed and CJ did not speak of it. Nor was the incident at breakfast addressed. Instead Jodie spent her time thinking mostly about all the tasks she needed to complete for her new job. The portfolio she needed to put together. The list of equipment and materials she would need and in her mind's eye she kept seeing Inspector Matt. His perfectly gelled hair, sun kissed face and fetching smile. Her stomach did a nervous flip. As much as she enjoyed having CJ's company, watching TV and having lunch while the storm clouds further darkened the skies and the rain hammered the windows, it was forestalling her scheme to leave the house. As hours passed the wave of frustration increased.

There was a rustling of paper and then the light knocking sound of the letterbox. Despite the heavy rain, the industrious paper boy was committed to delivering the local newspaper. He was head to foot in bright yellow waterproofs carrying a bright orange bag. Jodie spotted him from the lounge window as she got up to collect the paper and had a strange feeling of jealousy. Then as she picked up the paper her heart sank to the pit of her stomach. There was a photograph of Woodbank Road. Jodie immediately recognised the bend in the road and the parting of the foliage to the left where there is a dirt path leading up to Squirrel Hill. The headline read: *Double Tragedy as Two Teenagers Die in Hit and Run.* Jodie read on;

> *Double tragedy struck on the morning of 16 June when two schoolchildren from Kings High School were hit by a car on Woodbank Road. Mr Knight, a local resident of Mottrom Estate, was walking his dog when he discovered the children and called for an ambulance. Mr Knight said, "I was shocked that somebody could do this and just drive off."*
>
> *The schoolchildren named, Thomas Bradshaw and Kelly Jones were playing truant from school when they were ploughed off the road by a speeding motorist.*
>
> *Police believe the driver had reached a speed of around 80mph when the collision happened, but failed to stop. The*

> *children both aged thirteen years whom were being treated at Macclesfield Infirmary failed to wake from a coma. The severity of their head trauma has tragically cost them their lives.*
>
> *Police are appealing for any witnesses to the incident. Inspector Matt Campbell has said, "This is now a manslaughter investigation and we are putting all our efforts into tracking down the driver of a metallic blue S type Jaguar. We urge anyone with any information to come forward. I would also like to offer my sincere condolences to their families and friends who have suffered a terrible loss."*
>
> *Mr Miller, Head Master of Kings Comprehensive said, "We are all shocked and deeply saddened by the loss of two bright lovable children. It is unimaginable what the families are going through. Our hearts are with them."*
>
> *Local residents are now calling for the implementation of speed cameras and for tighter speed restrictions in the areas surrounding Squirrel Hill.*

Jodie read the article several times hoping that she had misread the names. But the ache that scorched through her body told her this was real. Her heart was in her throat making it hard to breath. She walked into the living room carrying the newspaper like it was a delicate artefact and handed it to CJ. Her eyes burning red with tears.

"Oh CJ ... I'm sorry ... I'm so sorry," she sobbed. CJ took the paper and his eyes fell upon the headline. And straight away he knew. The streaming tears stung his eyes so badly that he could not read beyond the first three lines. His face fell into the soft cushion and he sobbed uncontrollable tears of grief. Pain seared through his whole body. Pain that he had never experienced before. This was a hundred times worse that any pain Wayne Dear could inflict upon him and worse than any pain his father could cause. And he now knew what the dream meant. The boy and the girl on the boat, they were Thomas and Kelly. He could sense it stronger than ever. A feeling that something inside him had been ripped out of his body. His mother on her knees beside him, one arm resting on his shoulder and the other hand over her mouth silencing the sound of her own weeping. Sensing CJ's agony and wishing there was something she could do to stop him from hurting. Her muffled voice through her hand helplessly crying, "Oh I'm sorry … CJ … I'm so sorry."

A short time passed before Jodie managed to persuade CJ to move from the lounge up in to his bedroom. Grief had hit him like an incurable sickness. He lay on his bed still deep in shock, his mind full of questions swimming around his aching head. It was almost unbearable for Jodie to see her son in so much pain. She lay down next to him on his bed and gripped his arm in a vain show of affection and understanding, wishing there was something she could do.

If only they hadn't skipped school thought CJ. *If only I had talked them out of it. If it hadn't been for Wayne Dear they would never have bunked off school and they wouldn't be dead. It's his entire fault. Everything is his fault.* CJ struggled to put these thoughts out of his mind. Through his sobs be spoke of the frivolous things the three of them had done together. Tears were running down his face and he sniffed hard, struggling to talk to his mum of the distant memories of preschool, the three of them joining Theatre Works and their wild aspirations of being actors.

His mum listening attentively. Most of the stories Jodie already knew. CJ did not speak of Wayne. He skirted around the bullying paying homage to Thomas and Kelly. But the anger was very real, bubbling just beneath the surface of bitterness and sadness and one day it would rage up and CJ vowed one way or another he would make Wayne Dear pay.

After what seemed like hours of talking CJ eventually rested his head on his tear soaked pillow and slowly drifted off to sleep. He dreamed of walking through the woods with Thomas and Kelly in to a reminiscent reverie.

Jodie kissed him gently on the forehead. Then without hesitation she picked up the rug beside the bed, taking it to the car and threw it into the boot. She would take it to the dry cleaners the first chance she got. Then jumping in the car she reached under the seat and found the phone and top up card and added the credit to the phone. Then she pulled from her purse Inspector Matt's business card and dialled the number. She was sat in the car shivering and damp behind the steamy windows holding the phone to her ear eagerly waiting to hear the recognisable voice. Her heart beating wildly.

"Inspector Matt Campbell," said the voice at the other end of the phone.

"Hi, it's Jodie," she said. Her voice sounded raspy from crying.

"Jodie!" said Matt in a surprised and thrilled voice which quickly changed to one of concern. "Is everything okay?"

"I ... I ... no ...I wanted to talk to you ... it's about the hit and run ... the children I mean ... "

"Jodie do you have information? Can you come down to the police station?" asked Matt.

Jodie wished she had rehearsed what she wanted to say.

"No, no I don't have any information. It's just that ... I know the children. They are my son's best friends ... from school. We read the article in the Macclesfield Post today. I'm sorry maybe I shouldn't have called but ... I don't know ... I just wanted to tell you that. It's been a really bad day."

Matt could sense the misery in Jodie's voice. He had just learned that Jodie had a son. Why he felt this was a shock to him, he had no idea. He took a moment's pause as the truth of the situation unfolded. He was used to dealing with bereavement, the familiarity of events through years spent in the police force. But the connection he had with Jodie was one of confusion beyond his comprehension. Jodie felt cold and tried to find warmth huddled up inside her oversized hoody, but despite the bad weather a spark had ignited inside. She could hardly believe that she was finally on the phone to Matt, having been fighting the urge since yesterday afternoon. There was an uncomfortable silence and Jodie watch the tiny pitter patter of rain drops, amused by them unsystematically running down the windscreen and then Matt spoke and Jodie felt a flutter in her belly. She pressed the phone closer to her ear as though this would bring him closer, hanging onto his warm words.

"Jodie it's okay. Like I said, if ever you want to talk ... You can phone me anytime you want. I'm so sorry about your son. But I promise you, we will catch whoever did this and they will be looking at a very long stretch in prison." Matt spoke sincerely. He was even more determined than ever now to bring the culprit to justice.

"Thanks ... I ... " Jodie started to speak but was interrupted as Matt continued. He wanted to reassure Jodie that they were doing everything they can.

"It's not unusual for a hit and run driver to turn themselves in. Unfortunately people panic in these situations but there are some who have a conscience and come forward."

"So you think it was a local person?"

"Probably yes, based on the locations and time of the accident. But we have to cover all angles. We're also looking at possibilities of the car being stolen and working with other counties to see if there have been any reported stolen vehicles fitting the description and known joy riders. We have guys working round the clock. I think it's only a matter of time ...." Matt broke off for a moment. " ... I am so sorry that this has brought grief to your family ... your son ... what's his name?"

"Christopher ... Christopher John ... we just call him CJ for short. He's sleeping now. Spent all afternoon crying and eventually cried himself to sleep."

"And you? ... Sounds like you've done your fair share of crying too."

Jodie was oblivious to her sniffles down the receiver.

"Oh I … yes … it's been a big shock. And CJ … well he's in a bit of a state to be honest. I feel so helpless … I …" Jodie swallowed hard. She fought the urge not to start crying again.

"Listen Jodie, how about I call by sometime tomorrow afternoon. You know, just to check see if you're okay … and maybe I might have some more news for you."

"Sure, that would be nice … thanks Matt. I guess I should go … I er … need to …"

"Go check on CJ and I'll see you tomorrow."

"Okay. Thanks I will see you tomorrow … bye Matt."
Click

~~~~~~~~~~~~

When Jack arrived home that evening the heavy downpour of rain had turned to drizzle. The dark clouds hid the sun giving the illusion that the night had drawn in early. Behind the house the half-moon shimmered in the indigo sky. Small triangular leaves and spindly branches fallen from the silver birch lying scattered all along the pavement and driveway, shiny and wet. They reflected the dim street lamp that stood in front of the garden.

Inside was a wholesome and hearty smell of chicken casserole. This was all Jodie had managed to pull together for Jack's dinner. The despair that had overcome CJ after digesting the dreadful news of his two best friends seemed to have spread through the house and a chill hung in the air brought by the dismal wet day. She couldn't even face talking to Kat even though she had had a missed call from her followed by a text message saying the she knew who the victims were. She had recognised them as CJ's friends.

When Jack walked through the door to the delicious smell of stew Jodie was sure that even someone as unperceptive as he could feel an air of emptiness and sadness.

"Aha, chicken casserole … good … I'm starving," said Jack approvingly, checking that the carrots had been cut julienne style and not into circles.

Jodie's eyes were still puffy and blotchy. She had not tried to hide it. She had already decided that she was going to tell Jack the news as soon as he arrived home. She didn't care that he thought crying was a weakness. This was one sadness that she could not hide. Jack threw Jodie a droll look as she began serving him the casserole.

Jodie cleared her throat and in an odd serious tone she said, "Jack, y'know CJ's friends from school, Thomas and Kelly?"

"Erm ... yeah I think so," said Jack, further inspecting Jodie's cooking. Moving his fork around the plate.

Surely he must know his son's friends that he has grown up with thought Jodie incredulously.

"Well they died." She swallowed hard. Trying to speak the words was a battle. "They were hit by a car on Tuesday ... and they died ... it's in the paper." Jodie rested the serving spoon in the casserole dish so she could pass him the newspaper."

She took the seat next to him waiting for a reaction. After talking effortlessly to Matt, it made her realise what a struggle holding a conversation with her husband had become. The mood in the kitchen was peculiar. She did not care for criticism about her cooking. Whether or not the chicken was cut to the right bite size pieces. She did not care if the carrots julienne weren't all the same size. Although she had consciously made the effort, all these things that she would be ridiculed for and made to feel inadequate did not matter to Jodie today. The insignificance of Jack's petty gripes would wash over her. Her son had just lost two of his best friends. Friends that he had grown up with since nursery. Friends that he would never see again. Nothing Jack could say or do would make her feel worse but pale into insignificance. She waited for a reaction. Watching disgustedly as Jack put too much food into his mouth and chewed loudly.

"Why are you so upset? ... It's not your friends who have just died," said Jack coldly with a mouthful of food, placing the paper flat on the table so he could scan the story whilst continuing to scoff his casserole. Jodie could feel her eyes start to water again and dried them on the sleeve of her hoody. The upset and grief hurt like an open wound overshadowing the tension from Jack's presence. Jack read the article, stopping occasionally to shove more food into his mouth.

When he finished reading he turned to Jodie, a droplet of sauce on his chin, and said, "What's for dessert?"

Jodie did not know why she was completely taken by surprise. What reaction she expected from Jack, she did not know. She knew better than anyone he was not capable of showing compassion or even having a sympathetic bone in his body. He had never taken the time to get to know any of his son's friends. Or their parents. He was not made of the same stuff as a normal living human being. The next thing Jodie heard was the scraping sound of her own chair as she abruptly got up and went to leave the room.

"Oh great ... so some kid gets knocked down by a car and that means that I don't get any pudding ... Where's the logic in that?" snapped Jack.

Jodie stopped in her tracks, a whirling emotion of anger, rage, upset and disbelief.

"Not some kid Jack. Two kids ... two kids that happen to be your son's best friends."

Jack was more amused by Jodie's outburst than angered. A smirk shot across his face, that still bared the droplet of sauce, now a dry brown dot.

"Jodie ... CJ can't be that close to them. When did they ever come round here? I've hardly seen ... what are their names? Sally ...?" He looked down at the paper, "Thomas and Kelly."

"They did come here Jack." Tears fell down Jodie's face. "They came after school. You didn't see them because you were always at work. I can't believe you can be so blasé." Jodie sniffed and wiped her nose unladylike on her sleeve. *How could he not know his own son's friends? What sort of a father has such little regard for his own family?* Jodie didn't know what else to say to her husband. The expression on her face was one of utter astonishment in comparison to Jack's still baring the droll look.

"Okay Jodie ... forget the pudding. It's fine. I've only been working hard all day ... and what for? ... So you can mope around feeling sorry for yourself. Look at the state of you. You haven't made any effort to look nice. You look like a chav." Jack left the table and went to the drinks cabinet to fix himself a drink. "And where the bloody hell has all my brandy gone?"

Jodie was still, stood frozen in the kitchen doorway, contemplating her next move. Words racing around her head that she dared not speak. What she needed was a shoulder to cry on and a loving arm around her not someone who criticised her for having perfectly normal human behaviours and emotions. *Could he possibly make me feel worse than I already do?* thought Jodie. The answer was yes. Jack's intolerance to Jodie's feelings enraged her beyond comprehension. She suppressed the burning anger inside her for fear of what Jack would do to her. The only comforting thought was that she was going to leave him and he had no idea. Tomorrow she would start putting together her portfolio. Tomorrow would be another day closer to getting away from this man whom she had come to despise.

Jack was now walking toward her. The sound of ice clinking around the glass. She was half expecting a shove, but he passed with an irked look, walked through the hallway and into the lounge.

Jodie felt completely drained. The TV came on and she could hear the news.

"I ... I had some in my coffee ... I needed something ... to make me feel better," sniffed Jodie to herself, remembering Jack's outburst this morning. Though it seemed like so long ago. With all the energy she had left in her frail body she turned back into the kitchen and cleaned and tidied. She put the salt and pepper pot on the small shelf next to the cooker, folded the tea towel so the tag wasn't showing and hung it on the rail, wiped the place mat and made sure the picture was facing the same way as the other mats as she put it in the drawer. She closed all three roman blinds in the kitchen to the exact same drop. And after she had loaded the dishwasher, wiped all the sides and the table top and taken out the rubbish, she did a double take to make sure everything was orderly and nothing out of place. Her head was spinning. What will tomorrow bring she wondered. She had a plastic water bottle in her hand filled with vodka as she sluggishly made her way up to her bedroom.

Tomorrow will be a good day she told herself. Tomorrow I will see Matt and it will be a good day.

CHAPTER SIXTEEN

Friday Morning

CJ had woken early. His sleeping pattern had been completely messed up since Tuesday when he had cut his leg open. He had been falling in and out of sleep during the day and then lying awake when night-time had crept in, listening to the strange noises. The clanking of the water pipes, the rumbling of engines as the odd late night or early morning driver had passed the house. The hissing and snarls of cat fights and the more bizarre calls from foxes that had wandered down from the woods onto the estate looking for food. He had forgotten what a peaceful night's sleep was like. In the dim lit room he could just make out the hands of the clock sat on his dresser. It was 4.45 a.m. *Way too early to get up* he thought. Yet fatigue had passed and the painful reality of yesterday was dawning on him. Despite life in his bright green eyes his body felt numb and beat. His weakness had not only come from two traumatic days, but also from the lack of food, albeit the loss of appetite was from all the distress and shock.

Yesterday's rain had past. The grey clouds had dispersed and the sun was starting to make an appearance bringing promise of a pleasant day. And gradually as the dusk lifted, light peeped in through the slit where the curtains met. Soon he would hear his mum going downstairs to the kitchen and the aroma of coffee and toast would waft up the stairs enticing him out of his room. Normally his mum would wake him up for school and CJ would want nothing more than to curl up into a ball under his duvet and fall back to sleep again. But today he would be staying off school so he was not expecting his mum to come into his room to wake him up. Jodie wanted to make sure that CJ was fit and healthy after having the stitches in his leg. And he also needed time to grieve the loss of his two best friends. With his dad convinced that he had a stomach bug, he was no longer panicking over trying to hide his absence from school. But the comfort of knowing that he could relax in bed was bitter sweet.

CJ, now wide awake lay in his bed was reflecting on the 'Nomads' and the torment they had inflicted upon him and Thomas and Kelly. His mind was racing though his body felt sluggish and emotionally drained. As he lay, eyes wide open staring blankly up at the ceiling, he thought about all the lunch money Wayne had taken from them over the past six months. The new books they had to buy because Wayne emptied their school bags into a puddle. Clothes he ruined when roughing them up in the playground. The swimming kit he threw on the school roof that still remains lodged in the guttering. The list was endless.

I will make him pay. Don't worry Thomas ... Kelly ... I will make him pay for what he's done vowed CJ, whispering to himself, wiping his watery eyes on the sleeve of his pyjamas. He wasn't a physically strong boy, but he was smart. And he knew that there would be a way he could get retribution. He needed to think of something and fast.

He could hear movement which told him that his mum and dad were now up. The two and a half hours spent recollecting the maltreatment from the Nomads, particularly Wayne Dear had flown by and bizarrely CJ had felt better for it. His mind now having something to focus on. Something that he can change rather than dwelling on 'what ifs'. He made his way down stairs. He could hear the welcoming noise of the plates clattering, the tap running as his mum prepared to make coffee, the fridge door opening and shutting, the usual morning sounds that brought some normality to the Vickers' home. *Life goes on.*

He entered the kitchen to find his mum busying herself preparing the 'Royal' breakfast for Jack. His dad was still in his room getting dressed.

"Morning Mum," said CJ seating himself at the breakfast bar on the usual high backed chair.

"Hey honey you're up. You okay? You sleep okay?" Jodie said fussing over her son more than usual. The events of yesterday still vivid in her mind.

CJ shrugged and smiled loosely. He didn't know what to tell her. He hadn't slept well and he wasn't okay.

Unlike CJ, Jodie had slept deeply, after drinking all the vodka she had taken up to bed with her, disguised as a bottle of water. And today she was focused on her mental to-do list. Today nothing was going to distract her from her cause. Today Matt would be visiting her. She was already on her third cup of coffee. The first two she had secretly drank with brandy. She wanted to remain calm when Jack came down for his breakfast.

"You want some scrambled eggs on toast?" said Jodie as she began cracking eggs into a bowl.

"Yeah please Mum." The aroma of coffee and fresh bread toasting stirred his appetite. And scrambled eggs sounded good. He definitely was in need of some sustenance.

By the time Jodie was serving up luscious buttery scrambled eggs lightly seasoned with sea salt and black pepper (just how Jack likes his Friday breakfast) Jack had joined CJ at the breakfast bar dressed in an eye-catching blue-grey Valentino suit and red silk tie. *Must be an important day* thought Jodie as she admired the suit, sitting herself down on the heavy high backed chair.

Jack tucked into his breakfast and flicked through *The Times* newspaper without even giving Jodie eye contact. He did however ask, "How you feeling son?" with a small amount of sincerity in his voice. Jodie was unsure whether the question referred to Thomas and Kelly or the imaginary stomach bug. When CJ replied "hungry" she didn't know whether to laugh or cry.

The sun was now in full blaze in a cloudless blue sky. As the light poured in through the kitchen windows the wooden cupboards and floor panels glowed orange. Despite the warmth there was an eerie feel to the kitchen. Perhaps this was brought on by the heavy tension in the air that presented itself when

Jack was nearby. It seemed to ooze out of his very being and then vanish from the atmosphere at the moment he leaves.

Jodie was still on tenterhooks from the previous evening's episode with Jack. The brandy had settled Jodie's nerves momentarily. She planned today to replace the bottle and pick up some more vodka, brandy and whisky. That would mean going out this morning and leaving CJ on his own. She would need an excuse to leave the house. She pondered on this predicament as she sipped her lukewarm coffee and rather unenthusiastically nibbled on a piece of toast. The room was quiet but for the eating noises coming from CJ and Jack as they both polished off all the scrambled eggs and toast. It was extraordinary how they were both on opposite ends of the spectrum of feelings. Jodie would do anything for CJ out of unconditional love and she would do anything for Jack out of fear.

"Have you spoken to that dreadful woman?" asked Jack suddenly interrupting Jodie's thinking.

Jodie knew straightaway Jack was referring to Christine Hunt.

"Oh ... er ... yes ... As a matter of fact I did." Jodie couldn't help feeling rather pleased with herself. "She asked me get a price from Dickens. Maybe I can do that today." Jodie felt a sudden smugness. *Now I have an excuse to go out* she thought.

"Yeah, the sooner the better. Bloody tree. I've a good mind to chop it down," said Jack.

"Now that I would like to see," declared CJ.

Jack folded his newspaper, drank the remainder of his coffee and as he stood up to leave for work, he put his hand on CJ's shoulder, gave it a little squeeze and said, "Have a good day son."

CJ looked up, gave a nod and a forced smile, not quite sure how to respond.

At last thought Jodie, as she heard the door click shut and Jack leave the house. As if by magic the tension lifted.

CHAPTER SEVENTEEN

The Proposition

Jodie waited patiently at the Customer Services counter, listening to the man with a kind wrinkled face and blue twinkly eyes explain to his customer how compost and shredded bark helps contain valuable moisture during the hot weather. The customer then loaded a bag of multipurpose compost onto a trolley, already heaving with shrubs and plants and traipsed off towards the cashier.

"Jodie, my dear, how lovely to see you and may I say you are looking as beautiful as ever." Mr Dickens' blue eyes sparkled and Jodie smiled amiably. "And how may I help you on this beautiful sunny mornin'?" He was wearing forest green overalls with a light brown beret and had a cigar tucked behind his ear.

"Good morning to you too Arthur," said Jodie still smiling and she proceeded to explain her quandary with Christine Hunt's silver birch.

"Ah the lady of the wood is causing you a problem, I see. Well if the leaves are dropping off like you say they are, then our lovely Mrs Hunt has probably got an infestation. Them trees don't usually lose their leaves until October. Now we do have a tree surgeon who can come and take a look, prune back the branches and see if there are any aphids or fungi present. I'm getting too old to be doing oult like that myself. I will 'ave to see when he's free like," said Arthur. He placed a large book on the counter and started flicking through the pages, I mus' tell you though, they bleed, them trees. You'll 'ave sap seeping all over your drive for a couple o' weeks afterwards mind. You'll need to tell Jack. Not sure 'ees gonna be 'appy bout that.

"No. I ... I don't suppose he will be," said Jodie. Her jovial expression turning feeble at the very thought.

"But if it is an infestation, we gotta treat it quick or the tree could die. Ah here we are," said Arthur. "He's free on the 27th. It's a Saturday. You want me to pencil you in my love, in the morning? Charge for pruning is seventy pounds. Christine, alright with that?"

"Erm ... book the slot please Arthur. I will be seeing Christine tomorrow so I will let her know." Jodie had in mind the home watch scheme meeting.

Arthur wrote in the big book, closed it and popped it back underneath the counter.

"I've put you down for ten o'clock. Now my dear, is there anything else I can help you with."

"No that's all thanks," said Jodie. She said goodbye to the charming Mr Dickens whom she had grown very fond of over the ten years she had been a regular customer to the garden centre. She walked through the shop zigzagging around the rose bushes with pink, red, yellow and white colours, dahlias with vibrant pink tropical flowers in leafy stems and tall sunflowers with their large inflorescence. Hanging baskets spewing pansies, petunias and black-eyed Susan looked idyllic beneath the large sign at the exit that read 'Dickens Green and Pleasant Garden Centre' and the path to the car park was lined with a flush of lilacs and forsythia in attractive pots and blue, lilac and white flowering hydrangeas. The blast of scents was intoxicating, but Jodie did not feel any better for it. *Sap all over the driveway. That's not good.* She got into her car and drove down Hough Street to the Tesco Express with the intention to run in and grab a bottle of vodka, whisky and a bottle of brandy. She had promised CJ she wouldn't be out long and he had been as fine as she could have expected. She had not mentioned to CJ his father's lack of compassion and sympathy for the tragic event of his best friends, although the need to pour her heart out was brewing.

Jodie was stood in the queue at the checkout, getting some strange looks as she had only alcohol in her shopping basket.

She suddenly felt a warm breath behind her and a faint voice whispered in her ear.

"The police was asking questions about you."

Her heart skipped a beat. She jumped and turned round briskly, recognising the voice immediately. It was dirty Barry from the dry cleaners. She suddenly remembered that CJ's rug was in the boot of her car and she needed to drop it off. Barry was grinning at her showing his nicotine stained teeth. His two front teeth being slightly crooked. His light brown hair was shabby and his large brown eyes were all over Jodie. Besides beaming at Jodie as though he had just won her in a prize, which always made her feel uncomfortable, he actually looked quite smart. His white shirt was neatly pressed and tucked into a pair of designer jeans and he had obviously gone overboard with the Lynx as the smell was pleasant but a little overpowering and made Jodie want to sneeze. Fear had overcome Jodie at the mention of the police. She should have known that the police would check out her story.

"Who's been a naughty girl then?" he said light heartedly, but failing to amuse as he proceeded to place a pre-packed sandwich, a can of coke and packet of crisps on the conveyor belt. Jodie smiled weakly.

"You er ... on your lunch break Barry," she said playing ignorant to the mention of the police, even though she could not hide the look of dismay. She paid for her drinks as casually as she could, double bagging them. She wasn't even sure if Barry had noticed her purchases as he had not taken his eyes off of her.

"Just popping in early before the shop gets too busy," said Barry. "Glad I bumped into you though, I have something important to discuss with you. I think you should come to the back of the shop with me where we can ... " He paused for a second as his eyes bore into her breasts and he licked his lips ... "Yes ... where we can ...talk."

Both intrigue and trouble beset Jodie's thoughts. She had lied to the police and Matt was coming to see her today. Excitement had now become exhausted. *Had Barry told the police that she had not been at his shop at the time of the accident? Why had she not thought that they would follow up her story?* Panic had hit her hard. She had no choice. She had to know what Barry had told them.

"I ... er ... have something that needs cleaning," she said nervously. "I'll just go get it out of the car and meet you outside."

She waited as Barry paid the cashier and reluctantly she walked the short distance with Barry to the All Day Laundry still holding the carrier bag tightly so that the bottles did not clink as she walked, feeling foolish. Her nerves had got the better of her and she wondered to herself why she had not put her shopping in the car. Maybe subconsciously she felt comfort knowing that her liquid friends were close by. She was not thinking straight and tried desperately to clear her head. Barry said nothing as they walked. He carried the rug in an effort to impress, grinning and continuing to eye up Jodie. Two customers watched shadily as Jodie followed Barry into the back room of his shop. The air was stuffy and full of the smell of liquid solvent. Jodie felt nervous, but with a different apprehension than she felt with Jack.

"My assistant will mind the shop while we talk," said Barry dropping the rug on the floor and putting his lunch on the table. Then perched himself on the edge, his arms folded and his eyes running up and down Jodie.

"You said the police were asking questions ..." said Jodie prompting the conversation in the hope that she would spend as little time as possible in the back room with Barry.

"Apparently you used me as an alibi. Told the police you were in here picking up your dry cleaning around the time those two kids were knocked down." Jodie couldn't decide if his tone was one of annoyance or intrigue. She bit her lip and nodded her head. She couldn't deny that she had knowingly lied.

"It wasn't me ... " she said in vain clinging onto the carrier bag holding her drink in her arms, "...who run those kids over? It wasn't me." She was frustrated and had an overwhelming desire for him to believe her. This time Barry was looking straight into her eyes. Jodie could feel her eyes burning but she managed to hold back the tears. She was not about to break down in front of the man who cleans her husband's suits.

His eyes told Jodie that he believed her, but there was a look that she could not fathom.

"So ... what did you tell the police?" asked Jodie anxiously.

Barry was not enjoying watching Jodie panic. He thought she was a beautiful sensual woman but he had to play her, he could not let her see his soft side. Not yet anyway. He had manipulated Jodie into coming into his shop and was feeling very self-satisfied. Fate had dealt him a card that he could not ignore. He had fantasised over Jodie since the first time she had set foot in his dry cleaners. No other woman stirred the impassioned feelings that he got from Jodie. And now he had enticed her into the backroom, tricked her even. A small stuffy room with little more than a white melamine table, two chairs and an old stained kitchen worktop with a cupboard underneath and a jug kettle on top. Barry shifted off the table where he had been seated and reached over to the cupboard, pulled out two mugs that were heavily stained and placed them on the table.

"Why don't you pour us a drink and we can discuss your ... predicament," said Barry thinking that a stiff drink would relax Jodie and help stop his own heart from racing.

Jodie obliged. She could do little else. She had hoped that Barry had not noticed her purchases from the supermarket, but to her displeasure and embarrassment he had. She poured a measure of whisky into the mugs and took a big gulp. The burning sensation in her chest was gratifying.

"Please sit down," said Barry as he himself sat down on a chair and began drinking the whisky. Jodie seated herself opposite. She was incredibly hot and uncomfortable and fretful. She guzzled the rest of her drink and slammed the empty mug down hard on the table. The sound clanged louder than Jodie had expected.

"You didn't ask me here for a nice cosy drink," said Jodie angry and frustrated. "You want to talk, so talk ... please ...

tell me. What did the police say?" Her voice was getting a little frantic.

"If it wasn't you who ran those kids over why are you so worried?" said Barry concerned as he watched Jodie become agitated. Inside he was sympathising, but did not let it show. He could not and would not lose sight of his ultimate aim. Jodie did not have an answer to give. She had lied to the police because she wanted Jack to believe that she had done as he asked. How could she explain that to Barry? It would hardly sound plausible.

"I didn't run those kids over," she repeated weakly looking into his big brown eyes, imploring him with all her will to believe her. "Did you tell the police that I wasn't here?"

Barry paused as he contemplated his response. He took a deep inward sigh and finished his drink.

"Let's have a refill and I will tell you all about Wednesday's afternoon." he said, hoping as he himself was feeling relaxed from the fiery whisky, so to was Jodie.

She poured more whisky into the mugs.

"Go on," she said crossly.

"Well I must say I was very surprised when I had two police officers asking after you." Barry took a sip of whisky and continued calmly. "They told me that your car matched their forensic tests. Quite interesting actually. Did you know they are able to identify a car from tyre marks in the road? And there are traces of paint on the clothes of the victims. It's amazing really ... fascinating stuff."

Jodie raised her eyebrows showing her irritation and emptied her second drink. She didn't like the way the conversation was going and was perspiring. The thought of Matt Campbell and Barry having a conversation about her was bothersome.

"Anyway, forgive me Jodie I was sidetracking," he said leaning forward toward Jodie. She could smell tobacco on his breath mixed with the strong scent of Lynx. "Said that your car was one of nine in the area ... Blue S Type Jag. Am I right?"

Jodie said nothing as Barry stared hard giving the impression that he was studying her, but he was admiring her alluring features.

"Well I told them that I couldn't remember seeing you," he said leaning back in his chair, still watching Jodie with fascination. Her heart skipped a beat. "Told them that I would have to check the receipt book. But do you know what? I haven't seen my receipt book since you came in on Wednesday. Wouldn't know anything about that would you? Messed me right up that did. Spent ages going through all the orders and rewriting out the customer invoices."

"What are you saying?" asked Jodie.

"I'm saying that I couldn't verify to the police whether or not you were here ... when you say you were. Didn't have any records to prove it."

Jodie had been breathing heavily. She poured more whisky and polished off her third to try and relax herself. But she felt incredibly hot and her cheeks were flushed. The air in the room was humid and the smell of solvent was strong. She stood up and took off her cardigan. She didn't care for the faint bruises on her arms. She didn't care that Barry was ogling her breasts. He continued talking trying to fight the feeling of arousal as he caught sight of her cleavage. The bruising went unnoticed.

"You see the thing is Jodie. I do remember when you come in. I always remember when *you* come in." There was a glint of perverse exhilaration in his big brown eyes. "But you see the police don't know that... Do they? No ... But they did ask me if I was to remember anything then I am to give them a ring." Barry pulled a business card out of his pocket. Jodie recognised it immediately. It was Matt Campbell's. "All I have to do is to make one phone call to this nice policeman and tell him that I remember you called in here on Wednesday, not Tuesday at 11.30 a.m. and they'll be straight round to your house to arrest you." Barry felt a pang in his chest for saying these words. He realised they sounded severe, and to Jodie he looked cold and uncaring.

Jodie couldn't believe that Matt was enquiring after her. Surely he wouldn't pursue her alibi. The thought of Matt doubting her was wounding.

"But Barry, I didn't do it. You know I didn't do it. You know me." Jodie was desperate. She had been played by Barry just as he intended and now she felt backed into a corner. She could not let Matt find out that she lied. What would he think of her? And worse still what would Jack do if he found out not only she had lied to him, but to the police as well? Would he think she could possibly be the driver that ran down her son's best friends?

"You have to tell the police that I was here ... please," said Jodie.

"That's a big thing to ask," he said. "Perjury, I think they call it." Holding back his feelings for this woman was almost breaking him, but the manipulation was almost over. He was building up to the moment when it would all be worthwhile.

"Please Barry," begged Jodie almost close to tears.

"If I lie for you Jodie, I think it is only right that you should do something for me."

"What? What do you want me to do?"

There was a moment's frustrated silence. Barry felt himself stiffen, his erection pushing against his jeans. He exhaled deeply and replied, "Sleep with me?"

CHAPTER EIGHTEEN

Inspector Campbell

"I don't understand," said CJ. "Why are the police coming round again?"

"It's like I told you before. The policeman, I mean Inspector Campbell" Jodie corrected herself wanting to give Matt's' position in the force some credit, " just wants to check that we are okay. I spoke with him yesterday and he knows that Thomas and Kelly were very close to you."

"But Mum, that doesn't make any sense. Why would he want to know if we're okay? He doesn't even know us. Surely he should be trying to catch the person driving the car, not paying house visits."

"CJ, he is not the only officer working on the case. They have a whole team of people. And anyway he can give us an update on how things are progressing." CJ was watching his mum curiously. "I think it's nice," she added dreamily.

They were both sat in the kitchen at the breakfast bar. She was leaning forwards, her elbows on the table, hands cupped round her mug of tea. There was a plate of ham sandwiches placed in the middle of the worktop that Jodie had prepared for lunch. CJ was leaning back in his chair, half a sandwich held in his hand. He took a big bite and seemed to munch for a while deep in thought. He couldn't understand why the police would pay a social visit to their home. *Why are we so important? Surely the police should be calling upon Thomas's and Kelly's homes. Maybe they already have. And why was Mum talking to the police yesterday? And what did Kat want to talk to Mum about?* He saw his mum glancing at the clock on the wall. She had been wondering what time Matt would call round.

Jodie didn't know what to tell CJ. His questioning was more inquisitiveness than suspicion. Still chewing his food he finally said, "So Mum, you never told me what it was that Kat wanted to tell you."

Jodie hesitated. She was about to tell him not to eat with his mouth full but his dazed look and glassy eyes stopped her.

"Oh ... it was nothing ... just erm ... boyfriend trouble."

"Oh ... right ... is that all? And what about the funeral ... will this police guy know when it is?"

"Funeral? Oh I don't know." She reached across the table top and squeezed his hand gently. "Oh my goodness CJ. I should send a card and flowers." She had been so consumed with her own worries and goings on that she had not even taken the time to contact Mr and Mrs Bradshaw or Mr and Mrs Jones. The truth was she didn't really have the strength or will to visit them in person. Perhaps she thought they would need space to grieve and would not take too kindly to guests. Or perhaps she just wouldn't know what to say. Besides her feeling of qualm, going back out to the shops now was not an option. She didn't want to risk not being home for Matt. And CJ appeared unimpressed with her late arrival back home from the garden centre, she didn't want to exacerbate things.

"I'm sorry," she had told CJ, "the garden centre was really busy and then I had to queue for ages at the supermarket. There was only one checkout open. And I had to drop your rug off at the cleaners." Jodie hated herself for lying, but she couldn't tell him the truth. That she had sat in a stuffy room with the owner of the local dry cleaners drinking his father's whisky. The thought made her feel physically sick. She had brushed her teeth four times and gargled a quarter of a bottle of Listerine to disguise any lingering smell of alcohol before making lunch for CJ, apologising profusely for leaving him on his own.

CJ hadn't given the 'With Sympathy' card a second thought either. He too was too wrapped up in his thoughts. His mind full of anger towards Wayne Dear and he had spent many hours trying to think of a way he could get revenge. So far he had drawn a blank.

A few minutes later Jodie had made a phone call to the local florist and two bouquets of flowers had been ordered to be delivered to Thomas's and Kelly's parents.

It was late afternoon when Matt finally called on Jodie. The neighbours' curtains were twitching when a police car cruised slowly down Mottrom Drive and pulled up behind the blue Jaguar parked on Jodie's driveway. Jodie jumped out of her skin with the resonant sound of the doorbell. It didn't take much to make her jump these days. She had been deep in thought pondering over the painting of the mural that she hadn't heard the purring of the engine on the driveway. She still hadn't managed to prepare her portfolio due to recent events and this had been playing on her mind somewhat. CJ had relaxed a little after lunch and had been dosing in and out of sleep as he rested on the sofa. His sleeping pattern had become irregular. The TV was on. There was a programme about how leopards had become invisible. Neither Jodie or CJ had been interested in watching it. But the TV had remained on nevertheless. Jodie got up to answer the door. Despite the whisky consumed and the mouthfuls of vodka that Jodie had secretly drunk, the butterflies still presented themselves in her stomach.

Matt looked far more handsome than she had remembered. The sun shone down from behind the towering silver birch, casting a shadow on the doorstep. This made his face appear deeply tanned and his eyes darker. He looked well rested and refreshed. Jodie found herself momentarily speechless as though she was looking at a priceless piece of art. The snug fitting uniform was captivating and mesmeric. Her stomach was doing summersaults, but you could not tell. Jodie managed to control her nervous excitement and remained poised with the help of her liquid friend.

She appeared to Matt just as he had remembered her at hospital which was different to the jittery character he had seen when last visiting her home and the saddened Jodie that he had spoken to on the phone. It was a strange meeting. Slightly awkward, like a first date. Neither really knew what to expect. It was not a call of duty for Matt, yet not a social call either.

"Looks like I'm causing quite a stir in your neighbourhood," said Matt as he stepped inside. Jodie could smell a wonderful woody and vanilla aroma that could only be Matt's aftershave.

"Oh you have no idea," smiled Jodie, wondering if the scent was for her benefit. "I'm sure there will be a few of my neighbours having a good gossip later. It's not very often we have the police on Mottrom Road.

"No. I know. And twice in one week."

Unsure how to greet Jodie he gently touched her arm and asked in a soft concerning tone, "And how are you feeling today?"

Jodie wanted to say that she felt great. For at this very moment she felt the most elated she had felt for a very long time. A tall, dark and evidently handsome man had come to visit her. To see if she was okay. And he smelled gorgeous. Her jubilation was kept deep though. Only a day had passed since the death of her son's best friends and she didn't want to appear uncaring.

"The past few days have been cruel," said Jodie. "But I am hopeful that things will get better."

"The past few days? Do you want to tell me about it?"

"Sure. But first let me introduce you to CJ."

CJ was awake and curious. He was lounging on the sofa staring at the TV but not really taking an interest. He was tuned in to the conversation that was taking place in the doorway and was still intrigued to know why this strange policeman had taken a sudden interest in his mum's wellbeing. He stretched his head round toward the door without moving position on the sofa, so he could see his mum escort Matt into the lounge, using the least amount of energy possible. He was still weary. His face showed little colour and the dark circles under his eyes were an obvious sign of his worry. Unlike his mother, he couldn't disguise his anguish with make-up. In spite of his sorrowfulness, CJ had eaten well and was well rested and possibly looked his best since his unfortunate accident.

Matt gave CJ a firm handshake.

"Inspector Campbell, nice to meet you son. I'm really sorry about what happened to your friends. It's been hard on you ... I know, but like I've been telling your mum, we will catch the person that did this." Matt's voice was kind and reassuring. His presence brought a calming ambience and CJ immediately took a liking to him. CJ sat upright responsively.

"Thanks ... Mum said that you might have some news." CJ wanted to make polite conversation, but in his mind it was not the driver who was at fault for the death of Thomas and Kelly. It was Wayne Dear.

"Oh yeah sure ... well all I can tell you is," began Matt as he parked himself on the sofa beside CJ, "at the moment we're narrowing down the drivers' of the vehicle we believe was involved and are still checking out their alibis." Jodie shuddered at the thought of Barry being her alibi and the favour he had asked of her. "We're carrying out checks at petrol stations, monitoring cameras and checking out speeding tickets issued in the area. The usual kinda stuff," said Matt.

"Petrol stations?" asked Jodie.

"Petrol stations should have CCTV cameras installed so they catch anyone leaving without paying for petrol. So we should theoretically be able to see if anyone has gone through the car wash. Only, as we are finding out, not everyone is efficient enough to have film in their cameras. Or even switch them on for that matter."

Jodie's heart sank. She had not thought that she might be caught on camera. She was overcome with a sick feeling.

"And do you have any ideas ... I mean ... is there anyone you think might have done it ... anyone you are likely to arrest?" asked CJ.

Matt grinned showing his immaculate white teeth.

"Not yet son, we are going through a process of elimination. You see, every crime scene has clues that tell us what happened. We identify the clues and from this gather as much evidence as possible. This allows us to paint a picture of the whole incident and it's all put together rather like a jigsaw. At the moment we have a couple of missing pieces but I can tell you that it is all coming together. We are so close to finding the car and once this has been established, we can bring the driver in for questioning. Like I said, it's just a matter of time."

"So the cameras ... at the petrol stations ... are they a piece of the puzzle?" asked Jodie

"Unfortunately not."

"Oh, that's a shame," said Jodie with an immense feeling of relief.

"So ... what happens when you find the car?"

"Well once we have enough evidence we may need to get a warrant and then ... well ... we get our team working on the car to see if there are any signs of an impact. But, you see the thing is with the Jaguar, they are such robust cars ... it could be hard to spot."

"Do you need to check Mum's car?" said CJ innocently.

"Oh that's not necessary. Your mum has already told us that she was at the 'All Day Laundry'. I'm just waiting for the owner to confirm that. Seems that he's lost his receipt book. But don't you go worrying yourself son. Your mum is not a suspect. This is just a social visit. I'm not on duty." Matt was still smiling, the thought that Jodie could be capable of such a thing was ludicrous.

Jodie's heart had been racing, but the more information Matt freely gave the calmer she became.

"And the funeral? I don't suppose you know about that do you?" asked CJ.

"I'm sorry son. I don't. The hospital won't need to carry out the post mortem as the cause of death has already been determined, so I would imagine that the funerals would take place sooner rather than later."

Jodie watched and listened with high regard for the sincerity of Matt. His persona was as endearing as his look. She found it difficult to take her eyes off him. When eventually she did, she noticed the glazed look on CJ's face and the glassy eyes telling that it was not a good idea to continue the conversation. Addressing Matt she spoke feeling more relaxed, "Let me get you a coffee Inspector, would you like to come through to the kitchen?" Turning to CJ she added. "Honey can I get you anything?"

"No thanks Mum. I'm good," his voice a little shaky as he started to feel choked up. It seemed he had cried endlessly and just when he thought he had no more tears left he felt his eyes burned. CJ slouched back down on the sofa and stared at the TV absentmindedly, thinking about his own retribution.

Jodie took Matt into the kitchen. He admired her home. Gazing around curiously at the plush furnishings and décor he followed Jodie into the kitchen and sat down at the same spot he was at two days ago. He was on the edge of becoming part of Jodie's life and had a strange feeling of excitement and wonder. He watched admiringly as Jodie pottered around the room, opening cupboards filled with expensive crockery and filling the coffee maker with strong smelling fresh coffee that permeated the air.

"You have a lovely home," said Matt.

"Thanks," replied Jodie as she poured milk into a pan and placed it on the stove.

Matt watched inquisitively.

"Yeah ... Mottrom estate is a beautiful area ... but you know ....this house ... it feels like something is missing."

"What do you mean missing?" asked Jodie.

"Well it doesn't have a homely feel. There's an emptiness in the air ... like something is missing."

Jodie stared at Matt blankly.

"I'm not sure what you mean," she said.

"Jodie, forgive me if this sounds forward, but ... " Matt paused as though he was carefully choosing his words before he spoke.

Jodie handed him a mug of steamy coffee and sat down opposite him.

"But what?"

"Well this might sound odd. I've been in the police force a long time and whenever I go into someone's house I get a feel for the place ... I have an awareness ... I don't know whether it's been instilled in me since I have been in the force or if it's my natural senses ... but this house ... as lovely as it is ... there's a coldness. I get the sense that this is not a happy home. Am I right?"

Jodie wanted to be cross with Matt, but somehow warmed to the conversation as though she had just been given dispensation to divulge how miserable and lonely she felt.

"Well Inspector, Matt ... I don't know what to tell you. The past few days have not been happy ones. My son had an accident at school. Cut his leg open climbing through a window ... needed twelve stitches ..."

"What was he doing climbing though a window?" said Matt with a curious smile.

"Oh well ... from the small bit of information he's told me I think that he was meeting a girl. And then we have the neighbour from hell who's been telling everyone that CJ was attacked and now they want to start a neighbourhood watch scheme ... "

"Well it's always good to have neighbourhood watch," said Matt sarcastically.

"And then of course there are CJ's friends that have died. I still can't believe it," said Jodie incredulously.

"Ah ... so that's your cruel few days?" Matt nodded as if in agreement. "And when I saw you at the hospital, you were just visiting your friend Katrina?"

"Kat, yeah she er ... well it's complicated because I can't tell anyone." Jodie lowered her voice even though she was sure that CJ couldn't hear. "She wants me to take a contract with the hospital to be their muralist for the children's ward." Jodie sipped her coffee unaware of how absurd she sounded.

"And why can't you tell anyone Jodie?"

"I guess it must sound strange, but you see ... it's my husband ... he ...well he, well he doesn't like Kat ... or really anyone of my friends for that matter and since CJ came along he has this thing about me working."

"And are you going to work?" Matt was eyeing Jodie with interest. He had suspected that Jodie had issues with her marriage and wondered how much information she was willing to tell.

But to his surprise Jodie talked openly and freely. She told Matt about her plans to leave her husband, she told him that she was starting her own business in secret and she spoke about CJ's accident and how she has to keep it a secret from Jack. She told of her unhappy marriage and Jack's self-absorption as both a husband and a father. This was the first time Jodie had opened up to anyone, with the exception of her best friend Kat. She learned that Matt was a divorcee with no kids. He had married his high school sweetheart but their chosen career paths had lead them in different directions and they separated by mutual agreement. His ex-wife was an air hostess for Virgin Airways and lived in London.

The sun was still shining in a cloudless sky as though all in the world was blissful and for the time Jodie had spent conversing with Matt everything was. It was when CJ had come into the kitchen with a shady look on his face and asked if he could go into his father's study to use the computer that Matt decided it was time to go and Jodie realised it was also time that she started preparing Jack's dinner. *Back to reality* thought Jodie. As Matt said goodbye to Jodie he gave her an unexpected peck on the cheek and promised that he would be in touch. Christine Hunt watched in interest as Inspector Matt drove away, pruning shears in one hand and the other shading her eyes. Jodie couldn't help smiling in amusement.

CHAPTER NINETEEN

CJ Makes Tracks

The idea came to CJ very suddenly. Just popped into his head like a golf ball being struck and landing in a hole-in-one. So unexpected and fantastic was his idea you could believe that it was conveniently and prudently placed there from the afterlife by Kelly and Thomas themselves, in their quest for final payback to Wayne Dear. From nowhere and with an extraordinary feeling where sadness and joy entwined, CJ had a great urge to listen to his voicemail messages. He had forgotten that previous messages from Kelly and Thomas had remained on his phone since the half term break. He listened with mixed emotions churning around his delicate frame as the sounds of his deceased best friends spoke out from his mobile like disembodied voices. There were three voicemail messages that remained on his phone and in each message, there were words that lingered like the after taste of the most delicious melt in your mouth chocolate fudge cake. And as CJ digested these words he experienced an immense satisfaction as his plan for reprisal unfolded.

The first message was from Thomas;

'Hey CJ, it's Thomas ... d'you wanna come round later? We are watching John Tucker Must Die.'

Smiling to himself, he remembered the half term break when the three friends had hung out together. They had sprawled out on the huge sofa at Thomas's house with a stack of sweets and chocolates watching *John Tucker Must Die*. They had laughed so hysterically at the scene when John Tucker gets caught wearing a girl's G-string that an entire glass of Pepsi was spilled on the couch and they spent an hour trying to clean it up, hoping that Thomas's parents wouldn't notice the russet colour on the overturned cushions. He listened to the next message. This was from Kelly;

'Hi CJ it's me ... Kelly ... call me back. Just wanted to know if you are you coming round later?'

That was the day they first talked about hiding out in the classrooms and had spent almost the full day talking about nothing else except avoiding the 'Nomads'. CJ recalled walking to Hough Street and buying fish and chips from Chip 'n Dales and they had taken a detour past the recreation centre and sat on the swings eating their fish and chips and drinking root beer. The final message was from Thomas;

'CJ where are you, Kelly wants to know if you want us to come get you. Phone me back.'

In his mind's eye he could recall that day, Kelly's mum taking them to the town centre so that they could all buy new stationery for school. It all seemed so irrelevant now his friends were gone. Hiding from the 'Nomads', stocking up on school supplies and hoping that the stained cushions would go unnoticed. Reflecting back pained him and stirred feelings inside that he never knew possible, but at the same time he had to hold on to the memories. Thomas and Kelly were a part of him. They were alive in his memory and CJ would never let go and never forget them.

Realising it was almost five o'clock and his dad was expected home around seven, CJ didn't need any encouragement to get up off the sofa. The thoughts of Wayne that had angered him had cleared from his mind like dead leaves fallen from a tree. CJ knew exactly what he needed to do. His head now focussed on revenge and putting his plan into action. He had just enough time to save and edit those voicemail messages and then burn them onto disc before his dad was home.

His mum had given him permission to use the computer in his dad's study and within a short time he had already installed a free audio editor called Audacity and began working to save the voicemail messages. He quickly linked his phone to the computer using his dad's mini to mini cable, set his preferences, turned up the volume on his phone and clicked record, hitting the stop button at the end of the first message. A line of blue waves dashed across the screen represented the voice recording in a thick blue inky chaotic image. This was exported into a Wave file. CJ repeated the process for the other two messages then set to work editing. The audio recordings were split by track numbers. CJ marked the track numbers on the wave lines at the beginning and end of the words. *'You'* was numbered track 3, *'we are'* was given the name track 1, *'watching', 'must die', 'coming',* 'to' and *'get you'* were all given track numbers so that they would form a perfect string of sentences. Words that he would then use to haunt Wayne Dear. It was the perfect plan. CJ couldn't help chuckling to himself at the sheer thought of scaring Wayne half to death.

"What are you doing?" called Jodie from the kitchen as she was peeling vegetables.
"Nothing Mum. Just catching up on some work for school." said CJ as he continued saving the track numbers to I Tunes, making sure they were in numerical order before finally burning the recording onto a disc. When the recording was played back, the voices of Kelly and Thomas could be heard speaking the ghostly words; '*It's Thomas ... and ... Kelly. We are watching you. We are coming to get you. You must die.*' CJ then cannily proceeded to uninstall Audacity and delete all traces of the recordings, eliminating any evidence of his cruel yet worthy plan from his dad's computer. All CJ needed to do to complete his plan was to find out Wayne's phone number and then the tormenting would begin. CJ had no idea how he could secretly obtain Wayne's mobile number, but

instinctively he knew that somehow and soon he would get that number.

CHAPTER TWENTY

The Home Watch Meeting

Jodie was stood holding a basket of freshly baked butternut squash muffins. The sun threw down its welcome heat and a mild breeze blew lazily. It was a beautiful day. The sky full of wispy white clouds, the soft distance noises of children's laughter could be heard from neighbouring gardens and faint music rang out from an open window across the road. She rang the doorbell and waited for Christine Hunt to answer the door, admiring an eruption of flowers trailing from two hanging baskets either side of the porch. Lined up against the red bricks of the house oodles of flowers spilled from large pots. A bee flew leisurely in and out of the clusters of flowers. The sweet smell of flora was refreshing and homely.

This is a happy home thought Jodie as she remembered Matt's comment that her house had a cold feel. She had a nervous excitement about the home watch meeting. Partly because she was interested to know what her neighbours were saying about CJ's accident and the police visiting, and also this would be the first time she would get to see inside Christine's house and she was oddly curious. Not to mention she was able to socialise without consequence. Jack had not surprised Jodie by playing golf and she expected that he was now at the nineteenth hole. If she was lucky she wouldn't see him for the rest of the day. This prospect was pleasing.

"Jodie my dear, so glad you could come," said Christine opening the door to reveal a beautifully varnished wooden floor stretching through the entrance hall. "Please come in." A sea of deep burgundy carpet rose up the stairs and off into the many rooms. Jodie couldn't keep her eyes from wondering around as she stepped inside. The walls were papered with a floral pattern of large golden yellow flowers. There were more plants and flowers inside, stood grandly in the most uniquely designed pot or stand. Begonias, Dracaenas, Calatheas, Yukas, Ficas and even Bonsai trees took up corners of the rooms and window sills. And to add to the hordes of plant life, plug-in air fresheners filled the house with an overpowering smell of perfume, fused with the scent of flowers; it was a hay fever sufferer's worst nightmare.

Jodie followed Christine into her living room, peering around as she went. The layout was very similar to her own, albeit a mirror image. A rustic pine kitchen was on the left and the living room to the right. Entering the room, she had the feeling that everyone had been anticipating her arrival. A horrendous noise like a fog horn came from across the room as someone was blowing their nose. Jodie counted at least ten people that gathered there. Audrey and Albert were sat together on the sofa. There was Sheila, Maureen and Doreen, the three witches or the weird sisters as CJ liked to call them, huddled on another sofa. Jeff and Keith, the twins that bizarrely lived next door to each other and their wives, Mandy and Sharron who, even more bizarrely, were sisters. They were stood hovering in the corner. Keith was hugging a handkerchief and Jodie realised he was the one making the weird noises. And finally there was fat Pat, an American lady who owns Mother Clucker's chicken joint on the high street. Jodie had a waft of fried chicken as Pat stood close by next to the table of food looking as though she wanted to eat the entire lot.

Jodie thought this was a poor turnout considering the number of houses on Mottrom Road, but realised that Christine Hunt was not the most popular person in the street. Her intrusion into people's lives had probably upset a lot of the neighbours. Or maybe the timing was all wrong. Jodie didn't want to express her thoughts. The less she had to do with the meeting the better. She just wanted to make sure that the talk was not about CJ. Her protective mother instincts had kicked in when she learned from Christine that her neighbours thought he had been attacked.

A horrible silence had fallen among the guests and the clinking of cups being placed onto saucers and odd sighs were the only sounds to be heard. As well as the awful foghorn sound coming from Keith. Jodie had prepared herself for this kind of reception. She had drunk freely from her bottle of vodka and had lost count of the amount of brandy coffees she had furtively drank.

Smiling sweetly she raised the basket as if proudly displaying her baking skills and broke the awkward silence by asking, "Muffin anyone?" When Jodie had been drinking she could express a magical poise and smile kind enough to wash away any awkward silence, but each and every one in that room knew that Jodie was alerted to their tittle-tattle. Her quiet amusement spoke more words than if she was to shout down a megaphone and tell them all to stop talking about her behind her back.

"Well I think that's everyone here," said Christine joyfully, in her haste to break the sudden uneasiness, taking the muffins from Jodie whilst mumbling to herself how lovely they were. She placed them on a sideboard amongst some other baked goods and a large silver tray with a steaming pot of tea and dainty cups and saucers. "Please help yourselves, dears," she said pouring herself a strong cup of tea. Everybody began talking amongst themselves while Christine pottered around the room fussily making sure that everyone had drinks and were comfortable. Jodie squeezed herself on the arm of the couch beside Audrey and Albert, sipping tea from a tea cup so small she just managed to feed her finger through the handle. Christine seemed to be in her element. She was beaming so much, Jodie was sure new creases had appeared around her pale blue eyes beneath her small square glasses. She was stood in front of her guests beneath the large bay window that bathed her in golden sunlight. Everyone fell silent again as Christine began a speech. Her voice softer and less abrupt than usual. She was clearly wanting to make a good impression.

"Thank you my dears for coming and welcome to my home. Ooooh isn't it a beautiful day. You'd probably rather be outside in the sunshine I bet," she said with her hands clasped together in a gesture of gratitude. "So I just want to say that your time is appreciated. As you all know there has been some dreadful news in the local paper and we have lost two youngsters from the Mottrom Estate in a terrible car accident. Now this makes me think that we should campaign for speed bumps to make the roads safer, so I have started a petition that I hope you all agree to sign," she pointed to a sheet of paper on a console table, "and I will present this to the local council." There were lots of nodding of heads and whispered agreeing voices. "I think it is important that we get together to talk about the safety of our community," continued Christine feeling encouraged. Jodie was alone with her immediate feeling of grievance. *How could Christine talk about Thomas and Kelly with such a gleeful tone and expression as though she had some twisted satisfaction from the drama of the incident?*

"I read in the paper that they are already campaigning for speed restrictions round by Squirrel Hill. Why don't we put the petitions together? It will hold more weight."

"Yes ... thank you Pat. I will look into it."

"What about the mad man?" said one of the weird sisters.

"Yeah I heard that the police are patrolling the area looking for some guy with a knife," said another.

Jodie felt a pang in her chest anticipating a hoard of questions about CJ. She gave an inward sigh.

"Yes well let's not be too hasty. The police have been seen in the area, I grant you, but I have it on good authority that they have been looking for the driver of the car that ran down those two poor dears," revealed Christine throwing a glance at Jodie.

"Aye, that I 'ave too," announced Albert stroking his wispy bearded chin. "Jodie should be able to give us some information 'bout that. Eh Jodie? Been seen at your 'ouse ... so they av." Albert looked up a Jodie inviting her to speak. His eyes were sweet and genuine and completely innocent to the fact that he absentmindedly announced that he too had been gossiping to Christine. She threw Christine a scornful look quickly followed by a sweet smile as she remembered to keep her cool. This was the reason she came to the meeting, after all, so that she could give her neighbours the facts. The thought that the residents believed CJ to have been attacked by a mad man with a knife she thought was completely ridiculous. All eyes were on Jodie again and she hated being the centre of attention. But she had plied herself with enough alcohol to give her the confidence she needed to speak out and now the moment had arrived. Her head was a little fuzzy and she was unsure of whether or not to stand. She decided to stay seated, although the arm of the sofa was hard and uncomfortable she felt more at ease.

"Yes Jodie perhaps you have some information for us," said Christine interestingly, whom unlike Jodie was lapping up all the attention like some spoilt pooch.

Jodie cleared her throat.

"Well ..." she began, "I really don't know how much you already know," she said, looking around the room thinking that she was in the company of a strange bunch of people. The only common ground was that they all shared the same street. "But I can tell you that the police came to see me because they have identified the car that knocked down Kelly and Thomas as a blue S type Jaguar." Jodie heard a voice say *how the hell do they know that?* But chose to ignore it and continued, "And as I have a blue S type Jag they needed to eliminate me from their enquiries." The room began to fill with murmurs and comments that Jodie could not quite make out. "Apparently there are nine of these cars in the area," continued Jodie a little louder, now feeling more content with speaking, "... and I was told that they are close to catching the person that did this. And before anyone asks ... yes I have been eliminated from their enquiries." Jodie spoke prematurely, but she knew once she had given Barry what he wanted she would not be implicated with the investigation. A coldness ran through her body at the very thought. "So guys, there is no mad man, but there is a dangerous driver that killed two of my son's best friends. The police have been kind enough to keep me updated with the investigation purely because of my family's close connection with Kelly and Thomas." This was the first time that Jodie had managed to talk about their death without welling up and she had a proud moment that she was finally standing up for herself.

"Ah ... yes, I see Jodie. So that's why the police came again yesterday?" said Albert looking puzzled as he answered his own question.

"And long time that policeman was there too," added Audrey questioningly.

"So what did happen to young Christopher then?" asked Albert still intrigued by Christine's thoughts on the matter.

But before Jodie had chance to answer Christine interrupted. She did not want to highlight the fact that she had been gossiping about CJ, especially since Jodie had put her straight on the matter over coffee two days ago.

"Oh Albert we don't have to worry about young Christopher, it's got nothing to do with the police and why we're here, 'as it my dear?" said Christine, her cheeks flushing a beautiful colour pink as she quickly changed from a harsh look at Albert to a gentle smile at Jodie. Albert shook his head and muttered something under his breath that made Audrey snigger.

"Err ... no, CJ had an accident at school. Like I said, nothing to do with the police." Jodie felt a feeling of immense relief and enjoyed the moment that followed as the people in the room were glaring at Christine with a look of complete confusion. Christine attempted to regain her composure with success.

"Well I think that this has been useful ... yes I'm much obliged to Jodie for her valuable input to the meeting. Rest assured we are all safe on Mottrom Road. You see what happens when we don't have the facts. Oh mad man indeed," laughed Christine forcefully. "That's why we need to set up a neighbourhood watch scheme so we know exactly what goes on in the neighbourhood. Now I don't mind being co-ordinator, unless anyone else wants the job." Christine very shrewdly put herself back into the topic of conversation. "I can speak to the local police, they will have useful information ... so I'm told. They should be able to put me in touch with someone who can help start a scheme and direct me to other local resources at the local Neighbourhood Watch Association. Are we all agreed that I should go ahead with that then? As your coordinator?" Christine hesitantly scanned the group of bemused faces, her face down and blue eyes peeping over the top of her lenses, her cheeks still singed with colour. It seemed that everyone was happy to have Christine as their co-coordinator. There were lots of nodding and mumbles of agreement that made Christine smile as she pushed her glasses back onto the bridge of her nose.

"Wonderful. That's settled then. Let's all get together same time next week shall we and I can let you all know how I get on. Now everyone, please help yourselves to refreshments ... And then we can discuss any other business. I'm sure you've all got lots of questions ... Oh and I'd just like to say ... lets spread the word ... the more people we get on board with this the better."

Jodie did not know what to make of the meeting. But she had learned that not only was Christine Hunt a gossiping old bag, obsessed with gardening, she was also a bossy old woman and an attention seeker. Jodie thought it only polite to stay and have tea and cake, even though she wanted nothing more than to go home and make the most of the evening without Jack, assuming that he would spend the rest of the evening at the nineteenth hole talking shop, which was the usual routine. As she tucked in to one of her own homemade muffins she contemplated whether or not she would tell Christine that she did not want to be involved with her neighbourhood watch scheme. She didn't know how long she would even be living here for and if she had her way she would be moving out and leaving Jack during the summer break which was only five weeks away. As she scoffed her tasty muffin her thoughts then turned to CJ. She wondered if CJ had returned home from town. He had a pleasantly unexpected visit from Paul Barrett, who'd come to check on him after hearing on Friday at the school assembly an announcement of the fate of Kelly Jones and Thomas Bradshaw. Cake (as he was better known by his school friends) had not disappointed by bringing a large box containing a selection of donuts. And the two had ended up going into town together. This had given Jodie the opportunity to start putting together her portfolio. She had managed to scramble together some paintings of jungle animals, trees and flowers from the art magazine she had purchased and had also found some old canvases hidden away in the loft that she photographed and produced some printed copies of. Some of her pencil drawings and water colour paintings that she came across were also used. These were all neatly placed into the sleeves of a soft nylon presentation case that completed her portfolio which she'd hid underneath the car seat. Before phoning Kat to let her know that the portfolio was finished with the secret mobile phone that she also kept hidden under her car seat, she made sure that she had not left any traces of ever being in the loft. All the mess from cutting and pasting was thoroughly cleared away. She could not risk Jack suspecting she had done anything out of the ordinary. All she needed to do now, as Kat reminded her, was put together a quote for the work and wait for the confirmation from Revenue and Customs that her business was registered and then she could start painting. Excited that she was making progress, she'd felt compelled to share this information with Matt. And he had welcomed the call feeling privileged. The two were forming a special bond and the awareness on both parts was ever present.

As she took the last mouthful of muffin appreciative of her flair for baking, deep in thought and ignorant to all the talking going on around her she felt happy that it had been an eventful day. She had completed her portfolio, spoken to her best friend and Matt, told the nosey neighbours the facts about the police visiting and miraculously avoided having to explain CJ's accident. And for the first time in four days CJ was out with his friend from school. And she was about to enjoy a relaxing evening without Jack. The day could not have gone any better. It suddenly hit Jodie, she actually felt happy. It was a feeling that she had not experience in a long time. The happiness inside was real. The smile she was smiling was real. Life really was about to get better. Jodie could feel it intuitively. Turning to Christine she said audaciously, "Oh before I forget Christine, the tree surgeon will be coming on the twenty seventh, it's a Saturday ... around ten o'clock. It's gonna cost seventy pounds for pruning, but he thinks you might have an infestation. You surprise me, with your love of the garden, I thought you would be looking after that tree." Jodie was certain she caught a disdainful look in her sparkling blue eyes. "Lovely tea, thank you Christine," continued Jodie placing the dainty tea cup back on the silver tray. "Now I really need to get back." Not wanting to commit to regular meetings, Jodie added, "I need to check to see if I'm free next week, so I'll have to let you know if I can make it."

Jodie then left gracefully, leaving Christine with her mouth half open quite unsure of what to say. Jodie readily left the strange group of people. She had had enough of them, and her sense of smell had had more than its fair share of white lilies and lavender. She warmed to the thought of the scent of Matt's cologne. And as she left with a true smile, the sun shone brightly amongst the fluffy white clouds and the breeze blew lazily. The half opened flowers bowed down in the wind as Jodie closed the garden gate and went home. Christine however, was not happy. And no sooner had Jodie left, the gossiping commenced.

"Oooooh is it just me or could you smell alcohol on her breath?" said Christine turning to Pat. "I tell you that woman ... I don't think she looks after young Christopher ... do you?" Pat didn't answer, she was looking at the table of refreshments wondering what to eat next. "He's such a sweet boy," continued Christine in a menacing tone, "and I saw him go out earlier looking so pale and thin. I'm worried about him ... I don't think she is feeding him properly."

"Well hey Christine," said fat Pat in her boisterous American accent, picking up a large chocolate chip cookie, "if you're that worried then ... hey you should do something about it."

"Yes ... yes I should," said Christine, watching the crumbs fall on the floor as Pat devoured the cookie in the manner of a child. "And I know exactly what to do."

CHAPTER TWENTY-ONE

Morning Has Broken

Sunday had come and gone without event, except for learning that there would be a double funeral and ceremony for Kelly and Thomas on Tuesday, other than which, Jodie had spent the day feeling content and pleased with herself. She had managed to please Jack, in more ways than one acting as the subservient wife, keeping her spirits up and getting through the day with the aid of her liquid friend. CJ's mood too had been a lot more cheerful. His leg was healing well and he had enjoyed a huge Sunday roast dinner with all the trimmings that his mum had dutifully prepared.

But as the sun was rising on a dull and miserable Monday morning, Jodie woke with a feeling of terror. The dream had come again in the night. Walking into the warm sea and falling into an abyss of inky blackness, but this time the heat was even more intense. The sand had burnt her feet and her whole body felt like it was about to combust. Her heart was pounding violently, her body sweating and shaking with fright. So real were these dreams, Jodie was left feeling breathless, as though she had just died and come back to life.

In no time at all she was in the kitchen fixing herself a strong coffee with a good measure of whisky. It was all she could do to make herself feel human again, to stop the trembling and get on track for the day ahead. She took a couple of neat swigs from the bottle before placing it back in the drinks cabinet, enjoying the burning sensation in her chest.

The nightmare had caused Jodie to wake up earlier than usual, so she had ample time to prepare breakfast for Jack and CJ and do the usual kitchen rituals to keep Jack happy. It was always about keeping Jack happy. Once the whisky had warmed Jodie's heart and the shaking had settled, she began mooching around the kitchen, opening the blinds, setting the table and making a creamy batter for waffles. And as she did this with the everyday feeling of reluctance, she tried to remember what Kat had told her about the dream. *The heat ... what did the heat signify?* She thought hard, something about *being passionate and emotional ... yes that's it ... heat signifies passion and heated emotions.* Satisfied that she had interpreted the significance of the heat, she was convinced that this must have something to do with Matt. He was the only man she felt passionate about and he definitely sparked a flame inside her. Smiling at the thought trying to convince herself that despite the feeling of alarm something good was going to happen to her. She had to keep feeling positive.

Today she would be going to the dry cleaners and not just to pick up CJ's rug. And CJ was back at school. Jodie hoped that climbing through the window would not be blown out of proportion. She expected that after everything CJ had been through the school would think it was not necessary to punish him any further. She hoped hard, for she did not want Jack to find out about the accident and if he was going to find out from anyone it would be the school. The neighbours, she was not as concerned about as he had no time for them, but the school was a completely different story. Finishing her second cup of coffee, this time with brandy, she was wondering what was going to happen when she went to pick up CJ's rug from the cleaners. She shuddered and pushed the thought of Barry's proposition out of her mind *too much to think about* she reckoned, and went to wake up CJ.

"Hey honey, come on time to get up," said Jodie as she opened the curtains to let some light in the room.

Today CJ did not do his usual mumbling and hiding underneath the duvet. To Jodie's astonishment he woke with enthusiasm, eager to get to school. And was up and out of bed getting dressed before Jodie had hardly finished opening the curtains. He had his own agenda. Today he was going to, somehow, get Wayne Dear's phone number. And as strange as it seemed, he couldn't wait to get started. As though his body and mind possessed a strange power, spurring him on, like the revving engine of a Formula One car holding pole position at the starting line.

As keen as he was to leave the house though, he stayed seated at the breakfast bar tucking into blueberry waffles and lashings of maple syrup and gulping fresh watermelon juice until his dad had finished his breakfast, folded up his newspaper, tucked it underneath his arm and left for work, giving CJ a pat on the shoulder as he left. CJ liked to leave for school after his dad. His presence would placate his dad's tendency to torment his mum and more times than not he timed catching the bus perfectly. If his dad left early enough, CJ would have time to walk all the way down Mottrom Road and meet Thomas and Kelly at their bus stop.

But sadly those days were over. CJ would be getting on the bus on his own from now on, but oddly enough, he was not troubled at the thought of the Nomads sat at the back of the bus. Inside CJ's small and skinny body was the fighting spirit of a warlord.

Jodie kissed CJ goodbye and watched him stroll up the road with an inexplicable bounce in his step. It was a grey day, black even and the air felt cold. The sun was shadowed by dark clouds and glowed like a waxy ball of light in the sky. The wind blew hard throwing leaves around in a wild dancing frenzy, displaying as much dynamism as CJ, as he zipped up the road, rucksack loosely thrown over his shoulder and head held high. A bewildered Christine Hunt watched from her bay window with astonishment. *My word, has that woman given that boy drugs?* she thought forebodingly.

Jodie wished she had as much vigour as CJ, wondering at the same time where his unfound energy had come from. She would certainly need all the strength she could muster to face Barry. Even the amount of whisky and brandy she had consumed had not given enough burn to shake the cold dread that she felt. Grabbing the water bottle stashed away under the kitchen sink she listlessly trudged upstairs to get herself ready.

Before long the rain came. Then came the roars of thunder and flashes of lightning. The unforgiving storm was raging. Jodie looked out of the window. The silver birch tree was being battered by thrashing wind and the rain. Several branches were swept clean off and landed with a great thud on top of Jodie's Car. *Oh great ... that goddamn tree.* Jodie didn't know what to do. Her nerves were already getting the better of her in anticipation of seeing Barry today and now this. Jack would be furious. She would not be able to remove the branches by herself and did not even want to think about what damage was done to the car. *God damn it!* she thought as she drank the liquid from the water bottle.

CHAPTER TWENTY-TWO

What Happened With Barry

Walking into the 'All Day Laundry' Jodie felt anxious and was looking wet and windswept. She had been caught in the rain that was now easing off, running the short distance from the taxi into the shop. Dirty Barry was grinning from behind the counter looking shamelessly showing his slightly crooked and badly stained teeth.

"Jodie, I've been expecting you," he said with uncontainable excitement.

The shop was empty. Probably because of the storm. Jodie felt lucky that the looks of disgust she thought she might get when she disappeared with Barry up the back stairs and above the shop to where his flat was were averted. Even though she was certain no one would actually believe that she would sleep with him, she still feared people would see right through her.

"I have a meeting with this lovely lady," beamed Barry to Alex his young assistant without taking his eyes off Jodie. "I will be gone an hour. Hold the fort for me would you? Might get some customers in now that the rain is dying down."

An hour? thought Jodie in horror. *Why the hell is this going to take an hour?* Jodie did not join Barry in his joyous and thrilled attitude as she was trudging up the stairs behind him to his flat with as much enthusiasm as a fish with a hook in its mouth being dragged out of water.

Barry's home was screaming 'bachelor pad'. There was not a solitary item to accessorise the place. No rug, cushions, ornament or plant. The place was practically bare but for a TV on the wall and opposite hung a large framed print of Mary Magdalene above a small black leather sofa. Her red cape hung open over her shoulders, bearing her small breast and fair skin.

Jodie found it captivating, but she wondered if Barry liked it because it was revealing.

"Beautiful isn't it?'" he said catching Jodie looking intently. "Did you know that da Vinci never signed his name on any of his paintings? This one is simply called Mary Magdalene. Historians suspect it was painted by Da Vinci, but no one really knows for sure."

Jodie did not know what to say, although her extensive knowledge of art history would amaze him. She had not thought of Barry as being a sophisticated man. Maybe he did appreciate the picture for its innocence and charm after all. But that aside she still found him repulsive.

"I bought the print off Ebay," laughed Barry. "Mad really when you think about it. Brings a bit of renaissance to my flat. Don't you think?"

Jodie smiled flatly. She was not happy about the arrangement and could not bring herself to engage in conversation even if it was a subject of interest to her. But she did decide that she would look for a picture of Mary Magdalene to hang on her wall when she eventually left Jack and got a place of her own.

"I'm not religious or anything. I just find her beauty astounding," continued Barry. "She's the second most important female figure in Christianity, after the Virgin Mary, of course." Feeling that his eagerness to impress was unheeded, he walked to the bedroom and opened the door.

"Shall we?" he said revealing an equally bare bedroom. Jodie suddenly felt nauseous. All the windows were closed because of the storm, preventing any fresh air from entering the rooms and the smell of solvent was present. Although it was not as strong as she'd remembered being in the back room downstairs but all the same it made Jodie feel light headed. She just wanted to get it over with and go home and scrub herself clean, but first she needed a drink. Even though she had plied herself with alcohol she still felt the need for more. She didn't care that it was still the morning.

"Do you mind if perhaps we have a drink first? A strong drink?" asked Jodie nervously.

"Of course. Sure," said Barry as though this request was nothing out of the ordinary. "I think I have a bottle of white wine in the fridge." And he enthusiastically hurried off into the kitchen. "Pinot Grigio alright?" he called out as he banged about in the kitchen looking for a couple of decent wine glasses.

"Anything is fine," shouted Jodie from the lounge as she stood admiring the naked picture, in awe of the delicate paintwork and technique that captured the subtleness of the transparent veil over Mary Magdalene's abdomen. She was trying to convince herself that Barry on balance wasn't that bad. But in her mind's eye she couldn't help only seeing him for the lecherous creep that she experienced every time she came into his shop. And she couldn't forgive him for tricking her.

What Jodie didn't know was that Barry's plan was to make sure that she enjoyed every second she was with him. He wanted to please her, leave her wanting more. He wanted to be the best that she ever had. Jodie was not like the other girls he had slept with. One night stands with drunken women too eager to take their clothes off. Jodie was different. She was a real lady. A beautiful sophisticated woman and he was going to make sure that she was treated like one. He could feel a warm sensation in his loins, like a volcano that had been dormant and was finally getting ready to explode, bubbling up to the point of eruption. But he would contain himself. He had dreamed of this moment since he first set eyes on her. He had tricked her, yes, but he knew that she was out of his league. He would never be able to get her into bed any other way. He convinced himself that fate had brought about the situation and he was going to make the most of it.

"There you go Jodie." Barry handed her a cold glass of wine, filled to the top. She thought that was typical of him not to know a measure of wine, but she certainly was not about to complain."

"Thanks," she said taking a couple of big gulps that only slightly took the edge of her nerves. Barry was still grinning perversely. Jodie wondered if that was just the way he looked when he smiled. He definitely wasn't blessed in the looks department. She followed him back into the bedroom knocking back the wine as she went, her stomach churning. The bed was unmade, but other than that the room was generally tidy. She kicked off her shoes and lay down on the bed on top of the dowdy covers.

"Okay Barry, you promise that if I do this for you, you'll tell the police that I was in the shop collecting Jack's suits at eleven thirty last Tuesday?"

"Absolutely," said Barry moistening his lips.

"You do know that it wasn't me that hit those kids, don't you?" she said incredulously.

Barry didn't imagine Jodie capable of knocking down two kids and speeding off leaving them lying in the middle of the road. But at the same time he wondered why she was so desperate for an alibi. He imagined that she was up to no good, whatever her story was. Either way he was pleased that she was giving herself to him. The thrill of any moment seeing what Jodie looked like underneath her clothes, being able to finally touch her, taste her, after all the times he had watched her in his shop and wondered in lust, roused a passion in him beyond his own comprehension.

"I don't expect you did, but you certainly were somewhere you shouldn't have been otherwise you wouldn't be here now, would you?" replied Barry inquisitively, but decided against pressing her for answers.

Jodie fell into silence. She couldn't explain to Barry her reason. One lie had turned into a bigger lie and she was so scared of Jack that she had no choice. Barry was her only escape from the harm Jack would inflict on her. And the thought of being arrested for manslaughter; what it would do to CJ did not bear thinking about. And then there was Matt ... what would he think of her? No, she had no choice but to go through with it.

"How do I know I can trust you?" said Jodie.

"You have my word. You can even stay and watch me make the call and tell the police you were here."

"And that's it, right? No more tricks."

"I promise," said Barry with a strange perverse look of sincerity.

He had been planning his moves since Jodie had agreed to his proposal, and the first thing he wanted to do was the most important of all. He needed Jodie to trust him if his plan was going to work, for he knew that she felt scared and vulnerable. He had to get Jodie to overcome her fear. But he could not let himself lose the power of control. He took out a blindfold from his pocket.

"Trust me," he said soothingly, "I'm not going to hurt you." And tied it round Jodie's eyes. She was hesitant at first and heard herself say, "What are you doing?" Yet she did not refuse it.

"Just trust me."

Her head was spinning from knocking back the wine and breathing in the heavy air, but surprisingly the darkness was appealing. She could pretend she was somewhere else, pretend Barry was someone else. *It can't be any worse than Jack* thought Jodie trying to make herself feel better.

You're just gonna have to learn not to get caught!

Seconds ticked by as Jodie lay on the bed quiet and still in the darkness. Hesitant and anxious and disgusted with herself. She heard Barry draw the curtains then she thought she could make out he was undressing. His breathing had changed. It had become heavy and raspy as he became more aroused. She swallowed hard and bit down on her lip in apprehension as he knelt over her, the mattress gave under the weight of his body. He was bigger than Jack, his shoulders broader and his arms bulging biceps. She could smell his flesh and she knew he was naked.

Crouching over her, he slowly began unbuttoning Jodie's dress. Unwrapping his prize possession, taking his time to savour the moment when he could see what lies beneath. She could feel his breath on her skin as he moved downwards, slipping each button out of the eyelet. The smell of cigarettes reminded her of Jack. She was overcome with fear. Her heart was pounding fast yet she did not utter a word as the fabric of her dress fell away to the sides to reveal her slender body. She felt shy and ashamed as Barry gently stroked her smooth skin. She shuddered under his soft touch, her nerve endings twitching in irritation. Unlike Jack, the caressing felt affectionate, but as astonishingly tender as he was, she still hated it. It made her skin crawl. But it was a weird endurance for at the same time it felt wonderfully gentle beyond recognition.

Putting his strong arm around her and with surprising care, he lifted her forward to completely remove her dress and in one swift movement of the hand he undid her white lace bra before gently resting her back down, ensuring her head lay on a soft pillow. The bruises on Jodie had completely faded, her soft skin pale and fresh just like Mary Magdalene's.

Barry spent the next few moments just delicately stroking her breasts, running his fingers down her stomach and gently stroking her thighs. She could hear him mumbling to himself under heavy breath as she lay quite still in darkness, every part of her tense yet mesmerised at how delicate was the sensation. She had never been touched with fingers so featherlike and could hardly believe that it was dirty Barry. She was anticipating him to be rough, but as she relaxed a little under his gentle hands she realised that he was not going to hurt her and she felt remarkably safe. She allowed herself to trust him and gave in to the gentle caressing as it continued from the nape of her neck, to her shoulders, to her breasts gently flicking her nipples then down to her thighs giving an exquisite feeling and for a moment Jodie lost herself and let out a moan.

Barry smoothly removed her white lace knickers and parted her legs moving inside to stroke the dampness without losing the softness of his touch. So yielding were his hands Jodie felt a warm burning sensation with each stroke and a quiver of delight surged through her body. *No this is not happening* she thought with a deep feeling of erotica. Being deceived by her own body, Barry was instilling an intenseness that would not ebb. She didn't want to be pleasured. It was wrong to enjoy the sensation from someone she was not attracted to. Yet Barry's touch, his sweet caress was stimulating and tantalising Jodie beyond her control. Provoking and awakening senses that had been crushed by Jack's domination.

He noticed that her breaths had become shorter and harsher, but no longer from fear. She wanted to object, to protest, but she had become weak under his touch. Barry was working Jodie's body, pleasuring her into an ecstatic state of confusion. With each lungful of stale air she squirmed, her murmurs faint, her body trembling with excitement as Barry tasted her sap, his tongue moving in with relish. Lightly nuzzling and sucking, rousing and encouraging the juices to flow. She freely parted her legs wider inciting Barry to further explore, his hands continuing to caress sensually. Her face now scarlet, her eyes shut tight beneath the blindfold that had blinded her mind as well as her eyes.

Falling deep into the darkness she was no longer in Barry's flat. She was in the desert naked under a starlit sky with her lover. Arching her back and pushing down imploring the sensation, Jodie was on the brink of explosion. She moaned out loud as Barry retracted, she didn't want him to stop. Why did she not want him to stop? She had lost all sense of reason.

But then she felt him move to climb on top of her. He was big and strong, her hands now touching his flesh, gripping him, enticing him into her hollow opening. She could feel the tenseness of the muscles in his back and shoulders. Feeling helpless underneath his weight, yearning to be invaded some more she squirmed and writhed. Barry could feel that Jodie was reaching breaking point; his own sensations too were reaching their peak. He was gliding in and out rhythmically feeling the pressure build up within, reaching the inevitable release. And at the same time nuzzling Jodie's nipples, softly biting the hardness then licking and sucking. Jodie wanted to complain, but the intrusion touched the most sensitive parts.

The tingling ran through her body triggering her to press hard against his groin, meeting each thrust as the sensation of his erection slid in and out of her wet entrance, her body twisting and turning with guilty pleasure stretched to its limits. Then wave upon wave of orgasm came flooding in sublime motion. Every muscle extending as together they reached the pinnacle of climax. Jodie let out a blissful scream as the heat rose through their bodies, loins pulsating, panting and moaning euphorically. Juices mingling, their bodies in mutual movement as Jodie received all that could be given.

Jodie had fallen deep into the darkness. Barry's penis still throbbing hard inside her as her own spasm lessened and her used body became limp and motionless. His weight pressing down heavy on her, pinning her exhausted body to the bed so she could not move. He stroked her smooth bare skin and played some more with her breasts, sending even more twinges through her veins, prolonging the orgasm.

And when it was over and the blindfold removed the realisation of what just happened hit Jodie. As her eyes adjusted from out of the dark she was certain that Barry's grin of extreme pleasure was sweeter than one she had ever seen before. Her face still scarlet, her breathing calming as her racing heart slowed down to a normal pace, she was left in a state of confusion, trying hard to comprehend how prostituting herself had rewarded her with such immense satisfaction. She felt ashamed and embarrassed and loved all at the same time.

So overwhelming was this feeling, without warning or control, tears fell down her face. And in her confused and disorientated state she welcomed Barry's arms around her. Their bodies entwined, he held her with a warmth and kindness she had never felt before. And could never have imagined the man she had so despised was capable of giving her what she had desired and yearned for so long.

"I'm sorry I tricked you," said Barry after a few moments, handing Jodie a box of tissues. "I just had to have you. I'd do anything for you. I hated seeing you so upset the other day."

"You were the one who upset me … that doesn't make any sense." Jodie's head was mixed up. She wiped her eyes trying to clean off all the mascara that had run. "We had an agreement and that's it … This … what just happened … That doesn't change anything." But Jodie didn't sound convincing.

Barry's face looked amiable, his big brown eyes soft and kind. He was not the same Barry anymore.

"I know I upset you, I promise I will never pull a trick like that again, but are you going to tell me where you were when those kids got knocked down? Were you with a man?"

"No ... of course I wasn't with a man ... what do you take me for?" Realising how ridiculous that statement sounded she quickly added, "I can't explain it to you ... I told a lie ... a lie that I couldn't retract ... I was too scared to tell the truth ... you wouldn't understand."

"Are you in some kind of trouble?"

"Not exactly ... look I need to go."

"Before you go Jodie there's something I need to do," said Barry picking his jeans up off the floor, and reaching inside his pocket he pulled out his phone and Matt's business card.

"I made a promise," he said as he dialled the number.

CHAPTER TWENTY-THREE

Back to School

CJ couldn't fathom his own mood. He was rushing toward the bus stop. There was a fire burning in his belly anticipating avenging Wayne Dear. His drive for revenge was so heated that he could hardly recognise himself. He carried an expression of mischievousness too heavy for his frail body and his eyes were wide and full of resentment, which was indeed an oddity.

The day was grey and it looked like a thunderstorm was brewing and the wind blew eerily as it whistled through the trees that lined Mottrom Road.

CJ jumped on the school bus with puzzling enthusiasm. The driver smiled sorrowfully, his thick silvery hair puffing up as a gust of wind whooshed around the bus. CJ snatched a look toward the back. He wasn't certain but he thought the Nomads had a look of bewilderment. He took his usual seat at the front. The atmosphere on the bus was peculiar to say the least. There were whispers and soft voices going on all around him. It was clear that everyone knew Kelly and Thomas were CJ's best friends and bizarrely they were behaving as though they wanted to keep their distance. Then he heard a distinct voice from the back of the bus and he was sure that he heard the words 'slimy little maggot'. As far as he could guess Wayne and the Haywood twins were referring to him. *I'll give them slimy little maggot* he said to himself, hell set on revenge.

CJ did not feel the urgency to rush to the classroom today. A new strength had grown in him and by the time he was off the bus and through the school gates he found himself taking his time meandering along the school corridor. Noticing the Nomads walk right passed him without word or incident, he regarded them busily engaged, watching something on Wayne's phone and sniggering. CJ continued to look around. There were lots of mournful stares and then he noticed a familiar cheery face. Someone who hadn't wanted to avoid him, but instead had shared in his grief and given him his condolences, and doughnuts.

"Hey CJ, good to see you back at school," said Cake, his chubby round face smiling as they walked into the form room. *At last* thought CJ, *someone who treats me normal.*

"Now can I have your attention everyone?" said Mrs Edmondson firmly clapping her hands together to quieten down the class. CJ took his seat at the front of the class, feeling an immense emptiness either side of him, mindful of the vacant seats where Thomas and Kelly once sat. "I have something very important to say," she went on. Only half of the class were giving her their full attention. "I said everyone ... and that includes you three at the back." She was referring to Wayne and the Haywood twins who were still preoccupied with whatever was amusing them on Wayne's phone. "Now ... we are going to be holding a memorial service for Thomas Bradshaw and Kelly Jones. There will be a friendship bench brought in tomorrow in memory of them both. It will be situated in the foyer at the main school entrance, and you can leave messages, cards, flowers ... It will give you all a chance to say your goodbyes ..."

CJ raised his hand.

"But it's the funeral tomorrow Miss. I won't be in school."

Mrs Edmondson was sweet and sincere, smiling at CJ with kind eyes.

"I know Christopher," she said. "But for everybody else who won't be going to the funeral they will get the chance to say a proper goodbye." CJ thought he could see her eyes watering and then there was a complete voice change from sincere to a horrendous yell.

"Master Dear!" she bellowed making the entire class jump out of their skin. "Would you like to share with the class what you find so funny?" She was walking to the back of the classroom, shuffling along in her slip on shoes. "Hand over that phone right now young man ... Of all the downright rudeness ... I have never known anything like it. What do you think you are doing? Have you no compassion boy? And you two are just as bad. Detention for a whole week." Mrs Edmondson had completely lost it. Her voice had gone to a high pitch screech. So infuriated was she that there was so little regard for her two dead pupils that she was shouting like the class had never heard her shout before.

CJ's heart skipped a beat. The phone! She has Wayne's phone. This raised an excitement in him like a drug free high.

Suddenly there was a tremendous roar as thunder rumbled and darkness rolled in like a blanket completely covering the waxy sun. The lights flickered on and off in the room. It was creepy and unnatural. There was a chorus of gasps and nervous laughter. CJ watched with bated breath as the teacher strode back to the front of the class and shoved the phone in her desk drawer. A chill had filled the room and she hesitated, looking up at the florescent lights that seemed to have been affected by the storm.

Rain was now lashing the windows ferociously and lightning flashed in the violent storm. CJ looked out the window. A streak of lightning illuminated the playing field. There was someone outside. No, there were two people outside, just looking in. Two distorted figures.

"Miss, there's someone out there," CJ blinked, rubbed his eyes and then they were gone. *My eyes must be deceiving me* he thought. Doubt and fear shocked him. He looked back at Mrs Edmondson pointing out the window.

As quick as she had erupted in a rage her voice changed to one of calmness and she softly said, "Don't be ridiculous, who on earth would be outside in this weather? Now where was I? ... Ah yes ... CJ ... the funeral ... Yes it's tomorrow and I have already authorised your leave. Now if there is anything I can do you just let me know."

"Thanks Miss," said CJ. But she had already done more than enough, as CJ's eyes were fixed on the desk in front of him.

The rain hammered relentlessly and a fierce wind blew. The lights flickered again in the coldness of the room and then all of a sudden there was an almighty crash as something struck the window. CJ had been looking back out across the ground, expecting to see something or someone. He saw the lock come clean off in the force of the blow, yet did not catch sight of any object. He could not grasp what was happening. A cold chill ran through his body.

"What on earth is going on?" said Mrs Edmondson, clearly rattled but in her professional manner maintained calmness.

"Looks like a branch or something Miss."

"Cool ... maybe that big old oak tree has been struck by lightning."

The class gathered round all looking out the window, distracted by the commotion of the storm.

"Can we go home miss? It's freezing."

"No you certainly can't," replied Mrs Edmondson rubbing her arms up and down, clearly feeling the drop in temperature. "But I think it is much safer if we move to the assembly room. Gather up your things class and follow me."

CJ could not hide his look of horror. The window lock that was broken was right next to Kelly's desk. The very window that she had unlocked two weeks before so that the three friends could hide out in their form room during lunchtime. *It's just a coincidence* he said to himself. But he couldn't shake the fact that he had seen two figures outside. *No one in their right mind would stand outside in a storm like this. I must have been mistaken.*

It seemed that all the year seven students were rattled by the storm and they too were making their way to the assembly hall which was situated in the middle grounds of the school. CJ wondered if maybe this was the school policy. Similarly to holding the fire assembly stations in the school car park. The students seemed troubled and confused, but for CJ it was a blessing in disguise ... or a gift from beyond the grave?

Walking up to Mrs Edmondson casually he asked if he could use the toilet.

"Goodness me ... Oh alright," she said, "be as quick as you can ... mind."

"Thanks Miss," said CJ.

He was running through the school, back toward the year seven block that backed on to the sports field. Then down the corridor, passed the canteen and out the double doors. The rain lashed him hard and in a matter of seconds he was completely drenched. Hunched over he battled against the wind, the rain stinging his face and was making his way to his form room. Reaching the broken window he pushed it up.. There was a prickly sensation in his leg, but not allowing himself to be distracted by his accident he climbed in. The room was icy cold and he had goose bumps all over. Thunder was still roaring in the raging storm and the lights above him were buzzing and flashing, almost as if excitedly spurring him on.

Rushing over to the teacher's desk he opened the drawer and his eyes fell upon Wayne's phone. To CJ it was like finding treasure. He almost forgot that he was saturated and bitterly cold. Quickly picking up the phone he dialled his own number. *Gottcha* he said to himself smiling with satisfaction and relief as the water fell from him leaving puddles on the floor. He deleted his number from the call list then placed it back in the drawer before climbing back out the window. There had been nothing by the window. No branch or anything that could have broken the lock. Running through the storm, almost being blinded by the torrent CJ felt a chill run down his spine. *How and what had caused the window lock to break?*

CJ finally reached the assembly room. He was saturated from head to toe. All the students were sitting down and the headmaster was speaking to them. Walking through the door apprehensively he was spotted by Mrs Edmondson. She had been glancing over toward the entrance for the last fifteen minutes wondering what was taking him so long. As soon as she had spotted him enter the room she slipped out of her chair where she was sat with the rest of the teachers and hurried over toward him.

"Goodness me ... what in heaven's name has happened to you?" she whispered, careful not to interrupt the headmaster's speech.

"Did you fall down the toilet?" sniggered one of the students who was sat nearby.

"Miss there was someone outside. I had to see if they were okay."

"I see ... and?"

"Well ... I ... I couldn't see anyone."

"Yes...quite," said Mrs Edmondson. If she was satisfied with his answer she wasn't saying. "You had better come with me." And CJ was frogmarched off to the staff room. "Honestly CJ whatever possessed you to go outside?"

"I'm sorry Miss," he said through chattering teeth, his face red with cold, his cheeks were stinging and he was shivering all over.

Mrs Edmondson took CJ into the staff room and fetched down a large box from one of the shelves.

"Now there should be something in here that you can change in to," she said rummaging through the lost property box. "Ah now let me see ... yes ... this should do it," she said handing him a pair of navy blue pants. *Great this will replace the ones that got ripped and I won't need to ask Dad for new ones* thought CJ. "And you are going to need a top," she continued sifting through the whole box until finally handing him a tatty old PE shirt and a cardigan with one of the old school logos. "That's going to have to do I'm afraid. Ah wait ... here you go, take these as well." And she passed him two odd socks, one slightly larger than the other. "Now go and get changed before you catch your death of cold. Use the staff toilets. There'll be some towels in there you can use to get dry."

"Thanks Miss," said CJ shaking with cold and taking the clothes, thinking how disgusting they smelled.

A few moments later he was out of the staff toilets dressed in someone else's musty old clothes, but feeling all the better for being dry. With the exception of his feet. His shoes were soaking wet, making a squelching noise as he walked.

"Now CJ, I wouldn't normally do this, but here drink this. You need something to warm you up." And she handed him a hot steamy mug of hot chocolate.

CJ smiled gratefully. He cupped his hands round the mug and pulled it in close to his chest to warm himself.

"Thanks Miss."

"Oh dear me Master Vickers. Whatever is your mother going to say when she sees you?" laughed Mrs Edmondson. "I must say, you do look a sorry sight. But I'm afraid you are going to have to face the rest of day in those clothes. You've only got yourself to blame, mind."

CJ smiled agreeably, listening to his teacher as he enjoyed the sweetness of the hot chocolate. He was being told off, but in the nicest way possible. There was a smugness in his smile, for he didn't care how he looked. He had managed to get Wayne's phone number and for the moment that was all that mattered. But he thought he would push his luck further.

"Miss did you mean it when you said if there is anything else you could do for me then ... " He hesitated a moment. "Then just to let you know?"

"What is it CJ?" His teacher was looking at him solemnly.

"Well it's Miss Mendes." He paused for a moment then decided just to come out and say it. "Am I in trouble for climbing through the window?"

"Ah ... yes ... the window incident. I did wonder if you would bring that up and I'm glad you did. Hmmmm, are you in trouble? Well that all depends ... doesn't it? If you're ready to tell me what actually happened." She put her head down and looked at him over her half-moon glasses. Her blue eyes looked sunken and sad. He had not even thought that losing his best friends would have affected her too. Why had he not even considered it? Of course she would be distraught. "Your ears must have been burning that day." She gave a chuckle. "And how is your leg now? Twelve stitches was it?"

"Yeah ... it hurt a first, but it's okay now Miss."

"So ... are you ready to tell me what happened?"

"I think so Miss," he said.

"Go on then ... tell me everything mind ... and I'll see what I can do."

"Alright," said CJ giving an inward sigh. "Well its Wayne Dear Miss ... "

"Ah Master Dear ... what has he been up to now?"

"Miss ... I was trying to hide from him."

"Hide from him? ... Why on earth would you hide from him?"

"Miss ... he does things... him and the Haywood twins. That's why Kelly and Thomas bunked off school. They were scared ... had enough ... they wanted me to go with them, but I couldn't. So that day I was on my own and I knew that I had to make sure that they couldn't find me at lunchtime."

"CJ are you telling me that Wayne Dear has been bullying you?"

"Me ... Thomas and Kelly...and a load of other year sevens ... But me 'n Thomas 'n Kelly mostly, we were picked on the worse. Took the mickey out of Kelly's speech and everything."

"I see ... well that certainly explains a lot. CJ you have done the right thing telling me. You leave it with me and I will deal with Master Wayne and the Haywoods."

"No Miss ... please ... I don't want you to ... I can deal with it."

"CJ we have a zero tolerance to bullying. I will sort it, I promise."

"No miss ... please ... that won't help."

"CJ I've been a teacher for longer that you've been alive ... if there is one thing I know it's how to deal with bullying."

Her words gave bitter comfort.

"Miss please don't do anything ... that's not why I'm telling you. I just didn't want to get into trouble with Miss Mendes."

Miss Edmondson was studying CJ with stern eyes.

"Alright CJ, I will speak to Miss Mendes. I can't promise that she won't want to speak with you, but I will do my best to get her to drop the subject ... but as for the bullying ... I don't think I can turn a blind eye to that." His teacher didn't have to say it, but CJ knew that she was having the same line of thought that he was. 'Kelly and Thomas would not be dead if it had not been for Wayne Dear.' She was now staring blankly, her eyes weary and resentful.

"Ahh what to do? What to do? You certainly have left me with a predicament CJ."

"Please miss ... you can't say anything to the Nomads."

"Nomads?"

"Oh yeah ... it's what they call themselves."

"Oh dear me ... whatever next." She took a handkerchief from her purse, took off her glasses and dabbed her eyes. "I tell you what I'll do," she said. "I will watch Wayne and the Haywoods like a hawk ... like a hawk ...you understand? And the moment they put a foot wrong I will come down on them like a ton of bricks. But you have to promise me that if they do anything to you ... anything at all ... you come straight to me and tell me, alright?" She pushed her glasses back on her nose and gave a firm meaningful grin.

"Okay Miss," he said, now feeling a lot happier that his teacher was not going to get in his way and he could continue with his plan for revenge. And as he finished his drink, he noticed that the storm had passed and only the pitter-patter of light rain could be heard tapping the staff room window.

"Come on Master Vickers ... we better get back to the assembly hall," said Mrs Edmondson taking the empty mug from CJ and tapping him gently on the arm.

He followed his teacher out of the staff room and back through the school to the assembly hall. He realised that there would be comments on his attire, sniggers even, but he didn't care. He now had Wayne's phone number on his phone. He would write the number down and then delete the missed call and hide the number along with the disc when he got home. He was smiling inwardly to himself, looking offbeat, his shoes still squelching noisily with every step.

CHAPTER TWENTY-FOUR

Monday Afternoon

The taxi came to a sliding halt behind a police car.

Hell this can't be happening thought Jodie as she surveyed Matt busily pulling the broken branches and debris off her car.

Stepping out of the taxi into the light drizzle, CJ's rug under her arm she pushed the door shut with a thud.

"Inspector Campbell ... what are you doing here?" she said pleasantly surprised.

"Hi Jodie," he said through a pearly white smile. "I was in the area and ... well I thought I would stop by and see you ... and just as well I did. Looks like the storm got the better of that tree."

"Yeah ... No kidding ... Bloody thing." Jodie's face was flushed, her body still feeling tingly and excited after her orgasm. She hadn't noticed Matt quickly removing a pair of latex gloves and slipping them into his pocket.

"Do you want me to arrange to have it taken to the garage?"

"No really it's fine. Jack will do that." She had a hunch that Jack wouldn't appreciate another man sorting out his problems, even if it was a policeman.

"Can I take that for you," offered Matt reaching out for the rug.

"Oh, thanks." Jodie craftily crumpled up the 'All Day Laundry' tag and discreetly yanked it off as Matt took hold of the rug and shoved it in her pocket. Come on in ... I'll put the kettle on."

"There's a couple of reason why I wanted to see you," began Matt as he followed Jodie into the house, wiping his shoes as he went in. "I had a call from your dry cleaners ... the owner ... a Mr Barry Denholm ... seemed he found his receipt book."

Jodie was smiling at Matt. She knew what he was about to say.

"And did he tell you that I was collecting Jack's suits Tuesday morning?"

"Yes ... said that he hadn't remembered seeing you ... reckons Tuesday is the busiest day. But he has the receipt to prove it now, so ..."

"That bloody man ... he's hopeless. God knows how he manages to run that business. So I'm no longer a suspect?"

"You were never a suspect, Jodie ... It's just procedure. Anyway, I think we will be making an arrest today."

"Really?" said Jodie in surprise. They were in the kitchen now and she was filling the kettle with water.

"There's someone from Altrincham ... a guy with a record for dangerous driving and his wife lost her licence last year for drunk driving. Well anyway ... turns out this couple were travelling back from Chester Tuesday morning. They'd been there to pick up something ... bought something off of Ebay apparently. Well ... that morning seems they took a diversion, which would have put them on the Woodbank Road round about the time of the accident. It's all circumstantial at the moment, until the forensic investigators will be able to analyse the paint samples from their car and ... "

"Paint samples?"

"Yeah, trace evidence," Matt went on, "We have traces of paint from the victims' clothes and we can match it to the car that hit them. It's how we catch them nowadays. Cars may look like they are the same colour, but the reality is there is a difference so subtle that we don't see it, but under examination we can identify the actual car ... not just the make and model."

"Oh ... really? So even if ... just for argument sake...this guy says he has an alibi, you could still find him guilty?"

"Well, that depends how credible his witness is. Jodie are you alright? You look a bit peaky."

"I'm fine ... It's just ... you know ... I'm still getting over the shock of it all. And it's the funeral tomorrow."

"Well that was the other thing ... I was going to ask if you would like me to take you. Seems like you are going to need a lift now anyway. Your car is going to need to go in the garage for repair."

"You can do that? You not working tomorrow?" asked Jodie continuing to make the tea and wishing she could take a swig of vodka to take away the sickness in the pit of her stomach.

"Sure I can, I've just rearranged my shift. So long as you don't mind the ride in a panda car."

"D'you know what? I think I would like that, thanks," she said smiling and a dash of colour pinched her cheeks as she blushed and handed him a strong cup of tea.

"Well you're gonna need a strong arm around you tomorrow to get you through it," declared Matt. He blew into his mug and placed it on the breakfast bar and leaned back in the chair putting his arms up behind his head. His arms were certainly big and strong, just like Barry's and she couldn't help wondering if his fingers were as gentle too ..." And CJ, will he be going?"

"Yeah ... I said he could have the day off school ... and Kat will be there too. She knew Kelly and Thomas. She met them at CJ's birthday parties and she would come to the school to watch their plays. She gets on great with kids, it's a shame she hasn't got any of her own."

"Well that's good, because you're going to need to give her your portfolio."

Jodie's heart skipped a beat. Why had she not thought about her work hidden under the car seat? And the phone too. Jack would certainly have found it when he arranged for the car to be repaired. She recalled her dream ... *the feeling of drowning ... it means lacking of planning ... You're just gonna have to learn not to get caught.*

"I can't believe I didn't even think about it." She was leaning forward, elbows on the breakfast bar, covering her face with her hands then rubbing her forehead. "Why did I forget? And the phone too." Matt could see she was clearly rattled.

"Jodie it's okay ... I'll take the portfolio for you and we can give it to Kat tomorrow at the funeral."

"Thanks Matt." She took a deep breath trying to relieve the tight chestiness she felt in her moment of panic.

"No problem Jodie. I'm here to help."

"No really. Thanks. You have no idea what Jack would do to me if he found out I was planning to work. He doesn't even let me paint for fun anymore ... let alone get paid for doing it."

"I'm a cop," he said cheekily, "and if there's one thing I do know it's how to cover your tracks. That's why I'm so good at my job." He was smiling at Jodie, which always made her feel better. "Which by the way is why I am trying to get my badge for Chief Inspector ... even though I fall under the average age for a Chief."

"Promotion? Wow that's fantastic," she said. "I will keep my fingers crossed for you."

"Thanks ... and I will keep my fingers crossed for you too," he said. "Now what time is it?" he glanced at his watch. "Well Jodie I need to go. I have to get back to the station. I will pick you up tomorrow around ten ... now let's get that portfolio of yours out of the car."

"Sure ... and I need to find a new hiding place for my phone."

The phone she hid inside a box of Kleenex that was kept inside a tissue box beside Jodie's bed. The rest of the afternoon was spent putting together a quotation for the mural for the hospital. And once that was complete, Jodie got on with the housework, making sure that Jack had nothing to complain about when he got home, except for the damaged car. *Surely he won't blame me for that* Jodie hoped. Then CJ walked in looking like an impoverished kid who had just found some treasure.

"Mum what happened to the car?"

"It was the storm ... half of that bloody tree landed on it ... But never mind about that, what happened to you?"

"Oh Mum, I have had the most bizarre day ever."

"Oh," said Jodie, "That makes two of us."

CHAPTER TWENTY-FIVE

The Service

The stony path up to St Paul's church was still wet from yesterday's storm and the rolling grey clouds were masking a clear blue sky. The church steeple pointing skyward was reaching towards the heavens and the divine, with the tower and the belfry falling into shadow from the surrounding towering trees.

It seemed like there were hundreds of mourners making their way to the service. Dark clothed bodies with their heads bowed low moving slowly up the stony path. CJ walked on with Kat a little in front of Matt and Jodie. He wanted to see the open caskets before the service but his mum had not approved.

The two hearses that had brought Kelly and Thomas were parked outside the front of the church. And the church minister was stood at the entrance on the top step dressed in a long white robe clutching a small hard book greeting family and friends as they went in to the atrium.

A long line of flower bouquets and wreaths were bringing splashes of colour to the otherwise dull grey stone wall. Jodie placed a spray of lilies and roses against the cold hard stone. Immediately it was swallowed up by the hordes of flowers.

The sounds of tramping footsteps echoed inside the cold walls of the church.

"Hey Jodie," whispered Kat as they walked down the aisle to take their seats, "Don't forget to switch your phone off."

"Already done it," replied Jodie.

The church was full. All the seats had now been taken, yet still more people were shuffling in and standing at the back. The minister had now taken his position at the altar. Two coffins, side by side, placed on stands with purple drapes. And there was an easel where two large photos had been put on display. CJ recognised them as their recent school photos. Jodie's heart sank, sorrow overcame her and she sobbed. The dark shades that she had been wearing since Matt had picked her up were hiding her puffy red eyes. Matt put his arm around her to console her. It was exactly what she needed and she was glad that he had accompanied her.

The minister began the reading:

"Peace, my heart, let the time for the parting be sweet. Let it not be a death but completeness. Let love melt into memory and pain into songs."

Following the reading was the eulogy from a member of both sides of the families. It was almost unbearable to watch. The pain of trying to speak through tears, of the readers trying to control their voices when they are heart stricken, was agonising. Loud cries of grief, coming from all around seemed to fall on the grievers like a heavy weight. None more so that the wailing of the inconsolable mothers. And after the eulogies had finished and the kindest words that could ever be spoken to describe Kelly and Thomas had been marked on each and every one, the service ended with a prayer. There was not a single dry eye amongst them as they prayed:

"May the Lord bless you and keep you, The Lord make His face to shine upon you, and be gracious unto you. The Lord lift up the light of His countenance upon you, and give you peace, now and ever more. Let there be peace for all. Let there be peace. Let there be peace. Amen."

In unison voices repeated, "Amen." And then music of the Royal Scots Dragoon Guards filled the church as 'Amazing Grace' was played. The jubilant sounds of the bagpipes rang through the church, touching the hearts of all who could hear it.

One by one, friends and family members walked round the coffins in a procession, touching the casket, heads bowed low and saying their final words to the departed.

Jodie walked to the coffins with CJ, following the other funeral goers as they moved round, first touching Kelly's casket and then touching Thomas's, muttering, 'Goodbye'; 'I love you'; 'I miss you'; and 'I'll never forget you ..." As CJ took his turn to say farewell ahead of his mum he watch an elderly lady place a shaky hand on the coffin. Her skin was thin and shiny white. He was observing her closely, mesmerised and then he heard her mutter under her breath:

'Why is it you cannot rest? You must find peace. Rest now my dears, rest.'

"Mum did you here that?" he whispered softly.

"Hear what?"

"What that old lady just said."

"No honey. I can't hear much over this music."

They continued saying their goodbyes and by the time they left the church they felt emotionally drained.

"So what happens now?" asked Matt as they hovered around outside, a group of people were thanking the minister and passing comments that it had been a lovely service.

"We go to either the Bradshaw's house or the Jones's for refreshments," said Jodie. She was stood with Kat and CJ on the stony path. The sun had broken through the grey clouds and it was starting to feel a little warmer.

"So we don't go to the crematorium then?"

"No, they wanted the service at the church. It's just the minister that accompanies the bodies to the crematorium."

"Well that makes sense," said Kat. "Can't imagine having to go through another service ... It's heartbreaking enough having to sit through all that." She took out a handkerchief and blew her nose.

"Can we go then Mum? To Thomas's house?"

"Yeah let's go. I could do with a drink."

"Cup of tea it is then," said Matt. Although Jodie was thinking of something stronger.

"Great ... I'll follow you in my car," said Kat putting her arm round CJ and giving him a big hug. She wanted to ask if he was okay, but thought it was stupid question. *Of course he's not okay.*

CHAPTER TWENTY-SIX

At Thomas's House

The house should have been large enough to host a generous amount of people, but it appeared cramped and restricted. Many of the mourners spilled out into the back garden. They were helping themselves to refreshments. There was what looked like a pasting table covered with white cloth and weighed down with finger food. Everyone was just hovering around in a strange state of boredom, nibbling on sandwiches and cakes. CJ was just about to help himself to something to eat when he spotted the old lady he had seen at the service. She was dressed in a gypsy style dress with a black lace shawl wrapped around her bony shoulders. Her fine wispy white hair was pinned into a tight bun and she was wearing small round glasses. As CJ approached the bench where she was sat, he noticed her skin was thin, almost wafer-thin and shiny looking, and her pale blues eyes set deep in small folds of skin. She was clumsily sipping tea from a china cup with an unsteady hand. CJ was mesmerised by her. He had never seen anyone as old. His curiosity had gotten the better of him and he had to know why she thought that Kelly and Thomas were not at peace. Especially after his encounter at the school during the storm.

"Hi," said CJ politely and sat down next to her. He thought she had a strange smell which reminded him of mint humbugs, but she seemed sweet.

"Hello my boy, you must be CJ." Her voice was shaky and she seemed to slightly wobble her head as she spoke.

"Yes," said CJ in surprise. "How did you know?"

"Oh I've heard them talking about you, boy." She looked at him and her face seemed to appear even more creased as she smiled. "Thomas was my sister's great-grandson. She is no longer with us, God rest her soul."

"So your Thomas's great aunt then?"

"Yes ... yes I am. I'm Mable."

"Mable ... that's a nice name." CJ was going to say unusual but thought it might sound offensive.

"Well thank you. They said you were a sweet boy."

"Mable ... who's they?"

"Well Thomas and Kelly of course. Who do you think I meant dear?"

An icy chill ran down CJ's spine, *but they're dead.* He thought and then realised that she must mean before the accident.

"Mable can I ask you something?" began CJ.

"Of course ... what is it you want to know?" said Mable still smiling. Her eyes were pale and delicate yet looked sharply at CJ with interest.

"Well I was just wondering about what you said at the funeral. I was stood next to you and I heard you say something to Thomas and Kelly ... something about they are not resting ... What did you mean?"

"Oh my dear boy ... They were taken away from us too early. The poor dears." She took a handkerchief out from a black patent purse and wiped her eyes. "It was not their time to go."

"Is that why you think they are not resting?"

"Unfinished business CJ ... they have unfinished business my dear boy," she said still dabbing the corners of her eyes.

CJ's heart sank to the pit of his stomach and cold dread gripped his heart. *Wayne Dear ... they must want revenge before they can rest.*

"Mable ... can I ask? Do you know what it is ... the unfinished business?" CJ wasn't sure that he wanted to hear the answer but his curiosity had already got the better of him.

"Oh my dear boy ... you don't need me to tell you," she said now staring blankly into the open space of the garden. There was a moment's silence and then she went on, "It was a woman who was driving the car. The police think it was a man, but they are wrong. It was a woman."

CJ was observing her closely. He didn't know what to think.

"Mable, how do you know that?"

"Fishing," she said completely out of the blue. "Don't like it myself. All those slimy maggots that you have to put onto those hooks. Messy business if you ask me. Thomas's dad loves it though. Keeps all his fishing gear in the garage."

CJ was utterly confused. He wasn't sure if she was just a batty old woman or if she was some sort of clairvoyant.

"Well Mable ... I think I should go and find my mum. It was nice to meet you."

"Nice to meet you too Christopher."

CJ left the little old lady, his head was completely mixed up. He wondered if he should tell Inspector Campbell about the woman driver. *Would he think it was all nonsense?* He spotted Kat making her way over to the food table and decided that he too could do with some light refreshments.

"Hey Kat have you seen my mum?"

"Ah CJ ... wondered where you'd got to. Not sure where she is ... She was busy talking to the Bradshaws and then she seemed to disappear with Matt."

"Oh I'll go see if I can find her," said CJ grabbing a sausage roll. "Oh by the way Kat ... if you fancy some company while you're eating ... there's a nice little old lady sat on the bench called Mable. I think you might find her very interesting."

Being with Matt had given Jodie the sureness that she needed to express her sympathy and condolences to the Bradshaws. She had previously felt a shyness, cowardice even, and had not wanted to talk to them, but Matt seemed to have enough confidence and poise for the both of them. And he was already well acquainted with them as he was working on the hit and run case. She hadn't anticipated so many questions though, people asking why she had come with Inspector Campbell and not Jack. Matt had explained about the incident with the tree damaging the car and nobody thought anymore of it, although Jodie had felt like they had come as a couple.

When they had finished talking to the Bradshaws, they wandered into the kitchen. Matt had asked if he could have a private word with Jodie and he was looking for somewhere quiet. There was a door at the far side of the kitchen. Matt opened it and peeped in. It was the internal door to the garage. *Perfect* he thought and snuck in pulling Jodie with him.

"What are you doing? You're a policeman you can't go snooping around their house."

"That's exactly why I can go snooping around their house," laughed Matt. He quickly shut the door. It was pitch black for a second then the light flickered on as Matt found the switch.

"I have to talk to you Jodie," he declared suddenly serious and taking hold of her hands. It was the first time (other than the innocent peck on the cheek) that Jodie had felt intimate with Matt. He went on, "Today has made me realise something ... life really is too short. Those poor kids they were only thirteen."

"I know ... same age as CJ," said Jodie.

"Don't you think if you want something then you should just go for it before it's too late?"

"Absolutely." Jodie could feel a tingling sensation in the pit of her stomach, intuitively predicting Matt was going to make his move on her. She could smell the wonderful woody and vanilla aroma that she liked so much.

"I really like you Jodie ... but, the thing is you're married and it would be wrong of me to ask you out. But if your serious about what you told me the other day, that you're going to leave Jack, then I want to be with you ... that is ... if you like me too."

Jodie was becoming weaker at the knees and her belly was doing somersaults. She hadn't had any alcohol since breakfast and was now finding it extremely difficult to keep her cool.

"I ... I do like you," she said feeling more nervous saying the words than Matt," ... "And I am serious about leaving Jack," she continued, "I've never been more serious. As soon as I have the money for a deposit on a house then I will move out ... divorce him ... do whatever it takes to get him out of my life." She had not even thought about divorce until this very moment. It seemed like the right thing to say. She had to make sure that he knew she was serious. "I will be working at the hospital soon. Like I told you ... I will have the money for a deposit by the end of next month." There was an element of excitement in her voice. Looking into those gorgeous eyes and saying these words made it all the more real. All the more exhilarating. In truth Jodie was terrified. Filled with the same fear as stepping onto a colossal roller coaster. She was already strapped in, the train was slowly ascending to the first big gut dropping dip and there was no way off.

Matt was gazing at Jodie with his greeny-hazel eyes and Jodie still couldn't believe how incredibly handsome he was. She just wanted him to kiss her right there and then. It didn't seem wrong that it was in a dusty garage and that they had just been to a funeral. It seemed like there could not be a more perfect moment. Matt had been holding her hands the whole time, softly stroking them with his thumbs and then just as he moved forwards, his mouth edging closer, their lips about to meet, the garage door slowly began to open.

CJ had been wandering around the house looking for his mum. First peering in the living room, amused by the clean sofa (they had obviously found the Pepsi stain), then he looked in the dining room until finally strolling into the kitchen, but could not find her anywhere. He had not been able to shake the impact that Mable had left on him, the weird feeling that she seemed to know who he was and the talk of unfinished business bothered him in a creepy and daunting way. He was desperate to talk to his mum. Anyone else would just dismiss it as gobbledygook, but his mum would be more understanding. As he wandered from room to room he thought more about the fishing. *Why did she mention fishing and what was the reason for mentioning the slimy maggots. That's what Wayne calls us.* In the end he gave up looking for his mum and decided he would take a look in the garage. *There must be a reason she told me about the fishing gear.* CJ had no idea what he was looking for, but nevertheless he went out the front of the house and opened the garage door. There was a shuffling noise coming from the far side of the garage. CJ suspected that it could be a rat or mouse. He shuddered at the thought as he peered around the room. The light was already on enabling CJ to observe that the garage was crammed full of stuff. He thought most of it looked like junk. There was gardening equipment, tools, bikes, and boxes all different sizes stacked haphazardly. CJ could make out some were filled with old toys. On one side was racking fixed to the wall with plastic storage boxes and in the corner a big old chest and to the right leaning against the wall he spotted some camping gear and leaning against camping chairs was a fishing rod and some green netting. He made his way to the far side steering clear of where the shuffling noise had come from. He did not want to come face to face with a rat. As he got closer he spotted an orange plastic box. He opened it and inside were different size hooks, weights and reels and floats. Then out of the corner of his eye he saw something move. Only a subtle movement, but a movement all the same. There was a box, about the size of a regular lunch box, it was plastic and slightly transparent. He picked it up to take a closer look and sure enough inside were hundreds of wriggling white maggots. *Disgusting slimy little maggots.* CJ had no idea why, but he decided that he would take them. Perhaps to show Wayne Dear what a slimy little maggot actually looks like. He took the box and left the garage, the door rattled as he closed it. Looking round to see if anyone had seen him and seeing no-one he ran as quickly as he could to the school bus stop and hid the box in the hedge of the garden opposite and then ran back to Thomas's house.

Before he had chance to look for his mum again Mr Bradshaw came over to him.

"Christopher, can I have a word?"

"Err, yes Mr Bradshaw. What is it?" CJ was panic stricken he was waiting for him to ask what exactly had he been up to.

"You were Thomas's friend. A very good friend actually and I want to thank you for being there for him. You know you two never fell out and he never had a bad word to say about you. You're a good lad Christopher. This is as hard on you as anyone and I just wanted to say that if there is anything you want of his ... to keep in memory of him ... then you just say the word. In fact," he went on, "If you wanted to go in his room, have a look round see if there is anything you want to take ... I know he'd like that."

CJ stared in amazement. Mr Bradshaw's eyes glazed and watery, yet still, tears of sorrow were restrained.

"Thanks Mr Bradshaw. I ... I think I'd like that ... to, to have a moment ... if it's okay? ... in his room."

Mr Bradshaw tapped CJ on the shoulder.

"It's okay ... his mother and I have talked ... we can't keep everything of his ... Please it would be our pleasure."

Forgetting about trying to find his mum, and spotting Kat in the garden still sitting and talking with Mable, he ran upstairs to Thomas's bedroom. He was completely out of breath and sweating in a nervous flutter. Breathing deeply he opened the door and walked in. It was a heart wrenching moment stepping into the room. He almost expected to see Thomas sprawled on the bed playing on the iPad. *Well Thomas. What is it you would like me to have? I'll never forget you regardless, but if there is something that you want me to have, well now's your chance.*

He mooched round the room, picking up photos and looking through his Xbox games and DVDs, running his finger through the book case, eyeing up his box set of *Diary of a Wimpy Kid*, until eventually he noticed the mobile phone. It was inside a plastic bag tucked away on the book shelf. CJ realised that this would have been one of the items the police would have had used to help identify him. The very phone that Thomas had used when he sent all those messages ... that had since been edited and saved onto disc. Then the idea hit him. The last piece that he needed to finalise his plan for his revenge. He couldn't possibly use his own mobile to phone Wayne, or even his house number for that matter. But to use Thomas's phone number ... that was the icing on the cake. He took the phone out of the plastic bag. It was clearly battered and broken, but that didn't matter. He managed to get the back off the phone, took out the battery and then he slipped the SIM card out and popped it in the breast pocket of his black jacket and put the battery back in. He had to force the back of the phone on, but managed to get the pieces back together, placed it in the bag and stuck it back on the shelf. Then making a quick decision he picked up the DVD *John Tucker Must Die* and left the room.

"Well I never thought I'd be hiding from my son in his best friend's garage with a policeman," laughed Jodie as she stood up from behind the large chest.

"Er no ... I think we might have had some explaining to do if he caught us."

They were dusting themselves off from being crouched down on the grubby floor behind a large wooden chest.

"What the hell was he doing anyway?"

"I've got no idea, but I can't hardly ask him."

"We should get back inside before anyone misses us," said Jodie feeling like she was the thirteen year old. But just as she was heading towards the door, she felt Matt take hold of her hand. She turned round to face him and without hesitation he kissed her. The feeling of his lips against hers sent tingles running through her body. The smell of his woody aroma and the taste of him was exquisite.

"I couldn't leave without kissing you first," said Matt. "It's all I wanted to do since I first saw you."

Jodie's cheeks were flushed and her heart thumping like a runaway train speeding down the track. She didn't want to leave the garage, even though it was dusty and cramped. She would have been happy to stay there for longer in that moment of bliss.

"Come on Jodie, we need to get out of here before we get caught." Laughing like a couple of lovesick teenagers they slipped back into the kitchen unnoticed.

CJ spotted his mum and Matt making their way over towards Kat, whom had remained sat with Mable on the bench in the back garden. He headed toward them, grabbing another sausage roll on the way.

"Hey Mum, I've been looking for you," he said, taking a big bite of the sausage roll. "Could we go home now?"

"Christopher my boy, you should not talk with your mouthful," said Mable in her slow shaky voice, her head wobbling as she spoke. "Your mother does not like it ... do you dear?" She threw Jodie a look.

"Err, no, no I don't," said Jodie completely spooked.

"This is Mable," Kat told her. "We've been having a very interesting conversation. But I think I should be going too. Mable it was lovely to meet you," said Kat standing up to join Matt, Jodie and CJ.

"Lovely to meet you too dear." And then her eyes flickered towards Jodie, and she said in a gentle tone, "Things never turn out as you would expect them to ... do they dear?"

It was three o'clock in the afternoon and the sun had finally broken through the clouds. The grey sky had turned to a burnt orange with fluffy white clouds brushed with cadmium yellow. CJ and Jodie found themselves walking along Mottrom Road toward home after just saying goodbye to Matt and Kat. Matt had thankfully remembered to give Kat the portfolio that had been safely hidden in his car and Jodie had passed on the quote that she finally managed to prepare yesterday. CJ was glad of the walk. It would give him chance to tell his mum what Mable had said.

Jodie was in a dreamlike state. The effect of spending the day with Matt, hiding from CJ in the garage, and the kiss had turned her emotions of the sad day into a pleasurable one. This did however come with a feeling of guilt. She thought she had no right to be happy today.

"So Mum ... I was talking to that old woman ..." began CJ.

"Mable?"

"Yeah ... Mable. Anyway, it was weird ... she seemed to imply that she had been communicating with Thomas and Kelly."

"What do you mean ... 'seemed to imply'? What did she say?" Jodie was intrigued after the strange comment Mable had made just as they were leaving, not to mention that she knew Jodie hated CJ talking when he's eating. *How did she know that?*

"She said ... I can't remember exactly, but it was something about them not being able to rest because they had unfinished business ... It was weird though Mum, the things she was saying ... she knew who I was an' everything."

"Well I'm not surprised she knew who you were ... The Bradshaws probably told her all about you."

"Yeah maybe ... but is was kinda spooky the way she was talking." CJ didn't mention the maggots. He didn't want to have to explain the relevance to his mum. "She said that Kelly and Thomas told her who I was ... as though she only just knew. And there was this other thing she said about the driver who ran them down." CJ went on, "She said that the police are looking for a man, but it was a woman who was driving the car."

Jodie was stunned.

"Mum, do you think I should tell Inspector Campbell what Mable said?"

"Er ... no ... I don't think the police will take it seriously unless the information is from a reliable source. Matt met Mable, I'm sure she's a sweet old lady ... she just has an overactive imagination."

"But Mum ... I think it could be important."

"CJ ... Matt told me yesterday they were going to make an arrest. They already have a suspect and for your information it's a guy."

"Yeah ... well ... they could be wrong," exclaimed CJ in a defensive tone.

"Well if they have evidence to convict this guy, they're not going to listen to some crazy old lady ... are they?"

CJ smiled weakly as if to agree, but inwardly he sensed that, as crazy as Mable appeared, there was truth in what she had said.

They continued the walk home with CJ passing comments that he thought the nice inspector fancied his mum. Jodie brushing it off reservedly. But as they joked for the remainder of the time, CJ could not shake the thought about how Mable knew so much and Jodie was secretly mulling over the comment about the woman driver.

You could just make out Christine's silhouette in her bay window as mother and son strolled up the garden path, with a look of surprise when they noticed that the car was not parked on the driveway.

"Seems like your Dad has arranged for the car to be fixed."

"Cool!" said CJ, as they went inside. Both with a feeling of fatigue and extraordinarily gripped by the comments from the sweet and arguably crazy lady, Mable.

CHAPTER TWENTY-SEVEN

'Mother Cluckers'

"So I heard that Christine was going to report her neighbour to Social Services." A lady was speaking softly, almost a whisper.

"Why on earth would she do that?" said another lady, her eyes lighting up eager to find out more.

"Well Christine told me that she doesn't look after her boy properly."

A fat lady walked up and placed a large bucket of fried chicken on the table and sat down.

"That's right, I was at the home watch meeting when Jodie was there ... she'd been drinking ... or so Christine reckons."

"Well nothing wrong with drinking. Quite like a little tipple myself."

The three ladies were sat round one of the tables at Mother Cluckers' Chicken Joint tucking into a bucket of fried chicken. A man had walked in. It was lunchtime and the smell of fried chicken was inviting. He looked over to the table where the ladies were gossiping. He recognised Fat Pat the owner and gave an acknowledging nod and a smile then joined the queue.

The conversation went on.

"Well ... Christine reckons that she doesn't feed him properly; says he's as skinny as a bean pole."

"Yeah, have you seen CJ recently? He's ever so pale and thin ... you know I think Christine has every reason to worry."

"Well she only has the boy's interest at heart after all," said Pat, "And he was in hospital last week having his leg stitched up. Never did find out what actually happened."

"Well this is the thing." She was leaning forward waving a chicken leg at Pat. "The woman is so secretive, sneaking around all the time ... and Christine told me that she's always throwing away empty bottles."

"Empty bottles of what?"

"I don't know ... wine ... gin ... whatever it is that she drinks."

" ... and that husband of hers ... He walks about like he owns the place."

"Jack? O hell he thinks he's some big shot ... My Brad would give him a run for his money ... I betcha."

"So has Christine reported Jodie to Social Services yet?" She was still speaking softly.

"Well ... the thing is ... just as I was leaving this morning to come and open the shop ... I drove passed her house and Jodie was being escorted out of the house with CJ and into a police car. Jodie was wearing these dark sunglasses. Reckon she'd been crying. I mean, this morning was overcast ... Why would you need sunglasses?" Pat went on, "And the weird thing is the guy who was driving wasn't even in uniform ... he was wearing this black suit ... Looked all official and everything."

"Can't be from Social Services ... They don't drive around in police cars ... do they?"

"Who knows?" said Pat "But I tell you one thing ... if Christine is right ... it's no more than that Jodie deserves."

Barry had suddenly lost his appetite.

"You ladies should be ashamed of yourselves ..."

"You been earwigging Barry," piped up Pat. "This is a private conversation.

"And Jodie's life is private ... Who do you think you are to sit there talking about one of your neighbours like that?"

"Oh calm down Barry. And just remembered whose joint this is."

"I don't give a shit if you own this place ..."

Pat stood up to confront Barry.

"Now just a minute," she bellowed, but he was undeterred.

"I've known Jodie for years." Barry went on, "She's a good mum and there is nothing she wouldn't do for that boy. And I tell you she don't go bad-mouthing her neighbours behind their backs like you lot." Pat stood hands on hips, mouth open waiting to get her chance to speak, but Barry continued hollering. "Just because she keeps herself to herself you think you can go sticking your nose in ... Social Services? What the fuck is wrong with you people. Haven't you got anything better to do than mess with people's lives?"

"You don't know anything Barry," shrieked Pat, "You see her a couple of times a month when she picks up her dry cleaning. Why are you sticking up for her anyway?"

"Oh he's got a soft spot for Jodie, has our Barry," said the lady with the soft voice. Still seated with her friend, looking sheepish.

The argument had grabbed the attention of all the customers and they watched on with interest, sniggering.

"I know a damn sight more than you lot ... you're nothing but a bunch of spiteful old bitches ... the lot of yer ...and I'll tell you something else ... your fried chicken hasn't got anything on KFC ... and that's where I'll be going from now on and you can shove your rotten chicken where the sun don't shine." Barry stormed out of Mother Cluckers leaving three gossiping ladies speechless and a bunch of customers unsure whether they should follow Barry and take the extra-long walk up the high street to KFC.

Barry was not only livid, but overwrought with concern. *What sort of trouble was she in?* he wondered. *What was the lie she told? And who was she so scared of?* He hurried back to the dry cleaners. He had to get Jodie's phone number from his client book and check that she was alright. Rushing through the door he ran behind the counter and grabbed his address book, flicking through the pages as quickly as he could *V, V, V, Vickers.* He dialled the number with quivering fingers and held the phone to his ear. His breathing was hard and his heart beating fast. The call was diverted to the answer phone. *God damn it!* He redialled. Same thing again.

Barry could not focus for the rest of the day. And he had completely lost his appetite. He had to know that Jodie was alright. *That bloody meddling woman, Christine.* He was so angry that he wanted to go round and confront her himself, but he knew that would not help. He just had to keep calling and hope that Jodie and CJ were both okay.

CHAPTER TWENTY-EIGHT

Breaking Point

No sooner had Jack walked through the door than the tormenting started. There was something strange in his tone when he asked to see Jodie's phone.

"I've been phoning you today ... any particular reason why your phone's been switched off?"

"I was at the funeral ... remember ... I did tell you it was the funeral today," she said expecting his anger to abate. "I just forgot to switch it back on ... What was it you wanted me for?" She watched as he unzipped her handbag, took out her mobile and turned it on.

"The garage wanted to collect the car today." He threw her a disapproving look as her phone beeped several times. "Have you any idea how annoying it is when I'm trying to arrange for the car to be fixed and you can't even manage to keep your phone on? I had to take an hour out of work so that I could meet them here to give them the car keys. They are bringing it back here around twelve tomorrow." His eyes scanning the phone as he spoke with a hostile tone.

Jodie said nothing as she sat down with CJ in the dining room. There was no point in trying to justify to Jack why her phone was switched off. The fact that she had forgotten to turn it back in when she came out of the church was reason enough for her husband to gripe.

She had prepared dinner and CJ really wanted to tuck in to a hearty piece of steak with mashed sweet potato crumble and seasoned asparagus without listening to his dad hound his mum. He took a big mouthful, thinking how delicious it was, when his dad continued aggressively questioning his mum as though she was on trial.

"You have seven missed calls from the dry cleaners," announced Jack throwing her an objective look. "Any reason why Barry would be phoning you seven times?"

"I ... I don't know," replied Jodie, sounding frightened and nervous. Jack slammed the phone down on the table, took a seat and started carving up his steak.

"Shall I phone him back and see what he wanted?" asked Jodie fretfully.

"Well I'd like to know why another man has been phoning my wife seven times," he retorted with annoyance whilst chewing a piece of succulent steak.

Jodie anxiously took hold of the phone and called Barry. A dread of fear washed over her as the number rang. *What did he want? He said he wouldn't trick me again.*

"Jodie ... at last ... I've been trying to get hold of you all day. I thought you'd been arrested or something." Barry spoke in a troubled tone. "Where are you?"

Jodie's first thought was the hit and run. "I'm at home ... Why, what's wrong? You told the police that I was ..."

"No ... no Jodie ... I'm not talking about the accident. I'm talking about Christine."

"Ask him why he's been phoning," snapped Jack as he irritatingly shovelled food into his mouth. He was scowling at Jodie expressing his frustration while CJ sat silently.

"Christine?" answered Jodie. "What's she got to do with anything? Barry what's this about?"

"It's your bloody neighbour ... that woman's been gossiping about you Jodie ... I heard Fat Pat talking today in Mother Cluckers."

Jack was uttering *'What's he saying? What's he saying?'*

Jodie continued to listen intently.

"Jodie," Barry went on, "she's been telling people that you're not looking after CJ properly."

"I wanna know what he's saying," hollered Jack.

"Jack, please, I can't hear."

"Jodie ... I heard Pat say that Christine was going to report you to Social Services."

Social Services. The blood drained from Jodie's face, fear of Jack was now taken over with absolute hatred of her nosey neighbour. This time Christine had gone too far. Something inside Jodie snapped, a rage that she had never felt before, blood had reached boiling point and Jodie was about to explode.

"That bloody women," she yelled as she dropped the phone on the table, panic-stricken and went to run out the house. Jack was quick. He was out of his seat and had grabbed Jodie by the arm before she reached the front door.

"You tell me right now what's going on," he demanded

Jodie gasped as she felt his hand grip her arm tightly.

"Dad let Mum go," called CJ from the dining room.

"Get off me Jack." Jodie struggled to get her arm free. "Get the hell off me."

Jack was infuriated.

"How dare you disobey me ... you tell me right now what's going on ... or so help me you are going to live to regret it."

"Dad ... No ... Please don't hurt Mum," cried CJ, tears running down his face.

"I have to speak to Christine ... get off me Jack."

"Why?" Jack had hold of Jodie with both hands now. Her strength was no match for his. She was defeated.

"She's going to phone Social Services ... that's why Barry was calling ... " sobbed Jodie. She felt Jack release his hold.

"For Christ's sake Jodie ... why the hell would you be reported to Social Services ... What have you being doing?" he stood back, his fist clenched.

Jodie fell on the floor against the door. She glanced up at Jack. His cruel eyes staring down at her. Her long hair fallen on her face, wet from tears. Any moment she expected to feel a blow. She caught sight of CJ. He was stood behind Jack with a look of horror.

"I haven't done anything ... " Jodie shouted back at him. She feared that Jack would find out about the accident. She was enraged and terrified at the same time. Her emotions were in turmoil. The only action she felt worthwhile, and she had no idea why, was to confront Christine, even if that meant battling to get away from Jack.

"I hate you Dad!" screamed CJ as he turned and ran up the stairs into his bedroom. "I hate you! I hate you!"

Jack turned to see CJ belting up the stairs. He took a step back and Jodie seized the moment. She scrambled up off the floor, feeling for the door handle as she kept her eyes on Jack and without hesitation she swung the door open and ran out the house.

"I hope you're satisfied!" she screamed. The statement was directed at her neighbour as she darted into Christine's front garden.

"Jodie get back in the house now," hollered Jack, unable this time to get a hold of her.

"You get out here and face me you old interfering battleaxe. You like talking behind people's backs ... well let's see how well you do talking to my face."

Porch lights were going on all around as residents were stepping out of their houses to see what all the commotion was. Neighbours watched on, gripped by the scene that was unfolding.

Jodie had ploughed her way into Christine's garden and in an uncontrollable frenzy, began pulling up her flower beds.

"You got nothing better to do than spread rumours? Well I'll give you something to do." She was hauling up her phlox and hydrangeas and pulling out begonias from window boxes. Pushing over pots, smashed terracotta pieces scattering amongst the dark soil that spilled out on the paving slabs. She had lost complete control. Every ounce of frustration and hatred bursting out in an uncontainable hysterical wild explosive rage.

The next thing Jack was behind her. Jodie was struck hard in the face. Her lip was bust and the swelling immediate. She could taste blood. Then she felt her hair being pulled. Jack had hold of her hair with one hand in a tight ball and with the other hand he was squeezing her fingers with a strong painful grip. She let out an almighty scream in excruciating pain. He was dragging her up off the ground and forcefully marching her up the garden path.

"Get your hands off me," she bawled, kicking and screaming through angry tears.

Christine was now standing at her porch with a complete look of horror. From the state of her garden or the scene of Jodie being man handled and dragged off by Jack, you could not tell. The onlookers gasped in horror. They could not believe Jack's abuse nor the hysterical behaviour displayed by the usual quiet and reserved Jodie.

Jodie did not hear a car pull up alongside the house above her cries, but all of a sudden she was free from Jack and there was a thud as Jack hit the ground. She turned round to see Barry. His fist was still clenched and Jack was lying on the grass out cold.

"Barry ... what the ...?"

"I heard it all on the phone ... You never switched the phone off Jodie. It's Jack ... isn't it? Jack's the reason you were scared." He was panting hard and staring at Jodie. She only nodded, her eyes had become unfocussed and dreamy.

The police sirens got louder and louder as the car screeched to a halt beside them. Several neighbours had come out of their houses and rushed over to Christine, whom was startled and distraught.

"Why did you do it?" Barry spoke again but this time he was addressing Christine. His strong arm was around Jodie's shoulders. She warmed to his affection.

"What in devil's name are you talking about?" screeched Christine, as a group of people were now huddled around her.

"Call Social Services ... why did you do it? Look at the mess you've caused."

"I did no such thing," she hollered back.

"You told me ... You said that Jodie doesn't feed him properly," piped up Audrey.

"I ... you told me that too," said Albert. "Said you were gonna report her. Said she was an unfit mother and a drunk."

"Albert! How could you?" Christine was more distressed that Albert had spoken out against her than she was disturbed by the appalling state of her garden.

"I'm sorry Christine ..." Albert told her, "but if you go meddling with things that don't concern you ... well like I've said to you before ... you're gonna end up in bother."

Two policemen were surveying the scene before them. Jack was knocked out, lying on the grass, Barry was comforting Jodie who looked dishevelled and upset and a crowd of people were huddled around Christine in her front garden that looked like a herd of elephants had trampled through it.

"So is someone going to tell me what's going on?"

Jack was coming round from Barry's brutal punch. He mumbled and moaned, rubbed the back of his head and stood up. His legs were unsteady and his eyes focussing on the two uniformed police men who were stood before him.

"Officer, arrest this man." He pointed at Barry, his other hand still holding his sore head. "He just assaulted me."

"He did no such thing officer," screamed Christine. "We all saw what happened."

"Yes ... we all saw it ... " came several responses from the neighbours hovering around."

"Well I think your head is going to need looking at," said one of the officers and radioed for an ambulance.

"I ... he's got that right," muttered Albert sarcastically. "Christine my love ... you've got some explaining to do."

Christine walked sheepishly toward Jodie.

"I I might have said that I was going to phone Social Services ... but I was worried see ... about young Christopher ... But I didn't make the call Jodie ... I didn't phone them."

"You stupid old woman," Jodie's anger was still raging. "Stay out of my business ... Do you understand me? ... Or it will be you who they're carting off in an ambulance."

"I'll pretend I didn't hear that," said the officer. "Now calm down young lady ... and are you going to tell me how you got your lip bust?"

Jodie snatched a look a Jack.

"Will he be staying in hospital overnight?" she asked.

"I would imagine so. That's quite a knock he's taken to the head. And you all say that you saw what happened?"

Albert was the only one that spoke.

"Tripped ...so he did. Tripped and fell backwards and must have hit a stone or something."

The small crowd muttered and droned under their breaths, in agreement.

"Right ... I see," said the officer, getting nowhere further with his inquiry. "And what about the state of your garden, madam? I suppose it was a fox's party."

"Erm officer, that was me ... There's been a misunderstanding and I trashed the garden."

"I see. Right then ... you are?"

"Jodie Vickers."

"And your good name, madam?" he said glancing at Christine.

"Christine Hunt."

"And will you be wanting to press charges for criminal damages Mrs Hunt?"

Barry threw a vicious look at Christine. "No, No officer ... that really won't be necessary," she said ruefully.

An ambulance had parked behind the police car and two paramedics were now attending to Jack, whom had remained silent and disgraced.

"Well ... If no-one is pressing charges then there's nothing more for us to do here." The two police officers mooched around, assessing the damage to the garden and seeming perplexed by the whole incident.

"Okay folks ... I suggest you all go back inside your houses. There's nothing more to see here."

Slowly, one by one the neighbours disappeared off the street. No-one was concerned when the ambulance drove off down the road, carrying Jack to the hospital. And moments later the police car too had vanished.

Barry was walking Jodie back inside her house when another car pulled up outside. Jodie recognised it immediately.

"Jodie, are you alright?" Kat jumped out of the car and ran to Jodie. "CJ phoned me ... said he was scared and wanted me to come and get him. Oh my God Jodie ... has that bastard hit you again?"

"Again! So Jack's done this before has he?" said Barry wishing that he had punched him harder.

"Who are you?" asked Kat.

"Oh, er, Kat ... this is Barry ... from the dry cleaners."

Kat was looking confused.

"I'll explain," said Jodie as the three entered the house.

CJ suddenly came running down the stairs.

"Mum, what happened to you?"

Jodie's lip looked fat and purple.

"It's okay ... I'm fine."

"Where's Dad?"

"He's gone to hospital ... he had a bump on the head. Don't worry ... he won't be home tonight. It's safe ... We can stay here."

"Dir ...Barry ... What are you doing here?" CJ recognised dirty Barry from the dry cleaners.

"Well ... when your mum called me before, she didn't hang up. I could hear all the shouting ... so I came here to make sure she was alright."

Jodie was looking at Barry, smiling, although it looked distorted through her bust and swollen lip.

"Come on ... let's have a drink," she said and they all went in to the dining room.

"Jodie you sit down and I'll clear up this mess," said Kat as she started clearing away the dinner plates. Then she placed three wine glasses on the table and poured out a generous measure of wine.

"*Gaja Langhe Conteisa*," said Barry reading the label.

"Oh my God ... this is Jack's best wine ... Do you know how much this costs?"

"I don't care how much this costs," laughed Kat, "I care about my best friend. Now are you going tell me what the bloody hell went on?"

Jodie filled Kat in with the events that had just taken place. Her face was still flushed from her outburst and her top lip had trebled in size.

"Well good job you're here Barry. Give that bastard a taste of his own medicine," declared Kat grinning in recognition of a job well done. "Now are you and CJ going to pack your bags and come and stay with me tomorrow until we get your place sorted?" Kat lifted her glass in salute and took a mouthful ... "This is good stuff," she proclaimed. "Too good for Jack."

Barry looked doleful. He had learned that Jodie was in a violent marriage and although the knockout punch was gratifying and he was about to drink Jack's most precious wine, he needed to do more.

"If it's a place to stay you need Jodie, you can stay at my Mum's house."

"Barry that's really kind of you, but I'm sure your mum is not going to want a strange women and a teenager in her house," said Jodie. The wine was making her feel calmer and numbing the pain from her bust lip.

"Oh no ... perhaps I should explain. My mum died three months ago. The house is empty. I just haven't got round to putting it on the market yet. It's a small two bed terrace on Badger Street at the edge of town. Needs a lot of work doing to it, but if it's a place to stay you need, you are welcome to it."

Jodie could not quite believe that the man she hated only two days ago had not only been the man that had made her feel like a woman more than anyone else, had also rescued her from the cruel hand of her husband and was now offering her a place of sanctuary. Barry had become her hero, and as grateful as she was, she wished it was Matt that had saved her. Matt, who earlier on the same day had his strong arm around her shoulder when she needed consoling at the funeral. The man who had given her so much confidence and kissed her in the dusty garage. She sighed inwardly. It had been yet another strange eventful day.

"Are you kidding me?" piped up Kat. "Jodie that's brilliant. We can get you and CJ out of here before Jack's home from the hospital tomorrow. I can even check on him, maybe pull a few strings ... delay him leaving and give you time to move out.

"Well I'll drink to that." *This is too good to be true* thought Jodie lifting up her glass. Her eyes met Barry's as their glasses touched, and underneath his shabby hair and stained teeth, there was a sweetness and kindness so endearing, Jodie could not ignore that at that very moment her heart actually skipped a beat.

"So Mum ... are you leaving Dad? Are we going to move out tomorrow?"

CJ had been sat so silent that Jodie had almost forgotten he was there.

"I don't want to be here tomorrow when he gets home," professed Jodie.

"Neither do I Mum ... I hate him."

"Okay then ... tomorrow morning, CJ, will be the last time you take the bus to school, because I will be picking you up and taking you to your new home. Barry," continued Jodie, "... I would like to accept your offer ... but on the condition that we come to some arrangement with rent."

Barry gave an appreciative nod as he sipped Jack's wine, feeling both privileged and accepted.

Kat remained oblivious to the subtle glances her best friend and the strange man that she had just met had been sharing throughout the conversation. That uncomfortable feeling Jodie had of disdain had long abated and transformed into complete admiration.

"Then let's do it ... let's move out tomorrow. Here's to new beginnings." And Jodie raised her glass again.

And as the glasses chinked at that gleeful moment, Jodie recalled Mable's comment as she had left the Bradshaw's earlier that day: *'Things never turn out how you would expect them to, do they dear?'*

CHAPTER TWENTY-NINE

The Morning After

Jodie had slept like a baby. She woke up at the usual time. Kat was sleeping peacefully next to her. The events of yesterday were suddenly remembered. It had really happened. The feeling of the shame she felt towards Christine swam round and round in her head. The chaos left in her wake was scandalous, yet amusing. And then the realisation that her husband had been taken off to hospital with possible concussion made her smile with immense pleasure. She was leaving her husband today and the shakes she was feeling this morning were not out of fear, but nervous shivers of pure delight and elation. Already this day had come. She had thought this would not happen until the summer holidays once she had started work and managed to save some money. But she had underestimated how strong Barry's feelings were for her. He had offered his deceased mother's house as a place for her and CJ to move into … No tricks or propositions, but pure, unadulterated support.

She hadn't forgotten that Barry was sleeping in the guest room. But despite her warming to his incredible good nature, she showered, dressed, applied some make-up and pinned her hair up before feeling comfortable enough to leave her room. Even if her top lip did look like she had a collagen injection that had gone wrong.

Having both Kat and Barry in the house was reassuring, albeit bizarre. She rubbed her head. There was an ache that was probably from drinking the wine. Or maybe from the rough handling she had endured from Jack. Still, hangover or not, she needed to wake CJ up. It was a school day after all and after he had left the house, Jodie was going to start packing.

For the second time that week CJ had surprised his mum. He was up and getting ready for school without hesitation. He was keen to leave early this morning as he had planned to walk down the far end of Mottrom Road to pick up the maggots that were safely hidden in the bushes. Today was the day that he was going to get even with Wayne Dear. And somewhere inside his tiny frame was a catalyst whirling round on full speed goading him into action.

Grabbing a piece of toast and quickly saying goodbye to his mum, CJ was out of the house with the same strange spring in his step he had two days ago when he rushed out into the beginnings of a storm.

Jodie watched bemused at her son's eagerness to get to school. For the past six months he had little enthusiasm, and yet now that his friends were no longer with him he had so much drive that it was utterly confusing. *It must be a girl* thought Jodie. *The girl that he was meeting when he had cut his leg open.* There was no other explanation.

"Good morning."

Jodie turned to see Barry coming down the stairs. A sight that she thought she would never see, but for some strange reason she liked him being around. The perverse look had developed into a sweet sincere smile, or maybe it always was charming, she just hadn't seen it that way. Still, his hair was shabby and the nicotine stained teeth did not make him attractive even with the nice smile. But Jodie couldn't help recalling the way he made her feel with his gentle hands. *Could Matt make me feel the same way?* she wondered. *And what would Matt think of another man staying overnight at her house?*

Barry had noticed a change in Jodie too. The way she looked at him with acceptance and gratitude. She was no longer dismissive of his warmth towards her. And although she had not realised it she was smiling back with equal sincerity.

"Mornin' ... Can I get you some breakfast?"

"I would love some breakfast," he said following her into the kitchen. "And then maybe afterwards I can take some stuff over to my mum's house and you can have a look at the place."

"Sure that would be great," smiled Jodie as she started whipping up some batter for pancakes and making coffee. This time the smell that permeated the kitchen was relative to the love and warmth that was felt in the Vicker's household.

"I've already told Alex that I will be in late today so I'll have time to show you round, then maybe I can help you take some gear over. You can move in today. And if Jack causes you any problems then you just let me know and I'll sort him out."

"He's not gonna be able start any trouble ... is she?" said Kat with a big yawn as she walked into the kitchen. "He's not gonna know where you are for one thing. Any chance of a coffee? I need a caffeine fix if I'm gonna be any use in the hospital today."

"Help yourself," said Jodie as she was flipping over her pancakes. "Cups are in that cupboard."

"Where's CJ? Has he already left?" asked Kat.

"Yep, left first thing. He's been acting very strange you know. I don't understand it ... He seems so full of life ...like... oh I don't know ... like he hasn't really mourned the loss of his friends," said Jodie.

"People grieve in different ways though, Jodie. I've known people to actually laugh when they heard that someone close to them has died. Weird ... I know ... but true." Kat sat down opposite Barry. She had filled three mugs with hot steamy coffee and placed them on the breakfast bar.

"Well I kinda wondered if he has a girlfriend. You know what teenagers are like ... He hasn't really spoken about anyone, but I'm sure last week when he was in the study, he was chatting to someone. I could hear a girl's voice ... but he tells me that he was doing homework. And the day he climbed through the window, I'm sure he was meeting a girl." Jodie placed a stack of pancakes in the middle of the breakfast bar and set out three plates and a bottle of maple syrup.

"What's this ... climbing through a window?"

"Oh yeah Barry ... I guess you wouldn't have heard about CJ's accident."

Barry remembered the conversation at Mother Cluckers. He recalled Pat saying that CJ had had his legged stitched. "Oh ... I heard Pat talking about that the yesterday ... but I had no idea."

"Have my neighbours not got anything better to do then to talk about me?"

"Ha ... apparently not," laughed Barry, "So what did happened?"

Jodie explained the story of CJ's accident as they tucked into pancakes and drank coffee.

"Well if he was meeting a girl ... where was she when he cut open his leg? Sounds very strange, but who knows what goes on in the mind of a teenager."

"Maybe he was stood up?" said Kat.

"Maybe."

"Well I need to get to work," announced Kat as she finished her coffee. "So what's the plan today?... I finish my shift at six. I could come round to the house after work and help you unpack."

"Sure ... that would be great. I'm gonna pack my things now and Barry's going to run me round. My car's due back around twelve, so I can fetch CJ from school and go straight to the house."

"Right then ... so where is it?"

"Here," said Barry handing Kat his business card. "I've written the address on the back."

"Great ... thanks. I will see you later." Kat was just about to leave when she noticed the post had arrived ... "Hey Jodie, there's a letter here for you ...Look it's from HMRC ... you don't think? ..."

"It must be ... " beamed Jodie ripping open the letter, "Oh my God ... it is ... It's confirmation that my business is now formed at Company House."

"That's fantastic. Jodie. Listen, maybe I should take the letter into work with me, just in case they need the reference number from you to raise the work sheet ... and you don't want to leave it lying around in case Jack sees it."

"Hopefully I'll be long gone before he comes home." She shuddered at the thought of facing her husband. More so now than all the times before when she had been assaulted. Her behaviour would not be forgiven in Jack's eyes. She had disgraced him and she did not want to hang around to find out what the punishment was.

"If I can find out when he is able to come home, I'll give you the heads up. Let's hope that Barry's punch did some severe damage and he needs brain surgery. That should keep him out of the way." And Kat gave a friendly wave, got into her car and drove off.

"She really doesn't like him ... does she?"

"Mmmmm that's an understatement," Jodie said closing the door.

"Well Jodie ... looks like it's just you and me. Shall we get started in the bedroom?"

"What!"

"Packing Jodie ...What did you think I meant?"

CHAPTER THIRTY

Getting Even

Today was equally as overcast and cold. Beneath the dull sky, layered with murky grey clouds upon impenetrable white veils was a wonderful miss mash of colours spraying Christine's lawn in a chaotic mess. CJ had a wicked feeling of admiration for his mum as he caught sight of the state of the garden. Flower heads scattered across the vibrant green lawn, smashed pots that spilled dark soil and a wild array of leaves and plants dotted around and the flower beds were empty and cheerless.

CJ threw his rucksack over his shoulder and took off down the road. Hidden in the front zipped pocket of his bag was Thomas's SIM card with the disc and Wayne's phone number written down on a piece of paper. Before long CJ had the bus stop in his sight. There were several students hanging around. It was not going to be easy obtaining the box of maggots without being seen. CJ edged closer and closer wondering what tactics he could use to discreetly remove the box from the bushes and sneak it into his school bag. He was only footsteps away from the very spot, shuffling along trying not to look shady, when suddenly a car took a sharp turn round the corner, mounted the kerb and ploughed straight into a lamp post. Everyone turned to look at the wreckage.

CJ stole his chance and dipped his hand into the bushes, feeling around hastily, his fingers touched the plastic box. He seized it and shoved it quickly into his bag. He looked up to double check that he was not being watched. He could not be sure but he thought he saw two figures on the corner of the road. They stood like shadows next to the smashed up car. The car alarm was ringing and the driver was standing rubbing his head, a confused and dazed look on his face as he surveyed the damage. He appeared unharmed. CJ tried to focus on the two figures, but then the school bus came, obscuring his view. He took his usual seat at the front, threw a look out the window but they seemed to have suddenly vanish. Was his mind playing tricks on him? CJ did not know what to think. A cold shudder ran through his skinny body. He could not shake the feeling that there was something unnatural occurring.

He spent the bus ride preoccupied with trying to think of a way that he could play the ghostly message to Wayne and also deciding what to do with the maggots, that the chants from the back of the bus went completely unnoticed. He had no idea what he was going to do, yet felt strangely reassured, his inner voice telling him it would all work out, one way or another. Just as it had during the storm and at the funeral.

It wasn't until second break that the opportunity arose. The air was cold and damp. The sky had looked like it was going to rain all day, but by some miracle it had held off. Just as CJ was heading out towards the sport field to meet Cake the fire alarm bell went off. CJ turned and made his way to the year seven assembly point where Mrs Edmondson was doing a head count for her form.

"Ah CJ ... there you are ... excellent ... All present and accounted for," she proclaimed, ticking off names of her students on the register. "I need to take this list to the fire marshal." She went on, "So you lot stay here and stay out of trouble."

"So Miss is the school on fire?"

"No Master Haywood ... it is not," she said scowling. "Sorry to disappoint you but it is just a fire drill."

Their fire assembly point was at the front of the school at the far right side of the car park and a large crowd of students were now gathered there. CJ watched Mrs Edmondson approach another teacher who was wearing a red vest signifying he was one of the fire marshals. They were deep in conversation amidst a bunch of students and teachers that were supposed to be in some sort of orderly line, but just looked like a swarm of people eager to see some flames and smoke whirling out of the school building.

CJ found himself momentarily scanning the school. Even though he knew it was only a fire drill, there was a tiny part of him that maybe wanted to see some drama too. But then he caught something out of the corner of his eye. The strange sensation he had earlier when he thought he saw the two figures standing on the street corner crept up on him yet again. It was a questioning moment that had begun to frustrate CJ. The fence panels that concealed the boiler room were damaged and CJ was certain that he had seen something or someone through the slight parting. Some form or shape, he could not decide. His eyes squinting trying to recognise the shadowy movement as a human figure. It was the very same spot that Wayne had waited for CJ on that cold winter day six months ago before creeping up on him and giving him a bloody nose.

CJ's curiosity got the better of him again. He had to take a look. He could not comprehend the overwhelming urge that impelled him to leave the disorderly line that was his form. He moved undetected to the other side of the fence. Looking intently, expecting to see someone or find something that would give him reason not to question his own mind. But there was nothing. Not even a shadow cast upon the tarmac from the school fence, for the day was grey and dull and the sun had stayed hidden behind the thick gloomy clouds. There was a noise that suddenly caught his attention. It was a door rattling in the wind. As CJ walked closer he realised it was a fire exit, but for some reason it had been propped open with a brick. *Probably so that the staff could take a sneaky cigarette break* he thought.

It seemed clear to him that he should go inside. Although still he saw no-one. Whatever he thought he saw was either just his imagination playing tricks on him or could have been a cat innocently prowling around. Whatever had caught his eye his focus was now on wanting to know what was beyond the door. He shuffled through out of the cold and into the warmth of the school. This area was unfamiliar to him, it appeared that this part of the building was only accessible to the workers, yet still he wandered in undeterred. He found himself in a long corridor. He guessed the door at the end led toward the kitchen. There was a distinct smell of heat. The sort of smell you get from burning hot radiators and a humming sound like the whirling of a giant fan. There were several doors along the hall, painted in dark green gloss that were locked and labelled with numbered plaques suggesting to CJ they housed the servers, electrical fuses and a host of wires that must be for supplying power to the school. And one of them would be home to the boiler room.

But then on the left there was a small office. The window was dusty but CJ could still spot the computer. It seemed to jump out at him as if it was suddenly magnified, drawing him in to the tiny room. His heart was thumping in his chest and a nervous excitement stirred in his stomach. He realised this was his chance, maybe his one and only chance. The school was empty and Wayne was outside with his mobile phone in his bag. Without delay CJ went into the office. The temperature dropped sending a cold chill down his spine. CJ ignored the sudden coldness. As luck would have it, the computer had been left on and the screen unlocked. His focus was now solely on payback.

He zipped up his coat, quickly took out his mobile phone from his rucksack and replaced his SIM card with Thomas's. Then he put the disc into the computer and played back the track. '*It's Thomas ... and Kelly ... We are watching you. We are coming to get you. You must die.*' It was haunting even for CJ to listen to the voices of his dead friends, as if they were actually in the room with him. Their presence felt as though speaking the words at that very moment. Watching and waiting like invisible beings, boosting CJ in his efforts to get revenge like some concealed driving force behind every move that had led him to this moment. The apprehension in the air was strange and mysterious. *This is it* thought CJ. This was the moment that he needed. Without further hesitation, CJ dialled Wayne's phone number. His heart was beating wildly as he sat holding the mobile to the speaker in his left hand and waited for Wayne to answer the call, his right hand holding the mouse, his finger hovering waiting to left click as the curser was placed over the play button.

Wayne was sitting on the wall in the car park with the Haywoods, happily throwing foul comments at anyone who dare look at him. His chubby face smirking in delight at every dejected look he got. The Haywood twins, tall and skinny, yet strong and tough, were laughing joyfully at the vulgarity of Wayne's remarks. Then Wayne heard his phone ring. He answered casually with a feeling of self-regard.

"Hello."

CJ waited with intense hatred. His timing had to be perfect.

"Hello," said Wayne again. He looked at his phone and didn't recognise the number. "Who is this?" he asked.

Hearing the words, as if on cue, CJ clicked the play button.

"It's Thomas" then he paused the track and waited for a response. Wayne said nothing as he was digesting a dead person talking to him. His heart skipped a beat as every ounce of colour drained from his face. A moment's silence and the next track was played, *"and Kelly"*. Kelly's sweet tone was so distinct it sent shivers down his spine. The background buzzing noise amplifying the eerie voices. His heart was racing and his body trembling in horror as though a slither of ice was travelling from the nape of his neck down his spine.

CJ could hear the Haywood twins. *What's wrong ... who is it?*

And then CJ played the final track.

"We are watching you. We are coming to get you. You must die." Wayne's reaction was exactly how CJ had anticipated. Disembodied voices touching every nerve in his oversized body, cutting into his very soul.

A spine chilling screech pierced the cold air catching the attention of the crowd. The horrific cry was almost unbearable. There was not a single person who did not feel their skin crawl by the very sound of the bloodcurdling scream that was coming from Wayne, as though he was being gruesomely attacked. The affect was so gratifyingly evil CJ gave a sinister laugh which only added to the horror of the telephone call. Wayne threw the phone down and in a moment of shear panic fell backwards off the wall. He landed head first on the concrete pavement. He felt his head split and his greasy hair became sticky with blood.

"They're going to kill me," he shouted. His eyes wide, yet dazed and unfocussed.

"Oh my dear Lord ... Wayne are you alright? Somebody call an ambulance quick." Mrs Edmondson responded majestically and had rushed over to Wayne, pulling up her dress and flashing her fat knees, scrambling undignified over the wall, to reach her distraught and petrified student. Followed by a crowd that were now gathering round.

"Miss, they're coming to get me."

"Who dear ... who?"

"Thomas and Kelly." Mrs Edmondson looked perplexed as she witnessed tears of dreaded fear roll down his white clammy face. The crowd still swarming round in their sadistic eagerness to see what all the fuss was about. Pushing one another to get a look at Wayne. But no-one enjoyed seeing Wayne traumatised and scared more than CJ. His large body had taken an almighty thud with his head being first to hit the hard ground. There was a small pool of blood, deep red in colour spilling from the back of his head.

"Miss, I feel sick ... and cold ... I feel really cold." His voice dry and hoarse.

"Give him some room," yelled Mrs Edmondson at the onlookers as she waved her arms frantically in a vain effort to make some space. "And someone bring me some water."

"Ambulance is on its way." Somebody in the crowd called out.

Nurse Hettrick was now kneeling down applying a large wad of bandage to the wound and trying to reassure him that his parents had been contacted and the ambulance would be here very soon.

CJ had made his way swiftly back to the fire assembly point, his absence going unnoticed and was now stood among the crowd leaning over the wall looking down at Wayne. Wayne's phone that lay on the floor close by was now broken into pieces. It had been kicked around and stood on several times.

Mrs Edmondson was trying to get Wayne to drink some water, careful not to move him, for she could not tell the extent of his injury, although it was clear his head had been split open with the fall.

Nurse Hettrick was providing first aid care with a caring sweet smile and CJ heard her say, "My goodness you've got yourself a nice little wound there. You're going to need some stitches young man. Yep, trip to Macclesfield General for you laddie."

It was the moment CJ had been waiting for and it tasted sweet. But there was one more thing he needed to do to finish putting the fear of God into Wayne. The icing on the cake was the maggots. *Slimy little maggots.*

The other teachers were attempting to get the students in order and shouting out requests that they make their way back to their classrooms. It was a slow process. Most of the students were reluctant to leave the drama, but eventually the crowd dispersed. It was at this moment that CJ spotted Wayne's school bag leaning against the wall.

Sirens rang out on the distance, becoming louder and louder as the ambulance entered the school gates. Two paramedics rushed over to attend to Wayne and Mrs Edmondson was giving an account of what happened. Wayne was babbling inaudibly in terrorised shock.

CJ crouched down against the wall by Wayne's bag, watching as the students meandered toward the school entrance in their groups gossiping and sniggering excitedly as if they had just seen a major live performance. Teachers were yelling at everyone to get back inside. And from the other side of the wall he could hear talking amongst the paramedics as Wayne was being lifted onto a stretcher. They had provided pain relief and stabilised his neck and spine in a neck brace. CJ stayed back, just for a short time, just to be able to empty the entire box of wriggling revolting slimy maggots into Wayne's bag. Then with a feeling of immense satisfaction he ran back to the school entrance, glancing back as he reached the door just in time to see Nurse Hettrick passing Wayne's bag over the wall to Miss Edmondson.

"I did it," he whispered to himself, glancing up to the sky as if addressing the dark clouds as the heavens. "I told you I would get him back ... Thomas? ... Kelly? ... Didn't I tell you?"

CHAPTER THIRTY-ONE

At the Children's Ward

Wayne could not move a muscle. He lay there on the stretcher his body stiff, his head aching with intensity, listening to the sirens ringing out as the ambulance charged down Kings Road, past the Mottrom Estate and on to the D road that led to Macclesfield General. The blue light whirling and flashing as cars parted leaving the way clear for the vehicle to race Wayne to the hospital.

His immediate thought was that he didn't ever want to go back to Kings High. Such was the fear instilled in him that he imagined Thomas and Kelly lurking, waiting for the moment when they would strike. He was petrified. Frightened like he had never felt before.

"Don't worry, son," said the paramedic anxious that his patient was rambling incoherently and needing to restore some calmness, "you're going to be fine."

Once at the hospital Wayne had a thorough observation test. He felt like he was undergoing an examination by some alien abductor. Lights were shined in his eyes, he was tested for movement in his arms and legs, his blood pressure and heart rate were monitored and his temperature taken. Then he had a scan to see if there was any damage to his head. During this time the horror of two dead students talking to him did not cease. The voices still echoed in his rattled brain. Their tone so terrifyingly enthused with life and excitement, it was haunting. And that terrifying menacing laugh, unnerving.

It was hours later when he was in the children's ward with his parents that he was finally able to talk. He was already on his second lot of pain killers, his head was stitched and he lay comfortably with fluffy pillows and crisp white sheets. He had been falling in and out of sleep and was being closely monitored. The nurses were troubled by the constant mutterings; *'I'm sorry ... I'm so sorry... please don't hurt me.'* He became more alert when he heard his mother's voice. She sat in an armchair next to the bed, listening to the mumbling.

"No one's going to hurt you Wayne," she was saying in a confused voice when she caught his eye.

"Hey ... can you hear me?"

"Wayne nodded. His mouth was dry and he desperately needed a drink of water. He spotted his school bag on the floor next to the side table. He knew that he had a water bottle in his bag.

"Your dad's talking to the doctor now. They want to keep you in overnight, just so they can monitor you," his mum told him, "They said you kept losing consciousness ... it was quite some blow you took to your head, but you're going to be alright."

"Ah so you're coming round ... that's good." A nurse was passing by. She spoke with a strong Manchester accent. Her eyes hazel and her hair pinned up in a ponytail. She repeated the checks that he had had when her first got to the hospital. "Well your heart rate is still a little high, but your temperature is back to normal and your blood pressure is fine. I'm Nurse Katrina, now if there is anything you need you just pull this cord ... okay?" Kat smiled, filled in some details on her clip board and turned to Mrs Dear before moving on to see her next patient, "He's going to be fine ... he's just getting over the shock of the bang to the head."

What Wayne thought he needed was to get over the shock of the telephone call from beyond the grave. His body shuddered.

"Mum ... please ... get me my water bottle from my bag." Wayne's tone was raspy.

Mrs Dear unzipped the bag and reached inside for the water. Her hands felt something warm, slimy and fizzing.

"What the ...?" She peered in wondering what it was that felt so disturbing. Hundreds of tiny white wormlike creatures wriggling around in the bottom of the bag, slipping through her fingers like sticky rice that had come to life. She screamed and threw the bag. Kat came rushing over.

"Are you alright? What happened?"

Wayne was leaning over the bed.

"Mum what's wrong? What is it?"

"It's ... it's ... slimy maggots!" she bawled. Her flesh was crawling and she had goose bumps all over. She was sinking in the chair, pressing in her body and pulling her legs up off the floor, as if attempting to get as far back as possible away from the creepy insects.

Kat put her arm round her shoulders to comfort her. Then she realised Wayne had gone into shock. He was rigid in a sitting position, pointing at his school bag, mouthing the words *'slimy maggot'* over and over again, in between gasps of breath as his heart pounded in his chest. His pupils were large, making his eyes look so dark and scary. His body stiffened as every muscle in his fat oversized body tensed.

"It's ... it's ... it's slimy maggots ... they're going to kill me," he shrieked.

CHAPTER THIRTY-TWO

Home Sweet Home

It was only a small terraced house with two bedrooms that overlooked a narrow country lane and beyond the road were fields stretching out as far as the eye could see. Cows and sheep looked like dots in the distance and the beautiful shades of green and ochre brushed the landscape. At the back of the house was a small garden that backed onto a cul-de-sac and further still was a park that just touched the edge of town.

The windows were double hung, leaded, with weathered paint around the wooden frames. An open fire was the main feature in the tiny living room and the only source of heat for the house, although this was more than efficient. There was a comfy looking, albeit worn, pale blue fabric sofa and an armchair filled with scatter cushions. Nothing in the kitchen matched and the uneven floor tiles caused the little round table and chairs that filled the middle of the room to wobble. The bedrooms were small too and the ceilings low. In the main bedroom you could lie on the iron bedstead that was pushed up against the wall and look out over the beautiful countryside.

There was a small conservatory leading from the kitchen with just enough room to use as an art studio. The age old pipes rattled and knocked and chip board paper covered all the walls like a nuisance. The floor boards creaked beneath the worn out carpets. As Barry showed Jodie around it brought back memories of her own parent's house when they were alive. The house that she was brought up in. It had a warm welcoming feel to it. It was nothing short of cosy and once she had put her stamp on it, it was a place that she could call her home.

"I love it," she said. "It's just perfect." Which was just as well because Jodie had already decided, no matter what, she was leaving Jack today.

"Well in that case … we'd better bring in your suitcases," suggested Barry.

Once the suitcases were in the house Barry and Jodie took the thirty minute car journey back to Mottrom Drive. Jodie sped around the house, grabbing duvets, pillows, towels, books, anything she could think of that she would need, or miss if left behind. Even taking most of the food. She would not come back to the house after, so she had to be thorough and, as Barry kept telling her, *be ruthless.* Luckily Barry had a stack of flat pack boxes that he uses for his dry cleaning business, so they were able to put all the items into boxes. Suddenly there was a knock at the door and her heart sank.

"Afternoon Mrs Vickers, just bringing back the car." The mechanic handed Jodie the keys and she thanked him. Her voice a little shaky.

"Well now we have two cars to fill, you can take more stuff," said Barry, full of enthusiasm. He could not hide his elation that he had been in her company since yesterday evening and she was leaving her husband.

"Why not?" Jodie replied as she picked up the Carrera marble statue of the naked lady and threw it on top of a pile of bedding.

The cars were finally loaded up, and strangely there had been no sight or word from Christine. Today she was keeping a very low profile, but sooner or later she would need to sort out the damage Jodie had done to her garden.

Jodie was now following Barry back to her new home on Badger Street, when it suddenly occurred to her that she had not had one single drop of alcohol. Even though she has spent the day feeling extremely anxious. She had left the water bottles filled with vodka in the usual hiding places and imagined what Jack would think when he found them. In her mind's eye she visualised Jack's return home from the hospital. He would walk in the house expecting to find his obedient wife and instead he would see a sight so unexpected. Half of the household items would be missing: vases, rugs, ornaments, bedding, lamps, DVDs, books, cooking utensils and implements, the DVD player, pictures off the wall, computer from his study. She pictured him running up the stairs in to the bedroom to find all of her clothes gone and CJ's too. And at some point he would notice the last two remaining bottles of his finest wine that had been deviously placed back on the wine rack, were empty. Jack would be consumed with thunderous rage and the more Jodie thought about his reaction to her disappearance, the happier she felt. It was an image that would not falter for a long time to come and gave her a deep taste of joy.

Pulling up outside her new home she gave a wave of excitement and she desperately wanted to phone Matt and tell him. But there was a worrying aspect that the man who was helping her, was her alibi. So for the time being she decided she wouldn't make that call, just until she had made up her mind what to tell him, without rousing suspicion.

It took a long while to bring all the boxes into the tiny house and put the stuff into the right rooms before even starting to put things away. In her haste to leave, they had not labelled any of the boxes, so each one had to be opened before Jodie knew which room it was to go in. This was time consuming and before Jodie new it, school was almost finished and she had to pick up CJ. Barry had decided to take the full day off work. *'Perk of being you own boss'* he had told her. And he would carry on helping with the unpacking while she drove to the school to collect CJ. So she left without question. She had come to trust him implicitly since the Monday incident. Although, it was always on their minds the whole time, neither one mentioned it.

It was when Jodie was en route to the school, carefully driving on a snaking country road, when she received a call from Kat.

"Jodie, so sorry I didn't phone you earlier ... I had some problems with a kid on my ward ... just had to arrange for him to be taken to the psychiatric ward ... Anyway ... Jack left the hospital an hour … maybe an hour and a half ago …. just thought you should know. Please tell me that you are out of the house."

"Kat, I'm fine. Just on my way to get CJ now from school. The car was brought back … on time … which was great. And Barry has been helping me shift all my gear. So far so good."

"Oh that's great. I've been so worried. So, what's the new home like?"

"Small and cosy and in the middle of nowhere. It's perfect. Can't wait to show it to you later."

"Fantastic. So happy for you. Listen I can't talk for long, but I gotta tell you this … I've handed your portfolio and quote in to admin … they are issuing the work order today and you can start work straight away."

"Really? That's brilliant … but what about all the materials?"

"You've included them in your quote, right?"

"Yeah."

"So we'll go online and get them ordered. Soon as they arrive … get your arse over here and get to work."

"Right … will do."

"I have to go now. It's manic here today. But I will see you later. "

"Okay … bye Kat … and thanks for everything."

"No worries … see you later … Bye."

Jodie was approaching the school when she noticed a car. A car that was all too familiar. The Merc that was parked on her drive no more than three hours ago was now sitting right outside the school gates. Jodie's heart was in her throat. *Jack … shit.* Jodie did not stop. She drove on past the school, glanced in her rear view mirror. The Merc was still stationery. *Great he hasn't seen me.*

Jack's eyes were fixed on the main school entrance. As soon as he spotted CJ he would dart through the school gates and entice him into his car. By whatever means necessary. Although it wasn't in his nature to take out his anger on CJ, this time Jodie had gone too far. He had no idea where she was or who she was with. All he knew was that she had left and taken all her belongings and a great deal more besides. He wanted revenge. She had brought shame on the family and humiliated them in public. And he had not appreciated spending the night in a hospital bed, being monitored at what seemed like every half an hour after being assaulted, and only Jodie was to blame.

Although he appeared calm, on the inside he was seething with an intense rage. The only way he would lure Jodie back to the house was by using CJ as his weapon. He could not and would not allow himself to be beaten by his weak and pathetic wife. And when she came crawling back for CJ, then he would erupt and she would feel the full extent of his wrath.

Jodie had reached the traffic lights at the end of the road. There was barely five minutes to spare before school ended. She was beside herself with fear. She was shaking all over, her stomach in knots. She reached for the phone and quickly called CJ. No answer. She tried again. Still no answer. Then just as the lights changed to green she suddenly remembered that there was a housing estate at the back of the school with an alleyway that led to the side of the front car park. She quickly threw a right, raced as fast as she could to the roundabout and took the first exit in the Trees Estate. Weaving through the estate in a mad panic, she was running out of time. She needed to park up and phone CJ again before it was too late. Her body was trembling with fear. *How could I be so stupid? Of course he would come looking for CJ at the school.* She wished Barry was with her.

She spotted the parking bay opposite the entrance to the alleyway. There was an empty space, she zoomed in regardless of a car signalling to park up and did not care for the dirty look. School had now ended and CJ would already be out the doors and wandering around the car park looking for her. She was frantic. She grabbed the phone and called again. *Please, please ... pick up ... pick up.* No answer. Jodie tried yet again. Her eyes were burning with tears of dread. *Please ... please don't be with your dad ... please.* Still no answer. She wanted to scream out loud. Pressing the redial button for the fifth time the phone was ringing, on the fourth ring she heard CJ's voice.

"Mum ... Sorry I couldn't answer the phone, I was with my teacher."

"Oh thank God CJ ... Are you still inside the school?"

"Just walking out now ..."

Jodie spoke in an urgent tone, as fast as she could. She knew she had little time between CJ walking out the school and Jack seeing him.

"CJ, your dad is parked up right outside the school gates. Can you get to the alleyway without him seeing you?"

"Oh ... yeah ... I see him Mum." CJ was walking through the door with a team of other students. He kept his head down and stayed behind a couple of seniors and then sped off to the left and jumped swiftly over the wall. Jodie could hear a racket down the phone, but was unable to predict his movements. Then she heard his heavy breath as he moved hastily out of sight, his phone was pressed back against his face.

"CJ? Where are you now?" Jodie was frantic. She wondered if now was the right time to call Matt. Her spare phone where she had Matt's number stored was still hidden in the tissue box, but she did still have Matt's business card in her purse.

"Mum, I'm okay ... Just in the alleyway now," panted CJ as he quickened his step. "I don't think he saw me."

"Oh thank God. You'll see me parked up. I'm right opposite as you come out the alley. Be as quick as you can okay."

"Okay Mum, I'll see you in a minute."

Jodie pressed her head back against the seat, closed her eyes and took a big elongated breath. She was safe. For now. But would Jack be back again tomorrow? Or would he be back at work? As she waited the short agonising few minutes for CJ to make an appearance from the alleyway, she took out her bottle of orange juice, filled mostly with vodka and drank avidly, realising she would have to be on her guard. For the next few days at least. Perhaps this needed to be their arranged pick up spot for the remainder of the school term. Jodie did not feel completely at ease, until CJ was sat next to her in the car and the school was a couple of miles distance behind them.

"I wouldn't have gone with him Mum. I would have just run back in the school and phoned you," said CJ thinking out loud.

"So what were you talking to your teacher about?" said Jodie trying to change the subject. She did not want to dwell on what would have happened had Jack seen her or CJ.

"Oh yeah ... We had a fire drill today ..."

"What's that got to do with anything?" asked Jodie.

"Mum ... don't interrupt ... I'm telling you a story."

"Oh okay ... go on then."

"So, we're all outside at the assembly point ... right ... and there's this fat kid called Wayne who's sat on the wall and then all of sudden he falls backwards and cracks his head open."

"Oh my goodness ...that's awful ... So what happened, did he have to go hospital?"

"Yeah ... an ambulance came and took him off in a stretcher. He was freaking out and 'cos everyone was outside, we all saw it. They're all calling him Humpty Dumpty."

"CJ! That's just mean. The poor kid."

"Yeah ... it's awful Mum," said CJ trying not to sound sarcastic and inwardly laughing to himself.

"And so ... what did the teacher keep you behind for?"

"Oh she was just asking if I saw anything. Saw anyone push him. The Haywood twins were there and ... I don't know ... maybe she thought that they were messing around and he got pushed."

"Oh ... and did he?"

"No Mum ... he just fell ... It was wicked."

Jodie was on the country road only a couple of miles from her new home. She was enjoying the pleasant journey back and was looking forward to spending her first night in her own place, away from the control and domination of her husband. Her heart was not racing like it had been when she was at the school, but the nervous feeling had not abated.

"Oh Mum ... we've just passed Cake's house." There was a beautiful cottage set back off the road. "And just round this corner Mum is the bakers and a Spa shop. Hey, I know this road." CJ sounded excited. "How far Mum?"

"Two minutes," said Jodie.

In no time at all, the car was pulling up besides the house.

"Is this it?" said CJ, sounding a little unsure that his mum had chosen the right house to move into.

"I'm gonna fix it up. It'll be great. And like you said, Cake only lives down the road. You could bike it to his house."

"Mum, I don't have a bike."

"I'll buy you one," proclaimed Jodie.

"Hi Barry," said CJ as he burst through the door and spotted him in the kitchen, then ran up the stairs to check out his new bedroom.

"Everything alright Jodie?" asked Barry as she joined him in the kitchen.

"Jack was at the school," she said. "He was waiting right outside the front gate."

"What happened? What did he say?"

"He didn't see me. Thankfully. I parked on the Trees Estate and CJ cut through the alley," she told him. "But I don't think he's going to give up. He'll be mad as hell that I've left."

"Jodie, don't worry. He doesn't know where you are and I'm not going to let anything happen to you."

Jodie felt safe with Barry around, but it was little comfort as he wouldn't always be with her to protect her.

"I do have some good news though. I can start work at the hospital."

"What's this about work?" asked CJ as he entered the kitchen.

"I'm painting a mural for the children's ward."

"I didn't know you painted," professed Barry. "So you're not just a pretty face."

"Yeah Mum's really good. But she gave it up ... Was it because of Dad, Mum? Is that why you stopped painting?"

"Yeah ... he didn't like it ... Said that I would never make any real money out of it and that I should concentrate on being a mum and look after the house." Jodie had a sudden feeling of shame. All those years of being told what to do and never feeling that she could be herself. "I studied fine art at University and Art History," she told Barry, feeling very proud of her achievement, even though Jack had always thought her degree as worthless.

"Well Jodie I'm impressed ... and I look forward to seeing your work."

"Hey, the kitchen's looking good," said Jodie changing the subject.

"Yep, I've emptied most of the boxes and all the food is in the cupboards. The fridge is a bit dated though."

"It's perfect. Everything is perfect. And how do you like your room CJ?"

"Yeah ... it's cool. You can see the park from my window," said CJ smiling.

"Well Jodie, shall we have some tea and then I really should check that everything is okay at the shop."

"Sounds like a good idea."

As soon as Barry had left, Jodie sought her box of tissues and retrieved the hidden mobile phone. She switched it on and immediately saw that she had two missed calls from Matt. Her belly did a summersault in a nervous excitement as she called him back. CJ had taken to his bedroom and was finishing unpacking and sorting out his closet.

"Hi Jodie. So glad you called me back ... I've got some good news for you ... We've made an arrest of the driver of the hit and run," revealed Matt.

"Oh ... really? Wow that's great news. So all that forensic stuff you were telling me about ... there was a match?"

"Yep ... it's conclusive. I think it might be on the local news tonight. So be sure to let CJ know."

"Yeah of course."

"I have some news for you too. I'm actually phoning from my new home. I've left Jack. There was an ... incident yesterday ... and ... well let's just say Jack took a bump on the head and went to hospital ... So while he was kept in overnight I packed my bags and ... I left."

"I know ... Two of our officers were at your house last night. I saw your name come up on the report." Matt's tone trailed off from sounding happy to sad. There was a horrible silence. Jodie immediately knew something was wrong. And then she heard the words that she didn't want to hear. "It's probably not a good idea if we see each other for a while." Matt sounded dejected. "I'm up for promotion and if I'm seen to be involved with a married woman, who has twice had visits from the police about two separate incidents ... well ... unfortunately it would be frowned upon. You do understand ... don't you Jodie?" His voice sounded choked. He felt as though he was letting her down in some way.

For a while Jodie did not know what to say. This was a rejection she was not expecting. How could things suddenly change in two days?

"I wouldn't want to be the reason you don't get promoted," expressed Jodie graciously, even though she was on the brink of tears.

"I'm sorry Jodie ... I want to stay in touch ... and maybe in a month's time ... who knows what might happen."

"Yeah ... who knows," said Jodie. There was something more that Matt wasn't telling her. Another reason why he couldn't see her. She could sense it and hear it in his saddened voice. "Matt, good luck with the promotion."

"Thanks Jodie ... and good luck with you too. I hope everything works out for you. I'll talk to you soon okay."

"Yeah ... let me know about the promotion. Bye Matt."
Click.

Jodie felt weepy. She took a deep breath, fought back the tears that burned at the back of her eyes and pressed on with unpacking. *I'm not going to let this spoil things. I have my house and a job... I don't need a man as well. This is a good thing. At least I won't have to hide that Barry is my landlord. And I can see my best friend whenever I want. And who knows what will happen in a month's time* she thought, taking out the Thomas Moss clock from the box and placing it on top of the mantelpiece.

CHAPTER THIRTY-THREE

Kat's Story

By the time Kat arrived at the house, Jodie had decided she'd had enough of unpacking and she'd surprised her friend by cooking a generous portion of pasta bolognaise, thankful to Barry for persuading her to bring lots of food with her.

They were sat at the wobbly table on old wooden chairs that looked like they had been repainted many times over and the seats had been recovered.

"It's a bit of a fixer upper." Kat had told her in her usual honest way. "But if anyone can make this place look nice you can Jodie."

Part of the excitement of moving had been defused by the phone call she had with Matt. She tried not to dwell on it, but could not deny there was an empty feeling. The sort of feeling you get when you have lost something precious. And there was a definite sense that Matt was hiding something from her. Besides feeling deflated Jodie was intrigued about the arrest. She had told CJ, but he still seemed convinced that there was some truth in Mabel's theory that it was a woman driver. Jodie chose not to comment and was just glad that Matt had been able to get the evidence that he needed. Furthermore there was the dreaded fear of what would happen should she run into Jack. She needed to be cautious when she dropped CJ off at school in the morning. All these things seemed to suddenly weigh down on her. It was difficult for Jodie to unload all these worries and concerns on her friend with CJ present in the room., so for the time being she kept her thoughts to herself and asked Kat about her day.

"I have had the weirdest day," she told her. "There was this kid that came in to the ward ... Wayne ... his name was ..."

"Nothing like patient confidentiality," laughed CJ with a mouthful of pasta.

"Don't talk with your mouth full," snapped Jodie.

"Well ... this kid ... he had to be monitored every half an hour because he had a head injury." Kat went on, "So I give him the usual checks and he seems fine ... then all of a sudden his mum starts freaking out."

"Why, what happened?" urged Jodie.

"So anyway ... she goes into his school bag to get him his water bottle and the bottom of his bag is full ... and I mean swimming in maggots."

"Maggots?" said Jodie as she turned to look at CJ. "Didn't you tell me that the kid from your school was called Wayne?"

"Could be the same person," said CJ smugly. His plan for revenge had gone better than expected.

"So there were absolutely hundreds of them," continued Kat. "The mum starts screaming ... I guess you would if you were squeamish, but then the kid ... this Wayne ... he completely flips out. Goes into a trance and starts mumbling on about slimy maggots and they're coming to kill me."

CJ almost choked on his dinner and had to stop himself from laughing.

"We had to sedate him to calm him down and eventually he got sectioned ... they transferred him to the psychiatric ward."

"His last name wasn't Dear ... was it, by any chance?" CJ could hardly contain himself. *Wayne in a psychiatric ward. This could not have gone any better.*

"Yes as a matter of fact it was. You know him?"

"Is this the kid that fell off the wall, CJ?" asked Jodie

"Yep ... Aww I can't wait to tell Cake."

"CJ ... where's your compassion?" He was trying to be discreet, but he did not hide his enjoyment very well at hearing about Wayne's fate.

"Sorry Mum. Can I go do my homework now? I'm full up."

"Sure you can," replied Jodie happy that she would now be able to have the Venus talk with Kat that she desperately needed.

"Thanks Mum." And CJ left the kitchen singing 'Humpty Dumpty' under his breath. He returned to his bedroom, walked over to the window to draw the curtains. *Now Thomas and Kelly can rest in peace* he thought. *They have no more unfinished business.* But what was that? A prickly sensation was felt on the back of his neck as his hairs stood on end. CJ squinted his eyes as he peered out the window. *No, no it's just my imagination ... it can't be.*

CHAPTER THIRTY-FOUR

After Summer

"Come on CJ, time to get up." Jodie opened the curtains to reveal a grey dismal day. "Looks like it's gonna rain on your first day back at school. Oh well ... you still gotta get up babe. Come on ... I'll make you some breakfast. What do you want? Eggs? Waffles? Pancakes?"

"Ah Mum ... how come you're so happy? Glad to be getting rid of me so that you can spend time with your new man."

"Oh very funny. Actually I have work to do. I've got to get my canvases posted today and I have some more orders to do. And lunchtime I'm meeting Kat."

"What! Again?"

"Yes again. And my new man happens to be working today. Anyway, aren't you excited that you're going into year eight?"

"No not really Mum ... it's still school."

"Ahh, come on ... Where's your enthusiasm?" said Jodie as she pulled the duvet clean off the bed.

"Ohh Mum!" moaned CJ as Jodie left the room laughing.

In no time at all Jodie had made a plateful of pancakes, thinking very little of getting them a perfect round shape and all the same size. And the coffee was instant, with just a splash of milk. She laid the table, making little effort in making it look perfect. The table leg had been fixed, so the table no longer wobbled. Breakfasts were now pleasant and did not involve lashings of brandy or whisky in the coffee. Although, the urge sometimes surfaced, but the need was not there. And any broken plates were from CJ being clumsy and dropping one when he helped with the dishes. There was no nervous tension, being told what to do or who to see. Or even worrying about a nosey neighbour. But Jodie was still apprehensive that Jack could be back waiting for her at the school. She was still wary. Years of abuse didn't suddenly heal in two months. As Jodie was finding out. Healing her internal wounds would be a slow and long process. The school had already been told of their new address and their confidentiality was not to be compromised.

Jodie drove the thirty minute journey to school. The long and windy road through the countryside was very picturesque but slow. Often there were tractors or cattle crossings and it made the journey longer than Jodie would really have liked. Today though there were no hold ups, the first day back to school after the summer holidays. Jodie drove into the school car park, looking around for a silver Mercedes, but luck seemed to be with her today for there was no sign of Jack.

"Have a good day she called to CJ," as he jumped out the car. The sky looked gloomy and miserable. As if the heavens were about to open up.

"See you later Mum," he called back and disappeared amongst a team of people. Jodie felt a cold shiver and turned up the heat in the car. She thought she might light the fire in the lounge when she got home and hoped there were no bird's nest up her chimney. She gazed around in all directions, double checking that Jack was not parked up somewhere and about to follow her. She saw nothing, but there was still an uncomfortable feeling about being at the school. If he wanted to find her, and CJ, this was the place that she was sure he would start looking. She drove back home cautiously, checking her rear view mirror every minute for fear of being followed. And once she was home, she was constantly looking out the window half expecting to see a silver Mercedes parked up. *Am I paranoid?* she thought. *No. I have to be watchful.*

There was nothing to see outside the house. Just the dark sky, full of rain clouds getting ready to burst at any moment.

Jodie lit the fire and immediately the heat penetrated through the little house, warming it through. And the smoke seemed to pour out the chimney like and old steam engine. *No birds nest here then.* Jodie did several more checks out the window and saw nothing suspicious. Then the rain began to fall. The windows seemed to shake under the downpour.

She made herself a milky coffee and took to the conservatory to start preparing her canvasses for posting. She planned to stop off at the post office on the way to the hospital, before meeting Kat for lunch. Many of her customers that ordered from her website lived all over the country. So her paintings had to be carefully wrapped and handled with care. To keep up with the orders, Jodie was painting most days. And some days she would need to travel to people's houses so that she could paint murals on their walls. She was also close to completing a contract with a housing developer to help with the interior design of show homes. The business was booming. She was able to cover her bills and have plenty left over.

In the conservatory there were canvasses of different sizes stacked against the wall and an old pine table was laden with a watercolour block, paper, pallets and countless glass jars, some empty that were used for water and some crammed with paint brushes. A box underneath was filled with tubes of acrylic paints and watercolours and another with tissue paper and rags. A large roll of bubble wrap was leaning against the wall, a colour chart was hanging up next to a discoloured apron and an easel stood assembled in the middle of the floor.

Jodie used the bubble wrap to protect her paintings. Then she packaged them in several layers of brown paper. After she had finished parcelling her canvasses, she pottered around her tiny home tidying, cleaning, making the beds, putting on washing.

The walls still gave off a smell of fresh paint and the magnolia colour brightened up the house and the new beige carpet was soft under her feet. In the lounge, hung above the fire place was the stunning picture of Mary Magdalene. Jodie had truly settled in.

Before long Jodie was walking in to the hospital canteen. The sight of seeing Kat waving frantically, already with coffee and baguettes had become all too familiar. Yet a sight that Jodie would never tire of seeing. Jodie had become a known face in the canteen and all the staff knew her for her incredible artwork that she had displayed in the children's ward. The mural had kickstarted her career and for the past month she had enjoyed the attention. Contrary to what Jack would have had her believe, she was actually making money out of art and loving every minute of it.

"So, I hear that the handsome Inspector Matt finally got his promotion," said Kat pouring three sachets of sugar into her coffee.

"Yeah I know. Good news eh. I'm really pleased for him. Shame it means that he has to move away," replied Jodie sadly.

Kat caught Jodie watching intently.

"I need the sugar," she proclaimed, "for energy. You got no idea how knackered I feel at the end of my shift."

Jodie laughed, unwrapped her baguette and took a big bite.

"You're sleeping alright though?"

"By the time my head hits the pillow, I am out like a light. What about you Jodie? Any more bad dreams?"

"Actually I've had the same dream again ... well several times ... You know ... the one I told you about."

"What! Are you kidding me? You've been having reoccurring dreams and you've only just decided tell me?"

Jodie nodded.

"Well this is bad."

How to make me feel better thought Jodie.

"Well we both know that's not a good omen. It's a warning that something bad is to come."

"What ... like ... your prediction of potential danger? I think every time I'm out somewhere I run the chance of bumping into Jack. I don't need a dream to tell me that I might be in potential danger."

"But what if it's a warning about something else?" Kat firmly believed that your dreams could predict the future. If

Jodie was completely honest with herself, she did too. But she didn't want to believe anything else bad was going to happen. She was turning her life around and could finally be herself again.

After a short silence as they sipped their coffee, Kat finally changed the subject.

"Who'd of thought it eh? ... You with a nice new man, happy, and you two love birds have so much in common ... what with interest in art and everything. And the business is doing well."

"It's been amazing," piped up Jodie, brushing off the horrid feeling Kat had left her with from talking about her dream. "I can't believe how busy I am. And have you seen my website?"

"Sure. Looks fantastic ... Glad to see that you have included the pictures of the hospital. It was amazing seeing you paint those animals."

"So ... what do you think about Barry's new look?"

"Dirty Barry?" laughed Kat. "You would hardly recognise him with his teeth being whitened and he finally got a decent haircut."

"And he hasn't touched a cigarette in two months," added Jodie.

"Jodie, he's different man. Who would have known there was a handsome guy hiding away? Still looks at you like a slimy pervert though," she sniggered. "And it's good to see CJ looking so happy. Leaving Jack has made a world of difference to that boy. And he's even put on weight."

"Yeah, no-one can accuse me of not feeding him now. He still gets spooked sometimes though," said Jodie. "I'm telling you ... It's that bloody woman from the funeral ... reckons she's a clairvoyant ... Kept harping on about Kelly and Thomas having unfinished business. Says that it was a woman driving the car, not a bloke and that she had been drinking."

"Well maybe it's true ... His wife could have been driving," agreed Kat.

Jodie liked this idea. It would confirm CJ's theory about the accident. She certainly didn't want to have herself put in the frame.

Kat went on.

"And didn't Matt tell you that the guy's wife had lost her licence for drink driving?"

"Yeah he did."

"Well maybe she's the one who knocked them down. Would make sense if this old woman is right."

"It certainly makes sense alright."

"And it's amazing what you do to protect your loved ones," added Kat

"It certainly is," said Jodie.

Kat's words were still etched in Jodie's head as she drove to the school to pick CJ up and decided to park up on the Trees Estate and get CJ to walk through the alley. In her attempts to be cautious she had made CJ promise that he would always check his phone before coming out of the school so that any missed calls or texts could be checked. She did not want a repeat of almost being seen by Jack and suspected that he might still try and look for her at the school.

It was still raining hard and CJ was soaked by the time he reached the car. Jodie had apologise but made the point of asking if he would rather be with his dad or caught in the rain. It seemed a small price to pay if they were to avoid Jack.

That evening the rain was still hammering down relentlessly. The fire was lit in the lounge, the embers were giving off a warm glow and the tasty aromas of chicken curry flooded the house. The door opened with a creak.

"Hi honey I'm home," called a voice.

Jodie was met with a pearly white grin.

"Hi! she said. "Good day?"

"Yeah, not bad," replied Barry. His big brown eyes following Jodie around the kitchen as she began draining the rice and laying the table.

"I heard a rumour today that Jack lost his job," he told her. "Heard them talking in Mother Cluckers ... Apparently they don't take kindly to men hitting their wives ...Heard they were going to make him an associate partner as well. But his reputation is bad for business."

"I thought you weren't going to go in Mother Cluckers anymore?" said Jodie at the same time, in her mind, recalling the day when Jack wore an expensive Valentino suit all those weeks ago and wondering if that was the reason why he had dressed up.

"Of course... if it came from Christine Hunt then it's probably a load of old rubbish.," said Barry. "Although I do know that that bloody tree was lobbed down."

"Well I certainly don't miss that interfering old bag," said Jodie.

"So how was your day?"

"Good." Jodie paused for a moment to call CJ down to dinner. "I had a nice chat with Kat at lunchtime. She thinks your theory about the woman driving could be right," she , addressing CJ as he wandered into the kitchen and sat down. "What if the guy was taking the rap for his wife?" continued Jodie.

"Yeah that would make sense," agreed CJ. He had wanted an explanation for Mable's belief and this certainly would add up.

"So how was school today?" asked Barry as Jodie placed a scoop of chicken curry and rice on his plate.

"Barry, you need to learn the rules of communicating with a teenager. You never ask how school was. But seen as you're new to this I will give you dispensation ... Just today only mind...It was a pretty cool day." CJ had learned from Mrs Edmondson that Wayne would not be returning to the school. He was giving Barry a cheeky grin.

"Right okay," said Barry looking at Jodie and rolling his eyes. "You've gotta love this kid. And Jodie I've gotta tell yer, you make a mean curry."

Jodie sat down with her son and her new man and smiling to herself, oblivious to CJ glancing out the window and suddenly stopping in his tracks. His fork just reaching his mouth as he was just about to taste a mouthful of food. He couldn't be sure, but he thought that he saw two figures, through the rain, stood on the other side of the road, hiding in the shadows beyond the street lights. A shiver ran down his spine. He blinked and looked again hard. But they seemed to have vanished.

Jodie was still smiling to herself. She was relaxed and happy. The crackling of the fire in the lounge could be heard from the kitchen. The warmness penetrated through the tiny house and the infusion of the delightful smells of spices made the place feel homely and cosy.

As she sat tucking into her dinner feeling hungrier and looking more radiant than usual she thought to herself, *this could not be more perfect.*

EPILOGUE

Monday 29th June

"Well, Mrs Sibley …"

"You can call me Mable."

"Well, Mable … It's just as I expected … but you are not in any danger." Doctor Jenkins talked to Mable as though she was speaking to an adolescent. "I can tell you that the pain you are feeling in your back and abdomen is caused by dilation of the aorta. Fortunately it is not too enlarged and will not require surgery. But we will need to keep an eye on you. I would like to see you in a couple of weeks for another scan."

Mable smiled, despite her discomfort, and her bright blue eyes sparkled beneath her glasses. The doctor could not be certain if the sweet old lady lying on the bed understood what she was being told or the smile was simply an acknowledgement of something she already knew. Doctor Jenkins could not decide if she was drawn to the sweet adorability of Mable or unnerved by the peculiar impression that she bestowed.

"It's known as 'abdominal aortic aneurysm'," continued the doctor turning to look at the Mr and Mrs Bradshaw, assuming they would take account of her diagnosis.

"You'll have to stay with us Auntie … just for a bit longer," exclaimed Emma Bradshaw.

"Oh my … you don't want me to be extending my stay with you. Not after everything you've been through."

"Yes we do," piped up Andrew Bradshaw, "and we're not going to take no for an answer."

"I think it would be best if you wasn't on your own," agreed the Doctor as she helped Mable down from the bed.

Mable mumbled something incoherent as she wrapped her shawl around her shoulders and reached for a little black clutch bag. She looked unsteady and delicate. Age was against her. Yet her eyes were sharp and piercing and full of life.

The doctor handed her a piece of paper. "This is a prescription for some tablets to keep your blood pressure down Mrs Sibley. Now you need to take two a day. One in the morning and one at night time. This will help reduce the size of the swelling."

"Yes, yes dear ... I know ... I know. And call me Mable. Mrs Sibley sounds far too formal." Her tone honey sweet. "So if I'm to be staying with you my dears," Mable turned towards the Bradshaws, "would it be too much trouble to ask you to take me to Bingo?"

"No trouble at all Auntie ... it will be our pleasure." Emily Bradshaw took Mable's arm and began leading her out the room. Glancing back at the Doctor, Emily smiled amiably and thanked her.

It had been raining hard when they arrived at Macclesfield Hospital. Over the course of their time spent there, the ground had taken a pounding. Remnants of the down poor rested in ruts in the uneven pavement and the dampness hung in the air. Andrew Bradshaw had wisely parked close to the entrance. Ordinarily he would park along the side of the road to avoid the parking fee. But, he was much too concerned for Mable and the driving rain, that he chose a spot near the main doorway.

They took the longer route home from the hospital. This was the second trip the Emily and Andrew Bradshaw had taken with Mable to the hospital. The first time being an examination of the abdomen the day after the funeral. And this time was for a scan. As with their first hospital visit, Andrew Bradshaw could not bring himself to pass the spot where a speeding motorist had knocked down his son. He wondered if he could ever take the scenic drive home past Squirrel Hill ever again.

That night; Emily had given Mable her medication and settled her down for the night. The moon appeared full and bright in the indigo sky and the stars were out in abundance. Mable lay in bed sleeping peacefully and comfortably beneath a lilac floral duvet. Suddenly she was aware of a vast drop in temperature bringing a coldness to the room. Her languid breaths could be seen like smoke in the air. Slowly she opened her heavy eyelids as she lifted from sleep. Not quite able to focus without her spectacles she could just make out impressions in the emptiness of the space beside the bed. Two obscure figures, faint like milky shadows pressed up against the bed.

"Hey Auntie Mable, are you awake?" Thomas's voice sounded slightly slurred. A small hand brushed against Mable's cotton night dress. A cold electric charge tingled against her skin.

"My dears you were right about my stomach pains. You were right to warn me. But you need to go now ... go and rest my dears ... find your peace ... your place is not here anymore." Her eyes still unfocussed yet she was now wide awake.

"We got them Mable ... the Hayward twins." Kelly sounded clearer and more excited. Her voice filled with joy.

"My dears ... your place is not here anymore. You need to go to the light." Mable mumbled sitting up reaching for her glasses that rested on the bedside table.

"Not yet Auntie ... There's still more we need to do." Thomas's voice was coming through clearer.

"Jodie needs our help Mable," announced Kelly.

"Jodie? ... Christopher's mum?" said Mable putting on her glasses and suddenly being able to see more clearly. Kelly and Thomas appeared more solid and visible now. It was as though Mable had been looking into a steamed up mirror and the water vapour had immediately evaporated.

"Yeah ... Mable, she's in danger."

"Danger? Whatever do you mean my dear?"

"Jack will find her." This time Mable did not recognise the voice.

"Who's with you?" asked Mable. She was unable to focus on the third visitor. A transparent mist hung beside the bed. An intense pain abruptly surged through her skull and with it came a foul odour of algae and rotten fish.

"I was murdered ..." The distressed voice faded out the instant the bedroom door opened.

"Auntie, who are you talking to?" Emily and Andrew stood in the doorway.

As quickly as the pain came it went. The mist vanished and the stench no longer present.

"No-one my dears," replied Mable warmly. "I must have been talking in my sleep."

Emily and Andrew shivered as a cold flow of air spilled from the room. A look of horror and panic on their faces. Goosebumps from the nape of their necks to their toes as they observed Mable sat up in bed in the low warm glow of the landing light.

"But Aunt Mable, you have your glasses on. You don't usually sleep with your glasses on," declared Emily.

"Oh silly me ... whatever next ... I must have forgotten to take them off." Mable smiled her usual sweet smile and her eyes twinkled as brightly as the starry night sky.

THE END